"Who are you?" Dale demanded as he grabbed her arms and pinned her against a parked SUV.

"I remember only darkness, pain and your scent."

The woman wriggled away, lifted a hand to his face. Sexual energy jumped between them at the brush of her fingers. "Strong and courageous, is your heart, yet lonely and hurting...so much pain."

Dale lost all sense. Crushing her against him, he fisted a hand into her hair and kissed her hard. She responded back with a moan, her tongue tangling with his.

And then she began to struggle and nipped him on his lip, hard enough to draw blood. Dale jerked away in shock.

His mind fogged. Closing his eyes, Dale fell into a dizzying vortex. When he opened his eyes, the woman had vanished into the shadows, making him wonder if she wasn't a dream.

Or his worst nightmare.

BONNIE VANAK

fell in love with romance novels during childhood. After years of newspaper reporting, Bonnie became a writer for a major international charity, which has taken her to destitute countries to write about issues affecting the poor. When the emotional strain of her job demanded a diversion, she turned to writing romance novels. Bonnie lives in Florida with her husband and two dogs, and happily writes books amid an ever-growing population of dust bunnies. She loves to hear from readers. Visit her website, www.bonnievanak.com, or email her at bonnievanak@aol.com.

DEMON WOLF

—

BONNIE VANAK

Recycling programs
for this product may
not exist in your area.

ISBN-13: 978-0-373-88597-8

DEMON WOLF

Copyright © 2014 by Bonnie Vanak

H HARLEQUIN®
™ www.Harlequin.com

Printed in U.S.A.

Dear Reader,

Can a woman cursed with the darkness of demons ever find true love and happiness?

This was the question spinning through my mind after I finished writing *Phantom Wolf*. There's a scene in *Phantom* where Lt. Commander Dale "Curt" Curtis is tortured by a large black wolf who turns out to be a woman forced to do so by the demons who've enslaved her. After I wrote that scene, I knew I had to write Dale and Keira's love story.

Keira has been cursed by Centurion demons, who force her to torture good, brave men so the demons can steal their essence and become stronger. She's lived with darkness for so long that she is desperate to find any little bit of light so she doesn't lose her soul.

Dale Curtis is strong, brave and honorable. He's as pragmatic and disciplined as Keira is dreamy and hopeful. When he reluctantly hires her to help him recover from the terrible torture in the basement, he doesn't know of their shared past.

They must now join forces before an even greater evil is unleashed. Love and trust won't come easily to these two.

Happy reading!

Bonnie Vanak

To Robyn Lees. Strong, courageous and spunky,
you fought the good fight to the end and inspired us all.
You'll live forever in our hearts.

Prologue

Nicaragua, 1990

The Contra war was over, except no one had told these guys.

The crack of bullets and rattle of machine-gun fire echoed through the mountains of northern Nicaragua. Lieutenant Junior Grade Dale "Curt" Curtis crouched down behind a scarred oak tree and signaled to his men to wait. Heavy green and black greasepaint disguised their faces and the green camouflage uniforms blended in with the surrounding scrub.

Intel said nothing about fighting in this region. Could be a local turf war, but the sounds of that artillery to his seasoned ears warned this was a heavier engagement. Dale pulled his boonie hat low, scanned the terrain and cursed the godforsaken ass who'd assured them this area was safe to cross. But they were SEALs and accustomed to shifting gears.

He and his team of six operators had finished a successful op near the border. Now Dale had to figure out how the hell to get his men out of what was supposed to be uninhabited, safe terrain.

Motioning to his men to stay back, Dale crept through the jungle, making no noise. Four of his operators were norms. Then there was himself, a Primary Elemental Mage whose powers could blast through this jungle like a fire-bomb. And Etienne "Wolf" Robichaux, a Cajun from Louisiana, who was also a Draicon werewolf. Like him, Etienne used his powers sparingly around others.

The sickeningly sweet stench of decay assaulted his senses. Dale belly-crawled up a small rise, to a ravine and peered over. Revulsion and horror punched him.

Flies buzzed around a dozen naked bodies lying atop each other amid the dirt, grass and leaves. Women. Men. His stomach threatened to spill out the MRE he'd eaten.

In his five years as a navy SEAL, he'd seen his share of horrors. But this… The way the little group clung to each other, as if providing comfort in their last terrified moments, made him sick with anger.

A small whimper caught his attention. Dale raised his weapon and crawled down.

A black puppy, barely alive, hidden by the corpses. Dale's throat tightened. The little guy hadn't wanted to leave his mistress.

Or maybe it wasn't a dog. He called for Wolf on the radio. When Etienne arrived, the werewolf studied the dog, his eyes furious.

"It's a wolf, sir. Not a dog."

Stunned, Dale glanced at the corpses. "Your people?"

"Not Draicon. Our young don't shift until they reach puberty. I've never seen this species before."

Like Mages, there were different classes of werewolves.

"Who are they?"

"I don't know." Etienne wiped a trickle of sweat from his face, smearing the green and black greasepaint. "These carry a deeper, richer scent."

"This place smells of darkness. No wonder the intel was screwed up."

The sounds of battle ceased. Dale glanced around and made a decision. "Take the pup, head west and lead the men out of here. Use that nose of yours and flush out the smells of gunpowder, avoid the fighting at all costs."

"Curt..."

"It's not human. Whoever did this isn't human."

Etienne's jaw tightened. "All the more reason for me to stay with you, sir."

"I'm right behind you. I'm not leaving this area for some naive civilian to stumble into and get killed."

"If you ward it with magick, you'll drain your powers," Etienne warned.

Dale gave a cold smile. "You have no idea of the extent of my powers. Now go."

As soon as his men had passed, Dale lifted his hands, closed his eyes and began a low chant. The magick shield would prevent humans from entering the area, and save them from meeting the same fate as the wolves.

Slightly drained, he opened his eyes, and turned to leave. A low growl rumbled behind him.

The wolf was as large as a small Shetland pony. Sleek black fur stood on edge. Dale remained motionless, his gaze never leaving the creature.

Not even when the wolf opened its mouth, showing fangs as sharp as dinner knives....

Her world had shattered. Nothing mattered anymore. Her parents, her pack, they were all dead.

Simon, her little brother, whom the demons promised to spare in exchange for her slavery to them...dead, as well. The demons had lied.

She was only eleven, but already experienced in her powers as wolf. In wolf form, Keira stumbled through the undergrowth. Rage and anguish blinded her to everything. Soon the demons would return and force her to do their bidding.

Magick skimmed her fur, pinged off her muzzle. Light, good magick. She shook her head and growled and loped toward the source.

A tall man lifted his hands to the sky and chanted. He was clad in uniform, his face disguised, and the metallic scent of weaponry clung to him. Rage engulfed her. How dare he violate her people's final resting ground?

Blinded to everything except the red haze to hurt as she hurt, she stalked forward and growled.

The man fingered the gray metal weapon and she charged.

Knocking him down, she leaped on him and raked a sharp claw over his arm. But the man made no move to fire the weapon.

Confused, she backed off, watching warily as he stood. Their gazes met and she felt an odd connection, as if this powerful man of magick understood.

He regarded her quietly, sadness in his gray eyes. "I won't hurt you. I will not return evil for evil, for whatever was done to your people is making you react."

A giggle sounded nearby. Keira tilted her head, fear curling in her stomach. The demons were returning for her. Pure evil had infiltrated the region and it would never die. But this man who'd refused to hurt back, he was good. She sensed it.

She lowered her head, pawed at the ground and hit him with her muzzle, urging him to leave. The man's mouth narrowed.

"I won't leave you here alone."

Keira growled and head-butted him again. The man seemed torn, and glanced toward the west. She knew if the demons found him here, they'd enslave him, as well. He must not remember her, or he'd return. She sensed it.

So she bit him. He yelled and looked down at the wound, blood trickling with her saliva, saliva that carried the memory spell the demons infused into her. By the time he looked up, she was gone, fleeing into the forest toward her captors, vanishing from the man's sight and memory.

Giving him time to escape to safety.

While she charged forward straight into hell.

Chapter 1

If he discovered her true identity, the powerful Mage would kill her.

From across the bar, Keira Solomon studied her quarry. The glass of white wine gripped in her trembling hand rattled against the polished wood counter. She ignored the flirting drunk to her right and riveted her gaze to Lt. Commander Dale Curtis.

The navy SEAL commander of Team 21 sat by himself, his expression as lonely as she felt. Keira's heart went out to him, knowing she was the reason for his turmoil.

Careful, she warned herself. *If you let him get under your skin, you're a dead woman.* She concentrated on the man instead of her feelings, gauging how to approach him.

Though he looked no more than thirty-eight, the Mage was hundreds of years old. The commander had taut, angular cheekbones, a chin carved from granite, tempered by a full, wide mouth. His thick black hair, silvered at the temples, did not touch his starched collar. He looked like a powerful man of strong character, unaccustomed to compromise. But his most striking feature was his piercing gray eyes, shaded by thick, dark brows. Those eyes could become hard and unyielding, coaxing a confession out of the most tight-lipped prisoner, or turn seductive with promise, charming a woman into his bed.

She'd discovered all this about the man from listening to gossip in public haunts like this bar.

A severe khaki uniform hid a body firm with muscle that was now layered with deep scars. Keira knew the depth and width of each mark, knew how he'd endured, tight-lipped, as each one lashed his skin. And she knew the depth of his screams when the agony she inflicted became too much to bear when the Centurion demons forced her to hurt him.

No other man had survived such torture. Past victims had died from the force of her claws. Centurion demons had enslaved her to torture others. Now she had a rare chance to break free, because the man she'd tortured was strong enough to vanquish the demons for eternity.

"Hey, sweetie." Obviously determined to get her attention, the big, barrel-chested drunk put a paw on her arm. "Lemme buy you another drink."

Giving him a look of utter disdain, she pushed her glass aside. "No, thanks. I don't accept favors from gorillas."

The man narrowed his eyes as his companions chortled with laughter. "Ain't no ape."

"Okay, then. Chimp shifter." She gave him a singularly sweet smile. "I can't quite tell, but you all smell the same."

"Bitch." The shifter scowled. "I should drag you out to the parking lot, show you the meaning of respect. Flat on your back, your legs spread."

Demon blood surged. Keira held up a hand. Like flicking a switchblade, her claws emerged, each a razor-sharp talon. Ape Boy's eyes widened as she gouged the bar's surface. "Care to try?"

The men pushed away from the bar and fled. She sighed.

"I hate having to do that," she muttered to no one.

One day, she wouldn't have to worry about the demon

blood inside her. The key to her freedom lingered temptingly close, but it wouldn't be easy to fool him. Curtis's piercing gray eyes could see straight inside her, and discover who she really was.

And if that happened, no point fearing the demons capturing and enslaving her once more.

Because Curtis would have at her first.

Ladies' night at the paranormal Dive Bar.

Once a month, Tom dropped the magick shield blinding humans to the bar's presence. He announced two-for-one drinks and the human women streamed inside as if he'd offered marriage proposals to millionaires.

The custom was for regulars, who liked human women warming their beds once in a while. Tom's bar was a short distance from Little Creek, home to SEAL Team 21's elite Phoenix Force in Virginia. When in town, the secret force of paranormal SEALs crowded the seats.

Dale ignored the chatter around him. He sipped his beer, waited for his burger.

Scar tissue pulled and stretched uncomfortably, reminding him of a body no woman wanted to see naked. While in the hospital, his sometime girlfriend had visited. Melissa had taken one look at the blood and bandages and left.

No Mage female wanted him. No human, either, even if she didn't sense he was a powerful Primary Elemental Mage who could fry her to ashes with a single flick of his finger.

Dale knew he was better off alone.

"You okay, Commander?"

Tom always called him by his title. Dale nodded. It had been the ultimate bitch of a day, back at work only ten days after two long months of mandatory medical leave. Paperwork piled to his nose, submerged in long meetings, most of his team deployed to dispatch a last-minute threat overseas. Only Ensign Grant "Sully" Sullivan remained at base. Chief Petty Officer Sam "Shay" Shaymore was in North Carolina, training in close-quarters combat with SEAL norms—human navy SEALs. He'd taken his new wife with him.

Dale relaxed into a smile as he thought of the much younger Shay. Last month the SEAL had married his girlfriend. Dale had proudly escorted the fatherless Kelly down the aisle. A wedding he'd never forget, as he was glad to see the two Mages declare their love in a lifelong bond. Those two had rescued him from the dark, dank basement where he had only memories of pain and blood.

And the scent of a woman...he could never forget.

Across the bar, Sully flirted with a pretty, slightly tipsy blonde. The woman rested her hand on the SEAL's arm, giving him a suggestive look. Someone was getting something-something tonight.

Dale hoped Sully remembered to glove before love. A half-human bastard faced a lot of hardship in the real world.

Children. Setting down his beer, he closed his eyes. One regret he'd had in his eleven-year marriage. Kathy hadn't wanted any. The Mage had used one excuse after another and finally, she just left, but not before admitting she'd been sleeping in another man's bed.

You're a good man, Dale. But you're never around, not when I really need you.

Deep inside, he still craved a home life, a wife and a family. But what woman would want him now, his body looking like a road map to hell?

Someday, maybe, he'd find someone else. But first, he'd find the demon wolf responsible for scarring his body and when he did, that shape-shifter would pay. Such evil must be eradicated before innocents got hurt. Dale would do so gladly, sending the SOB straight to hell.

Tom slid a steaming burger, with fries piled high, before him. "Here you go, Commander. My treat."

"Thanks, Tom," Dale said, surprised.

"No, thank you, sir. If not for you…" Emotion shadowed the man's face. "What you did to free those kids, sacrificing yourself, hell, we're all grateful to you. I've got five kids and the thought of them enduring what you did…"

The cougar shifter's spine stiffened. "I'm proud to call you a friend. You're more than a SEAL. You're a damn fine officer and gentleman."

Holy hellfire, the man actually saluted him. Uncomfortable with the praise, Dale nodded. "No thanks necessary."

A few of the bar's regulars studied him like a moth pinned to a corkboard. Damn, all he wanted was a burger, not this scrutiny. Dale began to eat.

The brunette next to him spoke. "Come here often?"

Once in a while, against the ladies' room wall, pushing deep and hard, a woman's long legs wrapped around his thrusting hips. Dale nodded.

She gave a sultry smile, red lips moist and pursed. The tight blue dress clung to a body that had caught quite a few glances from the bar's male occupants.

"You're a SEAL."

Wonderful. Human frog hog. He swallowed a bite, shrugged.

"My second cousin's best friend is a navy SEAL." Now she slid over, her long red nails on his forearm. "I adore you guys. I can't thank you enough for what you do for our country, to keep us safe. You're so brave and strong, and I'd love to demonstrate my appreciation."

Hollow words, spoken by a woman who just wanted to bang a SEAL. Maybe one time he'd accept her offer, follow her home and show her the alternative meaning of *hooyah*. Not tonight. Tonight he felt every single one of his 420 years.

The woman's nose wrinkled as she studied his right arm. Dale automatically moved to hide the jagged gash. "That's a nasty scar. Did you get it in combat?"

No, I got it, and a rash of others, when I was tied up in a basement and tortured by a wolf's claws. Care to know more?

Appetite turned to dust, Dale slid his plate back. "Thanks, Tom."

Clear disappointment showed on the woman's face as he pushed back his stool. She turned to her right, engaged a member of ST 21's support staff, the vampire enthralled with the woman's long neck.

Nice night for a quick bite, Dale thought in sour amusement. Like every human here, she would recall only a pleasurable buzz the next day, assume it was alcohol-induced.

As he went to leave, a familiar scent hit him. Not the floral perfume of the human women, nor the heavy cologne of the males pursuing them. Something deeper, richer, more fragrant.

It reminded him of crushed autumn leaves, the burning richness of smoke on a hearth, the musky scent of pure…sex.

Dale whipped his head up, a memory pinging.

Her.

There, across the bar. An ebony-haired woman, a wineglass before her. Eyes blazing with fire and life glanced up. His gaze fell to her right hand.

Each finger was a sharp black talon.

Shock slammed into him. And pain. Distant memories… knives over raw flesh, biting back the screams that rose in his throat. Salt water dripping onto the fresh gouges, searing his skin with her tears.

He'd been tortured and left for dead, and recalled only flashes of memory. But that scent, it wound around him in an erotic ribbon, and pulled tight. His body hardened, blood pulsing to his groin.

Bleeding from a thousand cuts, the pain so deep he couldn't breathe, and that scent filtering through the agony, turning his cock to steel. Forgetting the pain, wanting nothing more than to roll her beneath him, spread her wide and drive hard into her soft, wet flesh.

He hadn't been merely tortured, but humiliated and debased, getting turned on, and then feeling something raking cold claws over his warm flesh....

This woman had something to do with those long, dark hours in the basement.

Dale went preternaturally still. The woman stared at him, wide red mouth parted in apparent shock. Then she slipped off the stool and fled.

Not so fast, he thought grimly. Dale raced after her. In the parking lot, against a parked SUV he caught her. Dale grabbed her arms, pinned her against the vehicle. The scent faded, leaving only the exotic smell of expensive perfume. But he hadn't imagined it. Wasn't going crazy.

"Who the hell are you?" he roughly demanded.

Fear clouded her gaze. "Not hurt, not hurt," she whimpered.

Gentling his voice, he loosened his grip. "Who are you? I remember only darkness, pain and your scent."

The woman wriggled away, lifted a hand to his face. The velvet of her voice stroked across his senses. Sexual energy jumped between them at the mere brush of her fingers. "Strong and courageous is your heart, yet lonely and hurting…so much pain."

Dale lost all sense. He lowered his head and did what he'd lusted to do all those long, anguished hours in the dark after he'd been turned into a pitiful, whimpering shell of a man.

Crushing her against him, he fisted a hand into her hair

and kissed her hard. She responded back with a moan, her tongue tangling with his in a fury of erotic heat.

And then she began to struggle and nipped him on his lip, hard enough to draw blood. Dale jerked away in shock. Son of a...

His mind fogged. Closing his eyes, he fell into a dizzying vortex, where memory was once more a clouded dream. When he opened his eyes, he was alone.

The woman, if there had been a woman, vanished into the shadows. Just like before, he could not recall her, making him wonder if she were a dream.

Or his worst nightmare.

Chapter 2

The moon hung like a silver nickel in the sky.

Hovering in the woods, Keira waited for Dale to arrive home the next night.

Other houses on the street showed signs of life. Lights flicked on. Children ran around their backyards, and then ran inside as their mothers called them in for supper.

Or their mothers threatened to zap them inside. It was a paranormal neighborhood, after all.

Hiding in the shadows, she felt a pinch of deep melancholy. She'd adjusted to loneliness during the infrequent intervals when the demons gave her brief freedom so she could find new men for them to torture. Keira had beaten the demons. She'd refused to associate with anyone, refused to give them new victims, but stalled them by promising them new ones.

They found one on their own. This last time had sliced off a piece of her heart. Dale Curtis had taken her spirit and turned it inside out. She'd almost killed him. And then, a miracle happened.

The commander's friend had arrived in the house where Curtis was being held prisoner and chanted a cleansing spell to vanquish evil. The spell had sent the demons temporarily to the netherworld and freed her, as well. But in a few weeks, as they always did, the Centurions would use their bolt-hole to this world and break back in.

Then the real fun would start. They would find her, find Curtis and force her to torture the SEAL once more, maybe until he died. The demons would steal all his strength and courage and become solid entities, able to taste the pleasures of the flesh once more.

Keira touched the valise containing the silver armband, which enslaved her to the Centurions. When the demons had vanished unexpectedly, the bracelet unlocked, freeing her from their spell. Only by enslaving herself to another could she escape them.

And Lt. Commander Dale Curtis was the only living person with enough power and courage to destroy the Centurions. She had to overcome her personal fear of seeing him again if she wanted to achieve her goal.

For twenty-three years she'd lived under the demons' control. No more. Emotion clogged her throat. Dale Curtis looked thin and haggard. The demons had sapped his strength, his vitality. If she didn't help him recover soon he'd weaken and die.

She needed him strong, needed his resources to find and destroy the demons' bolt-hole and imprison them forever in the netherworld.

Crouching down, Keira watched the commander's house. Beneath the light of the nearly full moon, she waited hopefully, and wondered if this brave man would be the one to kill her captors and finally set her free.

Another day of keeping the world free of paranormal terrors. At least free of the terror of paperwork.

Hell, he was so tired, he could barely function. Dale looked forward to a cold beer, a quick sandwich, a little light reading and then crashing. It was a lonely life, but right now, he preferred it that way. No complications or interference.

Yet as he drove home from the ST 21 compound on the base, Dale imagined a loving woman greeting him at the day's end. Someone who rushed to the door, eyes lighting up as he walked inside, the good smell of a delicious dinner cooking in the oven.

Instead of always coming home to an empty, silent house.

Dale snorted. He cherished his privacy. He didn't need a woman in his home, rearranging his life, turning things upside down.

Especially now, he needed to be alone to recharge and recover.

As he turned onto his street, he saw a white Lincoln parked in his driveway. He parked next to it, cut the truck's engine. His front door was locked. Once inside, he tossed his keys into the antique candy dish on the hallway table and relocked the door.

Someone was home to greet him, after all.

A light glowed down the hall. Mage instincts went on alert. He narrowed his eyes, took a deep breath and headed into his study.

"Nice of you to break in," he told the gray-haired man sitting in shadow.

"You're late."

Vice Admiral Keegan Byrne, pillar of support for SEAL Team 21 and a powerful Primary Mage, toasted him with a whiskey glass filled with amber liquid. Dale glanced at the built-in wood bar against the wall. The bottle of twenty-year-old smooth Scotch malt had been full until tonight.

"Had to finish up paperwork. I'm not asking how you gained access to my home without permission."

"You need a better security system, Dale. An infant could bypass that alarm."

"An infant armed with electromagnetic current. Did you fry the panel again?"

Byrne grinned. Dale sighed. Another visit from the electrician.

"Help yourself to more Scotch. Just don't take my beer."

Running upstairs in a light jog, he headed to his bedroom, removed the trident, the fruit salad and the insignias from his khaki shirt. Then he stripped and tossed the uniform and undershirt into a white wicker hamper. As he walked toward the closet, the dresser mirror showed the image he'd tried to avoid.

Dale approached, staring at his body for the first time in two months.

Reddened scar tissue raked over his chest, muscled torso, arms and long legs. Razor-sharp claw marks began just below his throat, continued down his belly, ending at his groin, and dwindled out at his thighs and calves.

A remembrance of white-hot pain surged through him. Dale braced his hands on the dresser, hissing through his teeth.

Jerking open a drawer, he sorted through folded shirts and found an old, frayed Virginia Tech T-shirt. Another drawer held gray fleece pants.

When he returned to the study, Byrne remained motionless, the glass of Scotch untouched. He steeled himself. If the old man wasn't here to socialize, it meant one thing. But he'd let the admiral set the pace.

Dale fished a beer from the minifridge, tossed the cap into the trash and took a seat in front of the fireplace. He knew Byrne would take his time.

Finally Dale gave him a pointed look. "Why are you here?"

"Have you used your powers since leaving the hospital?"

Stretching out a hand, he summoned the current simmering inside. Dale flung it at the fireplace, igniting the logs. "Happy now?"

Understanding and something deeper, and wiser, filled Byrne's gaze. "I wasn't talking about toasting marshmallows, Dale. I meant on assignment."

Surprised, he sipped his beer. "I joined my men on that op to extract Dakota and Kelly. I'm a paper pusher now, not an operator."

"Maybe it's time you took off with your boys, joined a mission to evaluate their tactics and skills in the field. Spend quality time, jaw with them, get to know them again."

Suspicion filled him. "What's the deal, Keegan? You lost faith in me ever since I got carved like a Thanksgiving turkey?"

Silence.

Anger slowly rose. "That's it, isn't it? You think if I were deployed more, I'd have fried my attackers' asses? Never mind the nine innocent children's lives at stake. You think I wasn't strong enough to beat the demons."

"Were you?"

Dale set down the beer, his hands shaking. "Screw you, Keegan."

"I'll leave that for the wife." The admiral set down his barely touched glass. "Dale, we've known each other for a long time and I have to say this. I'm concerned about you, son."

He hissed out a breath. "I'm not your son. I'm CO of the finest SEAL team in the United States Navy and a 420-year-old Mage."

"And I have enough years to make you look like a baby sucking on his momma's tit. Dale, you're losing touch. I've had reports of you being distracted, short-tempered and restless. I don't know if it's a residual effect of what happened to you in that basement, or something else."

"Reports from whom?"

"Your team."

"Renegade? A sulky SEAL denied leave because Shay was on his honeymoon and I couldn't afford another man out?"

"No," Bryne said. "All of them. The entire team. Even Robyn Lees, the new ensign who thinks you can do no wrong."

Dale sat back, trying to hide his shock. "Nice of them to tell me."

"They're worried about you. You've changed."

Almost afraid to ask, he groped for his lost composure. "You said it was my time in the basement or something else that's affected me. What's the something else you think is wrong?"

"A woman."

Dale raked a hand through his short, dark hair and laughed. "No woman's gotten to me." Or would want him, the way he looked. "I'm trying to catch up after being out so long. I had a difficult time healing in the hospital."

"You were almost dead when Shay and Kelly found you."

Temper rising, Dale straightened up. "Are you lecturing me on how I should have been smarter, knowing the waiting children were a trap? Maybe you should shake the demon's hand, pin a medal on his chest for catching me off guard."

Admiral Byrne gave him a long, level look. "If I found the son of a bitch who did this to you, I'd tear him apart with my bare hands. And then toss him to your team to deal with the remains."

The quiet—but strong— statement made Dale sit back.

"The boys worship you, Dale. They don't want another commander. They need you, but they're reluctant to say anything to your face because lately, you've been difficult to talk to. You're a damn good leader, a smart operator, a fine Mage and a close friend. So I'm saying it for them."

Byrne leaned forward, hands on his knees. "Get your shit straightened out, Dale. Get help from a private psychiatrist or a navy one. Or I'll assign a mind-melder to you."

Holy hellfire. A mind-melder, diving into his deepest memories, turning him into a whimpering mess when he barely managed to hold it together now? He didn't trust the shrinks, either.

"I don't need a witch doctor," he said, taking a long pull of beer, ignoring Byrne's scrutinizing look.

"You're too thin and haggard. Take a vacation, go see some sights…get laid and then come back and get help."

Nearly spitting out his sip of beer, he sputtered. "You came all the way from D.C. to tell me to have sex?"

A faint memory surfaced. Sitting in Tom's bar, a beautiful, mysterious woman staring at him. The memory became fog on glass. Damn it.

Lazily swirling the amber liquid, Byrne snorted. "Sure as hell didn't come here for this. Damn, twenty-year-old Scotch doesn't taste the same when you're 1,500 years old."

Then the admiral gave him one of his paternal, but knowing, looks. "What happened in the basement, Dale? You never talked about it. Who was that woman found with you, the wolf who vanished?"

Emotion squeezed his throat. He sucked in a deep breath. Byrne was right. He had changed, and denied it. His men deserved better. For two months, he'd hidden the truth, refusing to talk about what the demons had done to him.

"I don't remember. Everything's a blur. All I remember are smells and pain. The smell of a Roman orgy, this delicate, delicious female scent…and waking up to see Shay and Kelly standing over me."

And screams tearing from his throat, until he'd fallen unconscious.

"The Roman orgy was the Centurion demons who tied you up to torture you. Shay banished them with a spell. But the woman found with you, you don't recall her face? Or a black wolf?"

Dale shook his head, the knot in his stomach tightening. "She must be the demon wolf that tortured me. When I find her, she'll pay. She'll lead me to the others and I'll send them all back to hell."

"Remembering would help, but sounds like they infused you with a classic demon memory spell. Clouds the victim's brain in case he survives, he can't recall specific details." Byrne's expression sharpened. "So the demons can come at you again, and catch you off guard."

Right. Like I'd ever let that happen again. "I don't need you to watch my six. I'm not rushing headfirst into a sitch without knowing all the intel. Got it?"

Byrne's look remained steady. "I'm not watching your six anymore, my friend. But I am serious. Get help this week or I'm placing you on mandatory medical leave for another two months and it's going in your record that you're mentally unstable. Your team needs you."

The barbed wire knotted tighter in his stomach. Dale squeezed his beer bottle and felt it crack beneath his palm. He set it down, trying to regain his composure. Couldn't let Byrne see how rattled he truly was. He didn't trust him anymore.

Hell, he trusted no one. Not even himself.

The doorbell rang. He glanced at Byrne. "What is this? Another well-meaning friend?"

"Maybe a home invader," the admiral suggested.

Dale headed down the hallway. The double doors were warded with magick, but anything could be lurking outside. A Girl Scout selling cookies or a demon. Or a very human home invader.

After what happened two months ago, he never took chances.

Gathering his powers, he felt the current hum through his body. And pulled open the door

Not a Girl Scout or a demon, but a petite, ebony-haired woman clad entirely in black leather, except for a powder-blue T-shirt with some kind of business logo.

Chaos.

He gave an appreciative visual sweep of his visitor. Very curvy, with long, curly hair spilling down to her waist. She had a delicate, innocent face. Wide, full lips pulled down slightly at the corners, giving her mouth a cute pout. She looked no more than eighteen.

But deep in her green eyes swirled ancient knowledge, and a weariness he'd seen in the mirror these past two months.

Parked beneath a streetlamp was a motorcycle with a very flat tire.

The girl pushed back a lock of hair. "I'm sorry to disturb you, but do you happen to have an air pump? I've got a flat."

Neither the statement nor the soft, pleading words stopped him. It was the look of faint despair in those lovely, but sorrowful, sea-green eyes.

Dale glanced over his shoulder as the admiral strolled down the hallway. "She doesn't look like a home invader."

The girl glanced at the very intrigued and curious Admiral Byrne. Panic flared in her gaze and then her expression smoothed out. She ignored the admiral and stuck out her palm to Dale.

"I'm not. My name's Keira Solomon. I was visiting one of your neighbors two blocks away and my bike went kaput on your street."

He took her hand and shook it. Memories tugged…the fog temporarily lifting. Pain, so much pain, agony in each muscle, pulling off bone, shredded flesh…and a large black wolf panting in the corner, sorrow flaring in her green eyes, a long, low howl echoing his screams…

The memory died, leaving him grappling for it like a sleeper groping for wisps of a dream. Keegan looked at him, laid a hand on his shoulder.

"Dale? You okay?"

"Fine." He shook off his hand.

The admiral gave him a thoughtful look. "Have to get home. The wife is expecting me."

The woman politely stepped aside to let him pass. Suddenly he pushed her against the wall, his palm splayed over her forehead. Eyes opened wide, she stared at Byrne.

Dale remained motionless, watching with interest. The old man hadn't done a mind-meld in years.

When he pulled away two minutes later, the admiral didn't look worried or pleased. Just thoughtful. He glanced at Dale.

"She's a paranorm. Trust her." Something very old and sorrowful flickered in the other man's gaze. "She'll do you more good than you'll ever anticipate. You both need each other."

Keira's wide mouth wobbled precariously. Seeming to gather her composure, she shot the admiral a scathing look as he pushed past her and went down the steps to his car.

Turning to Dale she asked, "Do you have an air pump? Because it's getting late and I need to hit the road. If you can't help me, I'll knock on someone else's door."

The knight in rusty armor, he thought. *Can't help you with anything simpler than an air pump.* "Come with me."

He walked to the garage, where he opened a cabinet door and retrieved the pump and a can of instant flat-tire repair. Keira studied his garage. "Very organized. Everything labeled. Military man. I bet you're the type who irons your underwear and folds it neatly in the drawer."

He shot her a look, but she smiled at him, mischief dancing in her green eyes. That look turned him upside down. No one had dared to tease him in a long time.

As they walked back onto the street to her bike, and he set about fixing her flat, she plopped down on the pavement beside him. "I know this is a paranormal neighborhood. I'm a Luminaire."

Dale plugged the flat and reached for the air pump. "Witch doctor."

Keira laughed. "That's what some call me. I'm a psi therapist who helps paranorms restore their energy balance. Perfectly legit. Your neighbor, Mrs. Henderson, asked me to cleanse her home. Had a little issue with dark energy. And you are…?"

Although the admiral vetted her, Dale still didn't trust the girl. She looked like a pixie with her wide eyes and petite body, but pixies could be trouble.

"Dale Curtis. Don't know what you're talking about." He filled the tire and checked the pressure. Perfect.

She gave him a knowing look. "You should. I can feel the power emanating from you. I know you're a Mage, but can't tell what type. I have power, as well. I'll show you mine if you show me yours."

Her teasing, melodious voice almost coaxed a smile from him. Damn, how long had it been since he'd flirted with a pretty woman?

"You first," he told her.

Uncurling her fist, she displayed a tiny ball of white energy. The ball danced in the air and then slowly drifted upward, exploding into a shower of silver sparks. Dale went still. He hadn't shown his powers to anyone but Keegan in a long time. Truth was, his powers had gone south since the demons kicked his ass. No telekinesis. All he could do was shift into a wolf and toss a current of power strong enough only to light dry kindling.

"Not bad."

He focused all his energy and summoned a large ball of energy, which danced in his open palm. Bouncing it like a baseball, he sent it drifting upward, and it exploded in a much larger shower of sparks. Blood drained from her face, but she stood her ground.

"Yours is bigger than mine."

Dale's mouth quirked at the joke.

"You're a Mage—what kind?" she asked.

"Primary Elemental."

"Very powerful. But your aura is pulsing with dark energy. You need deep cleansing." She studied her hands. "Speaking of cleansing, may I wash up? I took a bit of a spill back there."

Mistrust flickered inside him, but he stood and nodded. She was such a tiny sprite, what harm could she do? Still, he took her hand and turned it over, his hand practically swallowing hers. Dale felt no darkness or negativity flaring from her, only a deeper, sexual spark igniting between them. Curious, he circled the scrape on her palm.

"You hurt yourself," he murmured. "Come inside, and I'll find antiseptic."

He picked up the air pump and can, put them back in the garage and let her into the house through the laundry room. Dale fished out a brown bottle of peroxide and bandages from a white cabinet. Keira winced slightly as he ran warm water over her hand, then treated it with peroxide.

"You're very good with your hands, but wow, the dark energy I feel from you, it's not you. Not normally you."

Dale glanced at her as he finished bandaging her hand.

"I use psi therapy, light and massage techniques to eradicate negative energy. High-frequency healing energy, using the natural elements. Harmonic meditation to calm the mind and soothe the spirit."

"Natural elements?"

"The power of the sun, wind, earth, even fire."

"I don't believe in any of that 'woo-woo' stuff." He replaced the bottle of peroxide.

"Of course. Because even though you're a Mage, you're very much a military man who believes in what he can see. You're a natural leader, a colonel or a captain. No, not army, not with the navy base so close." Keira wiggled her bandaged fingers. "Thanks."

His gaze narrowed. "Lieutenant commander. How did you know?"

"Simple deduction. The flag out front, this is a military neighborhood, although a paranormal one, and..."

Silently, she pointed to the uniforms hanging on the door, still covered with dry-cleaning plastic. "I'm really quite psychic. I have ESPN."

As she winked at him, Dale cracked a reluctant smile.

"Seriously, I can tell you need cleansing. You've been in contact with some pretty nasty demons."

His smile dropped. He gestured to the mounds of dirty laundry piled high in the overflowing hamper. "That's the cleansing I need. My housekeeper quit."

Sally had quit with the excuse to move closer to her grandchildren. They both knew the truth. Dale's nightly screams had fractured her nerves.

She traced a pattern in the air. "There's thick tendrils of blackness in your aura, blackness pulsing with the other colors."

"What other colors?" He didn't believe in Luminaires, but he knew about auras.

"Deep red, indicating you're a strong-willed and realistic person and a bright, vibrant red that says you're a powerful and extremely competitive individual."

"Bright, vibrant red also means someone who's very sexual," he said, enjoying the hint of pink spreading across her cheeks.

"Yes, that, too. And you have other colors as well, but they're so obscured by the blackness, I can't tell them apart. You've come into contact with great evil, evil that touched you deeply."

This was too close for his comfort zone. He folded his arms across his chest.

"Hire me and I'll give you a big discount. Only three thousand dollars in cash."

"That's all?" he asked drily.

Keira shrugged. "Work is slow right now."

"And what do I get from you for three thousand dollars?" He pushed close to her, getting in her face, crowding her. "And for how long do I get it?"

His brazen, suggestive words brought an attractive flush to her face. To her credit, Keira refused to back off or drop her gaze. "You get me, for however long you need me. A week. Or a month, or more, if you desire. I need a place to stay while I'm in the area."

Dale caught a faint whiff of an enticing scent that wound around his body and yanked hard. Oh, yeah…he desired. His body tightened, blood running hot and thick.

Their gazes met, connected. Something long dead inside him stirred to life. He reached out and with calloused fingers, touched her cheek.

Keira's eyes widened and darkened. Her lush mouth trembled.

Just as suddenly the connection broke. Dale stepped back.

"And why are you in the area?"

"I travel a lot across country. Never been to Virginia before. I like the beach."

She looked innocent. Guileless.

"What exactly are we talking about? What methods?"

"I combine aromatherapy massage and meditation with crystals to restore harmonic energy and fight evil. Light therapy, massage and reflexology." At his questioning look, she added, "I work with your feet on certain pressure points."

"Interesting," he murmured. He liked the idea of the massages. Maybe this could prove to be worth his time. How long had it been since a woman had grabbed his interest?

"I'll need you to sign a contract, of course. To protect us both," she said. Her gaze whipped around the house, so fast he could almost see her mind recalculating like a GPS. It was fascinating and disturbing, because he knew she was pushing him hard to go where he didn't want to venture.

Hiring Keira would get Keegan off his back. Keegan already voiced his approval of her. She was better than a navy shrink and ten times safer than a damn mind-melder. And much sexier. The surge of sexual interest flared again.

But he'd be damned if he let her try any of her woo-woo techniques. She could clean the house instead, cook his meals.

"I need a live-in housekeeper. You'd have your own room downstairs by the kitchen and I'll pay you the three thousand and you stay for the month. Come back tomorrow at oh-five-hundred with your contract before I leave for the base."

A tentative smile. "You sure?"

The hesitant words contrasted sharply with her earlier confidence. She almost sounded like a child hopeful for acceptance. Dale's curiosity was piqued.

He gave a rueful glance at his feet. "I'm not into all that New Age crap, but my feet could use some pampering."

"It's not massage. It's a technique to free the energy."

"You're not going to nibble at my toes? Damn."

Her mouth wobbled in a tentative smile. Dale chuckled, the sound rusty and grating. Hell, had it been that long since he laughed? "I'm teasing you. I'm not into having my toes nibbled."

At her widening smile, he added, "There are exceptions, if the mouth happens to be wide, and lush...and a tad crooked."

The most intriguing blush ignited her cheeks. Keira put her hands to her reddened cheeks as that lovely, wide and crooked mouth parted. "Oh five-hundred sharp. I'll be here. I'll even treat you to coffee."

She leaped down the steps, marched to her motorbike and with a kick start it coughed to life, and she took off into the night.

For a few moments Dale stood in the doorway, staring after her, feeling something tighten in his chest.

He shut the door and called his neighbor to see if Keira's story was true. After talking a few minutes, he hung up and then dialed Keegan's number. "Spill it. Tell me what you saw in her mind."

"Dale, it's late...."

"Tell me."

"I couldn't get a fix on her memories and who she is, but I'll say this, you need her. Trust me on this. Do yourself a favor. Let go and don't question, just go with your gut."

Right. Last time he did that, his guts almost ended up spilling out on the table where he'd been tortured. Damn, he hated coyness.

"Keegan...level with me."

"Already have, son. Find yourself help and get straightened out. I don't give a damn who straightens you out, as long as it's done. Hire a witch doctor if you must."

"Already did." He told the admiral about Keira. "You satisfied now? You'll get off my back?"

"You're doing the right thing, Dale."

He snorted. "We'll see. I don't believe in any of that woo-woo shit."

"Maybe you should. Maybe that's the only thing that can free you."

The admiral hung up, leaving Dale to ponder his cryptic words.

He went to the window and stared at the full moon, feeling the itch and pull of scar tissue. Or maybe it was the itch and pull of something deeper.

That wolf that hurt him, if he got his hands on the beast…

Dale went into the kitchen, opened the sliding glass doors and stepped onto his deck. A cool, refreshing breeze caressed his cheeks. He was a powerful Primary Mage, a Mage who could shape-shift into any life form. Right now the wolf called to him, the urge to run wild and free in fur. Closing his eyes, he stretched out his hands and called upon his magick, and shifted into a large gray timber wolf. He ran into his backyard, and leaped over the wood fence, giving a joyful yip as he raced through the woods. Senses filled with the night air, the sights and smells of the land.

Freeing and exhilarating, he relished the feel of leaves and earth beneath his paws. The wolf had no responsibilities, didn't have to visit a shrink to keep his job. The wolf had no scars, only thick fur. The wolf would never be tied down and helpless and vulnerable.

His wolf had power.

And if his wolf ever got his big paws on the demon wolf that tortured him as a man, that SOB would pay with Dale's claws.

The wolf grinned as he ran with the night.

Chapter 3

A gentle breeze stirred the American flag hanging next to the front door. Everything about this house, from the bright white paint to the neat black shutters and the truck in the drive, seemed normal.

But nothing was normal, especially not the man living inside.

Keira took a deep breath and steadied her nerves. When the door opened, she gave a bright smile.

"I hope you like your coffee black. Because I took you for a black-coffee guy."

She thrust a steaming coffee cup at the man in the doorway. Dale Curtis stood military straight in a starched khaki uniform, looking crisp and fresh and undeniably more handsome than a man should look at 0500 hours.

Those scrutinizing gray eyes showed a hint of a smile. "Thanks. Come in."

Carrying her valise, Keira followed him to the kitchen. Tension knotted her stomach. His older friend, clearly a superior, had done some kind of odd mojo on her last night. She remembered nothing except that his smile had been kind.

Still, she couldn't trust that the older man wasn't set-

ting her up, even though he whispered into her mind that
she was safe now. Right. Nothing was safe anymore. Not
since the Centurions had torn her world apart.

This arrangement troubled her. Living with him wasn't
on her agenda, but she needed to buck up his powers so
he could destroy the Centurion demons. Keira suspected
he hired her only to fulfill an obligation.

The commander set down the coffee, then sat on a
wood stool at the breakfast nook. His penetrating gray
gaze seemed to bore into her. For too long, she'd operated
alone, avoiding others, especially men. This close proxim-
ity unnerved her. Dale Curtis studied her, as if puzzling
out her real identity. Her hand trembled as she fumbled in
her case. Not this soon. She needed time, needed to gain
his trust. But instinct warned that was something this man
did not easily give.

He glanced at his watch. "Let's see the contract. You
have thirty minutes before I leave for base."

Tempted to take the watch and throw it into the trash,
Keira plopped the contract on the table. "In conveniently
large type, unlike most legal contracts. You can actually
read this." She glanced up at the clock. "Of course, I'm
sure you'll have to be at work soon."

Dale slid the papers closer and began to read, his brows
drawing together. Holding her breath, she tapped her fingers. But he was a fast read and finally came to the last
page.

"Sign here."

Keira handed him an old-fashioned quill. When he
scratched his name in bold, strong letters, she took the
quill and pricked her thumb. A droplet of blood spilled
over his signature. She licked her thumb and gestured to
the contract.

"I'll give you a copy. The contract states you are free to

break the agreement at any time by declaring verbally to me, 'I renounce you. I renounce our agreement.'"

She'd seen him pour over the rambling legalese in the document, but wanted to ensure that Lt. Commander Dale Curtis knew exactly what he was getting into.

Without telling him every single, small detail.

But cooperation was essential. No man could be bound to her against his will.

At his nod, she snapped open her case and withdrew a velvet box. Inside the red velvet bed was a shimmering wide silver armband. A large blue sapphire was in the center amid intricate runes studded with smaller sapphires.

"Please slide this on me, above the elbow."

She held out her bare right arm.

"This is a slave armband."

Suspicion flared in his eyes. Keira held her breath. So close, would he balk now? A man of reason, she realized. A man who questioned all because he left nothing to chance.

She shrugged. "Is it? The armband provides me protection while I cleanse your house, and assures you that as long as it remains on me, I'm bonded to you as your contractor."

And as long as you put it on me, I'm protected from demons. They can't touch me.

"Then if it protects you, why don't you wear it all the time?"

Smart. She wasn't accustomed to dealing with a man who had both valor and a piercing intellect.

Keira pointed to the gleaming sapphire. "Why would I wear it when there are more human thieves who'd harm me to steal the jewels, not knowing the armband's real value?"

Dale's full mouth pursed, but his eyes twinkled. "You have an answer for everything. Rehearse much?"

But he gently slid the armband in place. Feeling the warmth of her skin, the metal settled against her arm, not uncomfortable, more reassuring than restricting. She was bound to him. Her wolf could not attack him as long as the band remained in place.

He didn't remove his hand. Instead, his fingers brushed against her skin. Heat curled inside her body.

For a wild moment, she wondered what he'd be like as a lover. What would it feel like to at last surrender her innocence, give everything to a man as magnificent and powerful as him?

And surrender your heart, give total power over you, a small voice mocked. *After twenty-three years of guarding what little you have left?*

Dale stroked the skin under her arm along the band, and she bit her lip. Feelings surged, along with a delicious heat that made her toes curl. "This band bonds you to me. So it means you must do anything I tell you."

Keira fisted her hands to hide their trembling. "Not exactly. I'm no pushover, Lieutenant Commander."

With forefinger and thumb, he lightly clasped her chin. The spicy scent of his cologne swam in her nostrils. She became lost in the intense grayness of his eyes. Dale's mouth parted as he lowered his head.

But instead of a kiss, he nuzzled her neck, inhaling deeply. Dread filled her.

Mages couldn't scent the demon blood inside her. But he was a Primary, and much more powerful than an ordinary Mage.

"What are you, Keira Solomon? Why do I crave you? Every time I draw close, I think of sex," he whispered.

"They have support groups for that."

She backed away until her backside connected with the sliding glass doors. The commander advanced, a determined look on his face.

He would have answers, would wring them out of her.

"I thought you said you had to go to work." She mustered a smile and tapped his watch. "Better get going."

Please, let him be the kind of guy who's never late.

"The base can wait for once. This is more important."

Closer still he came, until his tall body overshadowed hers. He could overcome her with weight and sheer physical strength.

Inside, the demon blood surged, but her claws did not emerge. Because her wolf could no longer hurt him. Good for him, not so wonderful for her if he wanted to overpower her. Could he find out who she was?

Keira cringed and squeezed against the glass doors. He slowly stalked toward her.

"The admiral sensed something about you. I sense something about you. Something in my blood is calling to you. You're not who you appear to be."

She wriggled away as he reached for her. "Blood is for vamps. I don't like vamps. They like to sleep in and they never appreciate my cooking when I make garlic sauce."

He clasped her chin in one strong hand, his grip gentle, but firm. "I will have answers, Keira. You'd better hope and pray I don't find out anything I don't like."

Tightness constricted her chest, but she gave a small laugh. "Why? You'll feed me to the wolves?"

A slow smile touched his mouth. "Not quite."

"Too bad. Because I always liked to play Little Red Riding Hood, only with a big knife and some nunchakus. I don't fight fair."

"Neither do I." He pushed a strand of hair away from her face and tucked it behind her ear. "Not when it comes to chasing down something I want very, very badly. I can be quite ruthless. Like a wolf."

"And here I thought you were a puppy dog, Lieutenant Commander. A seemingly nice guy with too much starch

in your collar." She tried to duck beneath his embrace, but
he caught her and pinned her against the door.

"You don't want to know what I'm capable of, Keira.
And you'd better pray you can handle what I deliver, because I guarantee by the time I finish with you, you'll be
in no shape to fight me. I'll know every cell of you, every
inch of you. And there will be no secrets between us."

He lowered his head toward her. "None. I'll cull every
last one from you. So start now by telling me the truth."

She bit back a moan as he traced her lower lip with his
thumb. Oh, gods, this was a risk Keira knew she'd have to
undertake, but she didn't reckon with the magnetic power
of Dale Curtis's personality.

The force of his will.

Keira felt herself begin to crumble as the commander
stroked her bottom lip, his touch gentle and erotic. His
piercing gaze seared into her. *Please, don't ask the question, please. I don't know if I can withhold the truth....*

The commander would kill her. She knew it. Keira
tensed as he whispered.

"You're bound to me. The contract states it. Now, tell
me the truth. You must. Who the hell are you and why the
hell are you really here?"

Chapter 4

"I'm a Luminaire...."

"I know what you are. Who are you?"

His aura pulsed bright red, spiked with black. Sexual energy, as well as negative forces. Keira shoved lightly at his chest, breaking the physical contact.

"I'm your new housekeeper, a woman who needs a job, okay? I've been roving from town to town."

"Why?"

The man was relentless. "I like helping people. I search for individuals that need enlightenment and then help them heal. Ask your neighbor if you need a reference."

"I did. Odd how you showed up just when she needed you." He lightly clasped her wrist. Sexual current sizzled between them.

Keira closed her eyes and breathed deeply, channeling every bit of white light she could to fight the temptation to lift her face to his and kiss him. "I heard her crying. Psychic cries, not real cries. I'm a healer and it compelled me."

"Right."

"There's enough darkness and negative energy in this world. What's wrong with trying to eradicate it and make people feel better?"

"Maybe there's no hope for them." He dropped her hand.

Keira watched a shadow drape across his expression, then his face smoothed out. Dale Curtis was hiding deep pain, pain she knew well, because she'd caused it.

Suddenly he went still. Keira's heart dropped to her stomach as she caught the small, scampering sounds.

"Damn mice," he said. "One reason why my house-keeper quit."

"That's not a mouse," she said and bolted down the hallway, hooked a right and ran into a locked door. Keira jiggled the knob. "Open this," she told him as he pulled up short behind her.

A fierce scowl tightened his face. "That's private."

"If you want to get rid of your pests, open it. Now."

He looked shocked, as if no one ever talked to him that way.

Dale clicked a series of buttons on a brass plate and opened the door. She burst inside, barely noting that it was an office, with stacks of papers piled on the desk. Her sense of smell overtook everything. Those little, nasty creatures, smelling like a bad combination of bad breath and rotting cabbage...

"My report to the admiral..."

Ignoring Dale's mutterings as he sifted through papers on his desk, she dived to the floor by the credenza. Keira groped beneath the furniture and felt slicing pain scrape her hand. She peered down. The imp had affixed razor blades to the credenza's bottom, effectively making a protective nest for itself.

Two red, beady eyes glared at her. It started to lash out with its tiny claws and then backed away, obeying the hidden compulsion in the slave armband. Keira stretched out her fingers and summoned the power deep inside.

The creature squealed as it slid into her hand. She wriggled from under the credenza, clutching it tight.

"Jar," she gasped.

Dale stared at the creature as it wriggled in her hand. Blood seeped down her clenched fist. "What the hell…"

"Jar, hello, could use a little help here, get a jar, something to hold it. Please hurry."

He seized a heavy metal pencil holder from the desk, dumped out the contents.

Keira squatted down. "Be quick, they're really, really fast… I'll let go and you trap him. On three… One, two, three!"

As she released the creature, Dale slammed the pencil holder down. Damn, the man was fast.

He picked up a scrap of paper and tossed it down with a disgusted sound. "My report to the admiral… It's chewed to pieces."

"Uh, of course. They adore paper. Almost as tasty as flour." Keira examined her injured hand with a rueful sigh. "If he'd have gotten to your computer, your hard drive would be royally screwed."

To her surprise, he gave a small, wry smile. "Never did like anything royally screwed, especially my hard drive. I prefer the commoner's touch."

It took her a minute to realize the joke. And then to her enormous chagrin, she blushed. He gave his rusty, deep laugh again. And then he looked at her injured hand and stopped laughing. Dale took her hand very gently and examined it. His touch was absolutely gentle. Fishing out a clean, white square from his pocket, he wrapped it around her bleeding palm.

"Remind me to be careful dusting under there. It fastened razor blades to the credenza's bottom to keep anyone from going after him."

Dale focused his attention on bandaging her hand. "Even without a contract, you'd have to stay now. Can't have you leaving here wounded."

"It's not much. It'll heal."

"I always take care of my own." He looked slightly dangerous as he stared at the floor. The pencil holder trembled, but the creature was effectively trapped.

"What the hell is that thing?"

"Imp." Keira wrapped her hand tighter to slow the bleeding. Blood was bad, attracted bad things, and this house already had enough darkness. She couldn't risk drawing out more.

"A demon," he said slowly.

"A very minor one. Imps are drawn to negativity and darkness. They feed on it."

That and residual demon energy left on a victim, she thought.

Dale frowned. "That thing invaded my home because I've been in a bad mood?"

"Not exactly. You've been expelling dark energy. Something must have happened to you to suck out your white light."

He shot her an incredulous look.

"Imps tend to make a person bad-tempered and irritable. They make a bad situation worse. They're hard to kill because they're so fast. They can outrun almost anything."

He raised a dark brow. The commander opened a desk drawer and withdrew a pistol. Keira's jaw dropped as he chambered a round and pointed the gun at the pencil jar and fired. Shards of plastic exploded, along with a nasty splatter of gray demon blood. The stench stung her nostrils.

"Not a 9 mm," he said with satisfaction.

Sweat trickled down her spine. "Um, you're not very forgiving, are you?"

"No."

"I'd hate to be on your bad side."

"You would." His expression darkened. "Good thing you're not a demon."

Keira swallowed hard. "Yeah. Sounds like you've run up against them. It's the source of your dark energy."

"I'm only interested in one." A hard smile touched his mouth, making him look dangerous. "No matter how long I must wait. I will find her and make her pay for what she did to me."

The coffee soured in her stomach as she remembered how skillfully he'd wielded the pistol. Keira didn't relish him discovering her true identity. Holding back her nausea, she pointed to the mess on the floor. "If you'll show me where I'm sleeping and then where your cleaning supplies are, I'll get started on my first assignment."

He gently clasped her injured hand. "After I clean your wounds. Those are some nasty cuts."

"I can do it."

"I told you, I always take care of my own."

She was almost afraid to ask. "And those you consider your enemies? You take care of them, as well?"

Dale gave a slow smile. "The same way I did to the imp."

Keira didn't look at the splattered remains on the floor as they left his study.

After Dale left, Keira brought the saddlebags containing her possessions inside and set them on the floor. Then she sat on the bed of her new room, stroking the ecru duvet.

A real bed, with feather pillows instead of a thin blanket on the cold concrete floor. A brass reading lamp with a comfortable chair by a window that overlooked the wide backyard instead of a windowless basement. Her own bathroom, not a foul bucket in the corner.

Freedom, for the first time in years, not fearing that at any moment the demons would yank her back to captivity and imprison her once more.

Oh, how she longed to sit in the chair, crack open one of the books on his shelves and read. But she had a job to do.

Keira unpacked her kit and set about cleansing the house the way a regular housekeeper would not.

First, his office. Two wide computer screens took up most of a desk. Papers that had been neatly stacked and organized were scattered about the surface.

A map of the world was mounted to one wall, with several colored pushpins inserted into various countries.

She cleansed the remains of the dead imp and burned them in the stone hearth fireplace. Blood called to blood, and even imp blood attracted dark forces.

Keira then took a small box, opened it and arranged the crystals around Dale's office in a pattern. Then she closed her eyes and began the sacred chant. The crystals began to vibrate and hum, the music of elemental energy creating a harmonic vibration.

White light suffused the room, ribbons of light beaming out from each of the four crystals. Soothing and melodious, the light singing its own song of purity, drawing out the negative forces.

A dark cloud arose from the corner near Dale's computer. Ribbons of white light attacked the cloud, overcoming it, and the darkness evaporated. Keira watched, her chest tight. She lowered her hands. Why could she cleanse rooms and people and not herself?

Because of the demon blood inside me, she reminded herself. Until the Centurions were permanently vanquished to the netherworld, part of her would always remain in darkness. Lately it got more difficult to regain her inner light. Each time the demons returned her to captivity, her inner light shrank. Eventually it would go out all together, leaving her in the abyss.

Each time the Centurions allowed her freedom, Keira used the time to refresh herself with positive energy, using elements from the earth and her crystals. White light held the demons' darkness at bay for a little while, until the Centurions forced her wolf to torture a new victim.

Refreshed, she set about cleansing the other rooms, until reaching Dale's bedroom.

Keira hesitated at the door. She drew in a deep breath and stepped into the room, feeling the despondency and grief. The master bedroom had an attached bath. Large, with a glassed-in shower and a Roman tub big enough to fit four, it was sleek tile and slick chrome.

The darkness of horrible pain slammed into her temples.

Holding a hand to her head, she opened the medicine cabinet above the sink. Lined in a neat row were several prescription-pill bottles. All of them recently issued, most for pain, some for sleeping.

The bottles held a layer of dust.

Dale Curtis had not touched a single pill. Instead, he'd suffered.

Keira cleansed both rooms, feeling the light chase away the thick layers of suffering. With a much lighter spirit, she started on her housekeeping duties.

She worked steadily, leaving the basement for last. It still needed cleansing with her crystals, as well. Dread curled in her stomach as she finally gathered her courage and climbed down the stairs, clutching her most powerful crystal. Sweat dripped down her temples and she wiped it away with the back of her hand, the dust rag gripped in her fist.

You can do this, you can do this....

The basement ran the length of the house and was enormous, divided into two sections. The smaller section was unfinished, with a utility room, wood workbench and neatly arranged tools, the furnace and storage cubicles.

This section was separated by a wall with a solid door. She opened the door and went into the larger section. It was a comfortable living room covered with beige carpeting, a small, tiled kitchen with shining stainless-steel appliances, a dining table and chairs and a sectional sofa set before a flat-screen television mounted above a fireplace. Next to the stairs were eight bunk beds. She opened a door and found a bathroom with a tiled shower.

A shiver snaked down her spine as she gazed around the room. Another door was near the bunk beds. She opened it and found a small, windowless room with a narrow bed. No light switch. Nothing to chase away the darkness…

A sly, rollicking laugh echoed in her mind. *You will never escape us….*

Whimpering, Keira slammed the door and leaned against it, the crystal in her left fist squeezed tight. She raced up the stairs.

Maybe she'd tackle that room tomorrow.

Dale arrived home after seven. When he walked into the kitchen, Keira noticed the shadows beneath his gray eyes were pronounced and dark.

He flipped the light switch, flooding the room with overhead lighting. The man was thin and haggard, and looking worse each day. If he didn't regain strength soon, he'd lose the fight to darkness. Keira glanced up from the pot of stew she stirred on the stove. He brightened as he sniffed the air.

"Smells great, but you don't have to cook. I usually grab a sandwich at the commissary."

"I like cooking and making new dishes."

And you need more than sandwiches to get your health back.

He eyed the dining-room table, set with the china she'd found in the elegant cabinet. "I just eat in the kitchen."

"This is nicer, though, don't you think?" He had such

nice things. Keira wanted to relish and experience every good thing she could while she was free.

He sighed deeply, as if something hurt him. "It's been a long time since I sat down at a dining-room table."

Dale looked down at his uniform. "You went to a lot of trouble. Mind if I change first?"

"The stew will keep warm. Unless you decide on a hot bubble bath."

"I never take bubble baths alone, only with company. Saves on water."

He gave a real smile, showing white, even teeth. The smile lit up his face and chased away all the dark shadows.

Keira stared out the kitchen window as he went upstairs. Her pulse raced. First time alone all night with the man she'd tortured, a man of honor and integrity and tremendous power. She didn't underestimate his rough appearance. If he wanted, Dale Curtis could turn her to ashes with one flick of his hand.

A few minutes later, Dale returned to the kitchen, clad in khaki trousers and a navy blue polo shirt. Deck shoes covered his feet. He went into the dining room and returned with a sparkling crystal wineglass.

"What do you think?" he asked. He went for the built-in wine rack among the cabinets. "Red or white?"

She hadn't drunk spirits in ages and placed the glasses on the table more as pretty decor. It was dangerous to imbibe around him, dangerous to lower her guard. But he was acting more animated and she didn't want to spoil the mood. "Red, I think. You select it."

Dale opened a bottle and poured a small amount. "I haven't had wine since I got home from the hospital. Just beer, and I rarely finish the bottle."

Her heart skipped a beat. She watched him sample the vintage and nod. "Excellent."

"How long were you in the hospital?"

"Long enough."

As he carried the bottle and glass into the dining room, she ladled the stew into two bowls. He turned on the crystal chandelier hanging over the table. A lump rose in Keira's throat.

She had been forced to torture him in the dark. He never knew when she'd attack, never saw her coming, only felt the burning agony of her sharp claws.

Dale filled her glass with wine as they sat. Keira tried not to think of what she'd done to this man, but the stew tasted like cardboard as she ate.

He looked up, his brows arched. "It's very good. I taste thyme. Did you season the stew with it?"

Keira flushed under the praise. "Thyme and other spices."

Dale smiled, the sharp angles and plains of his face softening. "You're a good cook. I thought New Agers ate only wheat sprouts and fruit."

Keira thought quickly. "In all my travels, I had to adapt to various lifestyles, so I learned to enjoy their foods, as well."

He toyed with the stem of his wineglass. "You're a gypsy."

"With a Harley instead of a caravan. I like to travel and see the country."

"Why?"

"Because there's so much to this life to see, and experience." Keira spooned up more stew. "I want to relish every single moment I've been given and find the good in people, the good I know exists."

"It doesn't always exist. There is much evil."

"And good."

"That's not my job. My job is to find the evil and eradicate it, to keep the American people safe."

Keira's heart pounded like an excited dog's tail against

the floor. She set down her spoon. "You're too young to be so cynical."

"Old enough. Seen enough." Dale sipped his wine. "My family was insular. I chose against it."

"Why?"

"Because they cared only about money and status. When I chose to join the navy and become a SEAL, they were not happy. But serving my country, and keeping civilians safe, meant more to me than making millions, like my father wanted me to do."

"Who is your family?"

Dale raised a brow. "In all your travels, you've never heard of Curtis Mark Industries? The software empire, second only to Bill Gates and Steven Jobs? That's my father's company."

"You wanted to rebel against your father so you didn't work for him?"

"I wanted to do something with my life other than remain a part of a society that cared only for being seen and flaunting their power. There's an evil I wanted to eliminate to keep others safe. I have much power and what good is power if you don't use it to help others?"

Keira was touched at his dedication and selflessness. The Mage could have had a very comfortable, and very safe, lifestyle. She tilted her head, studying him. Why did she have the feeling she'd met him somewhere before, around the time the demons killed her pack?

But all those memories from Nicaragua were scrambled. The demons had seen to it by infusing her with four drops of their blood when they became temporarily corporeal.

"You sacrificed a lot to keep others safe. Your parents would be proud. I would be."

"They didn't understand. Neither did my wife. Ex-wife. Kathy was cut from the same bolt of social-excess cloth."

He seemed to catch himself and stared at his meal. "Damn. Sorry. Didn't mean to go there."

"Let me guess. She didn't like being the wife of a military officer."

He nodded. "We've been divorced a long time now. No children. Enough of me. What about you? Where's your family?"

The familiar lump rose in her throat. Keira struggled to swallow a mouthful of stew. She set down her spoon. "They were killed in a demon invasion while we were living in another country. I was able to escape."

His expression softened. "I'm sorry."

She shrugged to hide the tears welling in her throat. "It happened a long, long time ago. My pac—parents liked to rove around the globe, see the world and experience new cultures. Guess that's one reason I'm a gypsy. I don't have a real home."

Goodness, she'd almost revealed she once had a pack.

Dale ate with zest. "This is terrific. I haven't had a hot meal in weeks. Never bother cooking. No time, too much trouble."

She studied his lean frame. He'd lost weight since she'd last seen him. If he kept this up, Dale Curtis would resemble a walking skeleton, his powers useless, his body prime for takeover by other demons.

"You need more protein, real meals, not grabbing sandwiches. Now that I'm here, I'll cook dinner for you every night." Keira smiled, trying to lighten her mood. "I promise if I find another imp, I won't throw him in the stew pot. Besides, those little buggers can take the heat."

"How do you normally kill them?"

"Not with guns, though yours did the trick."

Dale smiled, looking less severe.

"Usually it's best to blast them with white light. They're

so small, it's easier than trying to kill a demon with white light. With demons, you need the big guns."

Those startlingly gray eyes met hers. Beneath the mild look was an exacting scrutiny. Uncomfortable, she realized he was sizing her up, digging beneath the surface to find out what her deal was. Not a good idea.

"How do you know so much about imps and demons?" he asked.

"I studied them."

"Most women wouldn't want to get near a demon, even an imp, if they lost loved ones to dark forces. Yet you knew exactly what was in my office, and where it would be hiding."

Guilt surged through her. "I studied demons and their minions. Wanted to know what my enemies were capable of doing."

"I do the same, only I'm trained in combat and weaponry."

"Did you know imps love to invade kitchens, food supplies, even liquor? Once I found a dozen of them in a liquor cabinet. They'd managed to break open a bottle of brandy. Have you ever seen a drunk imp? Not a pretty sight."

She set down her spoon. "And I'm rambling. If you want, I can eat in the kitchen, leave you in peace to digest your meal."

"Stay," he said quietly. "It's nice to share a meal with someone. I get tired of eating alone."

"Me, too." The words slipped out before she could catch herself.

Warmth shone in his eyes. For a moment, she indulged in the fantasy that this was her real home, and she could cook here every night. A real home, with someone to belong to.

The lump returned to her throat. Keira gripped her spoon. If she allowed melancholy to consume her, she'd dim her white light. Think positive. "Tell me about the piano. Do you play?"

He nodded. "Not for a long time, though."

"Classical or contemporary?"

"Only the classics. I once wanted to be a concert pianist, but wanted to fight our nation's enemies more." He gave a crooked smile. "You can't kill the bad guys with music."

"You've never heard me play."

Dale gave his deep, husky chuckle. "And you've never heard me sing."

They were deep into a discussion of classical music versus rock when a clear thud sounded downstairs.

"Something's in the basement." The spoon rattled against the table as she set it down.

Dale wiped his mouth with the linen napkin. He stood, his expression shuttered. "Or someone. I have quarters down there for my men when they run into trouble. But they always ring the front doorbell."

"I don't like your basement. It's a bit spooky," she admitted.

His gaze turned troubled. "I haven't been down there… in a while."

Keira didn't want to go down those stairs. Not now, as shadows draped the house and the darkness pushed away the sunlight. Her pulse raced. And then she looked at Dale and thought about how he must feel about basements.

He dragged in a deep breath and went into the hallway. When he returned, he carried the same pistol he'd used to shoot the imp. Dale slid the chamber back, the racking sound echoing in the room.

"Stay here."

Something vulnerable flashed in his gaze. Keira's heart kicked. As much as she loathed and feared what lay below, she couldn't let him go there alone.

"I'm coming with you."

"No."

"Bullets won't stop a demon."

"My powers can."

"You'll need extra help. White light can aid and enhance your powers." She fished her white quartz crystal from her jeans pocket.

Dale narrowed his eyes. "Fine. But you stay behind me at least five steps, and if I order you to run back upstairs, run."

She followed him. He opened the door to the basement as she squeezed the crystal tight.

Keira swallowed hard, seeing the steep, gray steps swallowed by inky blackness. Anything could be down there. She'd failed to cleanse the room with white light. Her breathing ragged, she prepared to descend with him into the darkness.

Chapter 5

Dale hadn't been in his own basement since before the incident. Cupping his gun, he crept down the stairs. Sweat trickled down his temples. This was his home, damn it, and he'd tolerate no intruders. But his pulse rate tripled and he struggled to swallow past the panic rising in his throat.

Memories assaulted him. The terrified little boy held in a demon's cruel grip. "His life for yours," the demon had cackled.

And then Dale had willingly become the Centurion's captive, as they tied him down and tortured him until his voice grew hoarse from the screams....

A soft whimper sounded behind him. Keira was just as terrified. Dale straightened and motioned for her to stay back. Damn it, he was a navy SEAL, not some wimpy ass scared of entering his own damn basement.

He flipped on the light switch. Soft white light illuminated the downstairs. When he reached the bottom step he heard singing.

"I don't think demons sing," Keira whispered.

He lowered the gun, relief making his knees weak. "That's no demon, but an imp from hell. What his mother calls him, anyway."

Dale rounded the corner to the section he'd built as quarters to house his men when the Phoenix Force needed to discuss ops in private. He flipped the safety on his weapon and shoved it into the waistband of his shorts.

Grant "Sully" Sullivan lay on the carpet, singing a bawdy song. Dale inhaled and recoiled.

"Jesus, Sully, what the hell?"

The ensign struggled to sit up, and fell back, the odor of whiskey clinging to him like cheap perfume. "Sorry, Curt. I'm a little…little drunk."

"And you came here to sleep it off? Or escape from a lover?" Dale squatted down beside the young SEAL.

Keira entered the room and looked at Sully. Dale sighed. "Keira, meet Ensign Sullivan, one of my men. Sully, this is Keira, my new housekeeper."

Sully opened one eye and held out a hand. "Pleased to meet you, ma'am."

Her mouth quirked. "It's a pleasure since you're not a demon." Her gaze whipped to Dale. "Although I've heard you're an imp."

"That's what Mom says. Of all her eight kids, I was the worse. Worst."

Dale wiped his clammy palms on his shorts to hide them from Sully. Even drunk, the man was sharp. Of course. He'd trained the SEAL himself. "Why did you teleport here?"

"My sis. Cassandra's worried about you. Made me promise to warn you in person, Curt."

"Who's Curt?" Keira asked.

"It's my team nickname." Dale glanced at the kitchen. "Could you get him a glass of water?"

As Keira headed for the sink, Dale sat beside Sully and lowered his voice. "I told you, I'm fine."

The last thing he needed was Sully's well-meaning but

nosy older sister fretting about him. Did the whole world have to fuss over him?

"Cassandra saw a vision in her crystal ball."

Keira handed the glass to Sully, who gulped down the water. "Your sister has a crystal ball?"

"Just for fun. Doesn't need it." Sully set the glass down and looked slightly more alert. "She sees her visions in her mind. She came to my place and yelled at me for drinking too much. Jeez, I hate when she yells at me. Like I'm eight again and she's my bossy older sister nagging me. Well, I was a mess, but damn, I didn't expect company, sorry for swearing, ma'am...."

Trying to follow a line of conversation with Sully when he was soused was like trying to read Latin backward. Dale pointed two fingers at his eyes. "Focus, Sully. Why was your sister at your apartment?"

"Cassandra was worried about you. Came to tell me. Saw a vision in her crystal ball of you dancing with a demon. Not your ex-wife, either."

Dale's mouth quirked. He glanced at Keira to see if she absorbed the joke, and saw blood drain from her face.

He wondered what it meant. Then she smiled, but it seemed strained.

"What kind of demon?"

Sully frowned. "She started bitching... Sorry, ma'am, I mean, complaining, about how messy my place was and how I drank all the whiskey."

"The demon?" Dale asked.

"My sis."

"Why did you drink so much?" he asked gently, already knowing the reason.

"Ever since Miranda broke up with me, my life's been a wreck. I loved her and no one will ever be as sweet." He sighed. "'Cept maybe Paulina. She was amazing...."

Keira gave him a questioning look. "How did you break in?"

"Teleported. Never break in."

She gave Dale a questioning look. "He teleported over. Sully's a Light Mystic."

"Which is Curt's polite way of saying I'm the bastard son of a Mystic Witch and a psychic human. Unlike Cassandra, who's a pure-blood Mystic." Sully rubbed at his face.

She tensed visibly. "Mystic Witches have visions of the future."

"Cassandra's are usually spot-on, which is why I need to know more about this one." Dale turned back to Sully. "What did your sister see?"

"Oh, Dale, let the poor man sober up. He looks hungry." She smiled at Sully. "Have you eaten?"

Sully ran a hand through his thick hair. "No, ma'am. Was gonna grab leftovers or something out of a can."

"I made stew. There's plenty. Would you like dinner?"

Dale shot her an incredulous look, but she ignored him and focused on Sully, who brightened, his boyish face lighting up like a Christmas tree. "Gee, thanks. I love real home cooking."

He didn't like the idea of Sully dining with them. Dale ruminated over this. It wasn't the thought of Sully treating him with kid gloves or asking him again and again how he was healing.

Dale disliked the idea of sharing Keira's company with another man.

Interesting. He rubbed a spot on his chest, his scars itching suddenly. Or was the itch much deeper, the burning wish to enjoy a quiet conversation with a woman who didn't look at him with either fear or desire in her eyes?

Sully scrambled to his feet, swayed a moment and then caught himself. Dale stood as well, wondering about Cassandra Sullivan's cryptic message. Her visions in the past had proved correct. But no way in hell would he ever dance with demons.

Dale headed for his study and locked his weapon in the safe. When he returned to the dining room and retook his seat, Keira had set a bowl of stew on the table before Sully.

The SEAL began to eat. "Wow, this is terrific," he said around a mouthful of stew. "Maybe if Curt fires you, you can cook for me."

She sat, looking amused at Dale's scowl. "I just got hired. Why would he fire me?"

"You're not his type. Too nice." Sully waved his spoon. "He likes tall, model types with sharp tongues."

"Ensign," Dale warned. "Tell me about your sister's vision. What did this demon look like?"

Keira choked on her wine. Dale glanced at her. "You okay?"

"Fine." She coughed. "Drank too fast."

"Sis said the demon's face was blurred, but she had pretty hair. Silky." Sully squinted at Keira. "Kinda like yours, ma'am. No offense. Didn't mean to compare you to a demon."

"No prob," she said quickly. "Care for some wine?"

"Think I've had enough to drink. Wouldn't wash down well with the finest whiskey this side of—"

"Ensign," Dale interrupted. "The vision?"

"Cassandra said that the demon is closer to you than you'd ever realize…a demon in disguise—"

"More stew?" Keira persisted.

Sully shook his head. "Could use coffee, though, if you have any. Need to sober up."

Her smile was bright. "Sure. Would you like dessert? I made chocolate cake."

"From scratch?"

Keira had already vanished into the kitchen. "Dale, would you help me? I can't carry this by myself."

He went into the kitchen and carried out the cake as she set up the coffeemaker. Keira scurried after him into the dining room.

As she began to cut slices of the thick cake, Dale shook his head. "I'm full. I'll save it for later."

He aimed a stern look at the ensign. "Sully, your sister's vision."

"A sad demon. Weird. A demon who liked to dance and invaded your house to get close to you, the devil in disguise. She said your future depends on vanquishing the demon." Sully dug into his slice of cake. "This is great. Thank you, ma'am."

"Keira," she said. "Dale, I think the coffee is ready. I couldn't find anything to serve it in. Do you mind?"

Dale bit back his impatience as he returned to the kitchen. Damn it, why couldn't Cassandra have clear-cut visions instead of sounding like a Chinese fortune cookie? What demon? Why would he allow a demon into his own home?

Then again, he'd changed since the time in the basement. Dale pressed a hand to his temple. Things that were normally clear before had grown muddied in his mind. He needed to get his act together.

When he returned, carrying a silver service and three cups, Keira was eating her slice of cake. Sully snapped his fingers.

"That's what Cassandra said. I forgot. She said the devil you dance with is the devil in your house, the demon you'll fall hard and fast for, the devil you'll bring to your bed…."

"Oh, my God," Keira cried out.

They both turned. She was licking frosting off her fork, her tongue slowly stroking the tines. Dale's jaw dropped. Holy crap, the woman turned eating cake into carnal art.

"Oh, my God, this is so good! Chocolate," she breathed. "I haven't had any in months. You must try this. I used dark *and* milk chocolate."

Keira took another bite. Eyes closed, expression ecstatic, she looked like a woman in the throes of orgasm.

He forgot all about Cassandra's vision. Forgot about why Sullivan came to his house. All his focus centered on the woman eating a slice of chocolate cake with such sensuality, his blood thickened.

Dale hungered to see her looking this way again, only naked beneath him, her pleasure visible to his eyes only.

Sully stared at her with wide eyes, a pulse beating wildly in his throat. The man was clearly turned on. She licked the fork slowly, and Dale had the oddest feeling she was truly savoring the meal, but also distracting them.

Why? Did she see Mystic Witches as a threat?

Keira flicked her tongue over the tines and slowly slid the utensil into her mouth. Out. Then in again. Sweat trickled down Dale's back. He gulped down his wine, his gaze riveted. Beneath his shorts, his cock hardened.

Stunned, Dale set down his wine. He hadn't experienced arousal since his torture. Now his new housekeeper, with her innocent air and pouting, full mouth, had given him an erection. He narrowed his eyes at Sully.

Leave us alone. Now.

The SEAL wasn't stupid. Sully suddenly pushed back his plate. "I'll be going. Thanks for the meal."

He stood and stretched out his arms as if to teleport, but began to sway. Dale bolted out of his chair. Damn it, he was so tuned into Keira's little display, he'd forgotten his first responsibility—to his men.

"Downstairs, Ensign. You're not headed anywhere. Either I get you a taxi to your apartment or you stay here. Last time you teleported someplace drunk, you ended up inside the lingerie department of a department store."

"I do love the ladies in silk." Sully sighed.

Dale helped him down the steps and watched him collapse onto a bunk bed, covered him with a blanket. Then, as an afterthought, he left a lamp burning.

No one should be left alone in a basement with the lights off.

No one should be left alone in a basement with the lights off and the sound of his own blood slowly dripping onto the cold concrete floor.

His erection deflated. Dale climbed up the stairs, needing to return to the brightly lit kitchen.

A soft, sweet voice hummed a tune he recognized from the sixties. Keira's arms were plunged into a sink filled with soap suds. Disappointed, Dale cocked a brow. He wanted to watch her eat more cake, with him as her only audience. He wanted to slide chocolate frosting over her mouth and slowly lick it off, then trail his tongue down her neck and lower...

What the hell was wrong with him? All he could think about was sex. This was the woman he'd hired to clean his house and keep Keegan Byrne the hell out of his personal life. Dale drew in a deep breath, then another, and folded his arms.

"I have a dishwasher," he told her.

At her questioning look, he pulled open the stainless-steel door and slid out a rack. A most becoming blush tinted her round cheeks.

"Runs on electricity, saves time," he added.

"Some things are done best the old-fashioned way. Save the planet."

His irritation grew. "Hope you're not into only candle-light and battery power like most New Agers and I'm going to wake up to find organic sprouts for breakfast instead of bacon and eggs. I don't eat sprouts and I'm not into peace and love." Dale fetched a clean dish towel and began to dry the plates she stacked on the drainer.

Keira's lovely mouth wobbled. "Are you making fun of me?"

His stomach churned at her woebegone expression. He set down a plate. Damn it, had he lost all his manners? Since when had he been so rude?

He took another deep breath, wrestling for control, feeling his life was spinning away from him again.

"I'm sorry. I'm rather bad-tempered these days."

Especially when facing a woman who really turned him on, and made him feel even more out of sorts because each time he was around her, all he could think about was getting her naked.

Her peaches-and-cream complexion looked creamy and smooth, like fresh milk. The pink-and-green-flowered frock floated around her calves, hugging every inch of her curves. With her huge green eyes and the dark curls tumbling down her backside, Keira looked more like a forest nymph than a housekeeper.

"Why?"

That voice, it stroked over his clammy skin like velvet. So lush and melodious. Seductive and yet without the artifice of his sometime girlfriend, Melissa, who knew how to use her feminine skills to get her own way.

Keira was his housekeeper. It was none of her business why he was bad-tempered. She was his employee, nothing more.

Dale braced his hands on the counter and looked her in the eye.

"I told you before that I was in the hospital. It's only been two weeks since I returned to active duty. I'm still trying to find my feet again and learn to be civil." His mouth twisted. "Hard to be social and polite when you spend days and nights bare-assed, needles and tubes snaking out of your body, nurses waking you up every hour to check and see if you're still breathing."

Sympathy shone in her green eyes. "Why were you in the hospital?"

He dragged in a deep breath. Sooner or later, she'd hear the rumors. "I was tortured by demons."

She flinched.

"But I made it, and thanks to one of my men and his girlfriend, who saved my ass and got me airlifted to a hospital in time, I'm going to be fine. Great. Terrific."

"Do you remember anything?"

"Not much." Dale picked up the dish towel and began folding it into thirds.

"The man and his girlfriend who saved you, do they remember anything?"

He frowned. "Shay and Kelly told me there was a girl in the basement, but she vanished. His memory and Kelly's both got fogged. But he'll never forget the girl's face."

She drew in a deep breath. "Where is this Shay and his girlfriend? Maybe they can help you."

"They got married. Shay's away on training, took Kelly with him to live near the base. They won't be back for a few weeks."

Keira's expression remained shuttered. He stared at the counter, willing the memories to become stronger.

"I remember the little boy the demons threatened to torture and kill and how they said they'd make him die slowly if I didn't take his place. I'll never forget his name. Joshua."

"Josh," she murmured.

Dale studied her and Keira flushed again. "Most boys with that name are nicknamed Josh. What else do you remember?"

"There was a wolf there, a black wolf. And a woman. I think. I remember her scent." He rubbed an aching spot behind his throbbing temples. "Citrus and wood chips. No, maybe it was lilies and honey. It's a blur now."

Keira rummaged in the freezer, found a bag of frozen peas and handed it to him. "Here. This will help your headache."

"Thanks." He pressed it against his pounding skull. "How did you know my head hurt?"

"Your face is all compressed."

The cold bag felt good against his throbbing head. "I thought you were going to say my aura is red and black."

"It is." Keira dried her hands. "But I know you're not into that woo-woo stuff."

He had the grace to feel ashamed.

Dale tossed the peas back into the freezer and stuck out a palm. "Let's start over. I'm Dale Curtis, lieutenant commander of the best team of SEALs in the U.S. Navy, sometime classical pianist and foot-in-the-mouth jerk."

A tentative, sweet smile touched her mouth as she offered her hand. "Keira Solomon. Roving gypsy, Luminaire and quirky New Ager. Oh, and I happen to detest bean sprouts."

Her palm felt soft, the bones delicate beneath his big hand. Dale caressed it very gently, feeling the bandage he'd placed there, feeling loath to release her. The delicious scent of cookies, vanilla and almonds drifted from her, tendrils wrapping around him and invading his senses. She smelled like freshness and innocence.

She smelled like home.

Dale hadn't been home in a long, long time.

His guts clenched as he dropped her hand. She did not move but moistened her mouth, staring at him.

Riveting his gaze on her mouth, he moved closer. Closer still, his own lips parting. Hungering to sample her, see if she tasted as delicious as she smelled.

Dale reached for her, ready to cup her cheek and lower his mouth to hers.

A sharp scream cut through the air. Keira blinked, and paled.

Downstairs. Sully.

The SEAL never had nightmares. Ever.

"Oh, God, get it off me! Please! Someone help me!"

Chapter 6

Keira's gaze widened. "I never cleansed the basement with white light."

"I have to get down there." Dale ran into his study and removed his SIG Sauer 9 mm from the safe. Adrenaline pumping through his veins, he grabbed a flashlight and then bolted for the stairs. Keira raced behind him, two large white crystals clutched in her shaking hands.

More terrified screams. Sully was a stalwart SEAL. He'd faced down terrorists and fire demons. What the hell was down there? Dale toggled the light switch, but nothing happened. The basement remained dark.

Dark as the night the demons had tied him down and giggled, and then the hot, razorlike claws had gouged his torso...

Loaded pistol in one hand, flashlight in the other, he climbed down the first step.

Another haunting scream cut through the air. Fear slicked his throat. Immobilized by it, he could not move.

And then he heard Keira's ragged breathing behind him. With every ounce of his strength, he started down the stairs, pointing his flashlight at the steep steps. One of his men needed him.

Soothing white light suddenly cut through the darkness from behind him. He stopped and turned.

White light pulsed from the crystals Keira held. She bit her lip and handed him a crystal. "Take this. It will amplify your powers."

Another bloodcurdling cry cut through the air. Dale tucked the crystal into his pocket. He believed in his powers as a Mage and the gun's bullets, not magick stones.

Sweat beaded his forehead as he advanced toward the bunk beds.

The stench of sulfur and rotting flesh assaulted his nostrils. Dale gagged and forced himself to push on.

He swept the flashlights beam over the room. The lamp he'd left burning so Sully wouldn't be alone in the dark lay shattered on the floor. Dale ran to the wall. While in the hospital, he'd hired an electrician to install floodlights on a separate circuit breaker, in case of emergencies.

So the basement would always have plenty of light.... He flipped the switch, turning on the lights, revealing a nightmare.

Dale dropped his flashlight and stared.

Still lying on the bunk bed, Sully thrashed wildly, fighting with a gray, scaly thing atop him, yellowed fangs sinking into the ensign's neck. Blood slicked his gray T-shirt.

"Get it off me!" Sully screamed.

The ensign's cry was a sharp slap to his terrified mind. Dale pointed his gun, feeling helpless all over again. His SEAL was being shredded by a demon and he could only stand there with a gun in hand, looking for the best shot.

"No!" Keira cried out. "I'll place the crystal on the demon's back and that will break its hold. Then you grab it and throw it to the floor."

Grab it. He pocketed the pistol, stretched out his hands and reached for his powers of telekinesis. Nothing. Drier than the Sahara, damn it.

As Keira advanced toward the demon, memories flashed. Fangs sinking into his side, the burning agony searing his flesh, his voice hoarse from screaming…

"Curt, please!"

The ensign's voice snapped him from immobility. He ran forward as Keira touched the demon's thick, sinewy tail with the crystal. The demon pulled his fangs from Sully and released a high-pitched screech like glass grinding in a blender.

Dale seized the demon, ignoring the stinging lash of its razor-thin tail whipping against his arms, and threw it on the ground. He withdrew his SIG and fired.

The bullets vaporized in midair. Damn! He spotted the poker by the fireplace and grabbed it.

The demon turned and hissed. Sully's blood covered its mouth, making it a red oval. Dale brought the poker down, slamming it on the triangular head.

Another banshee shriek. Dale hit it again. And again. Grayish blood splattered his bare legs, but he barely noticed. Hands wet with sweat, he kept a death grip on the weapon. The poker descended over and over. Had to kill it, make sure it would never hurt again.

"Dale! It's dead."

Keira's soft voice sliced through his frenzy. Dale stared at the floor. Quarter-size dents gouged the carpet. The demon had vanished, leaving behind a pile of gray goo. The poker clattered to the floor and he wiped his hands on his once-clean polo shirt, turning to Sully.

Keira had taken strips of the white sheet and was pressing them against the ragged gash on the ensign's throat. She also held the crystal against his neck, the stone's white glow fading.

Sully gripped the makeshift bandage, his gaze wide. "Thanks, Curt. Thought that thing was going to rip my throat out. What the hell was it? One minute I was passed out, the next this foul breath was in my face, and something burning my skin in the dark."

"It's an espy," Keira said. "Minor demon that sucks on its victim's blood. Prefers dark, damp places to hide and lie and wait like a spider. Goes after those who are helpless, likes to take from drunks." She gave Sully an apologetic glance. "Favorite prey."

Dale wiped his hands on his shirt again, wondering how she knew so much about this demon.

Sully shook his head. "Screaming like a baby. Feel stupid."

He dropped to the bunk bed and clapped a hand on the SEAL's shoulder. "You had a demon gnawing on you like a dinner bone. Nothing to be ashamed of."

Dale had screamed plenty in the dark, dank basement when the demons came after him.... He focused on Keira, who was staring at the mess on the carpet.

When her wide-eyed gaze met his, he gave a rueful smile. "Don't worry. Not going to ask you to clean that. I'll cut out the section and replace it. I doubt my carpet cleaner can remove demon blood."

Sully removed the stained makeshift bandage. The jagged gashes on his neck had knit together. "Amazing," Dale murmured. "The crystal heals."

"White-light therapy."

He still didn't embrace all this crazy stuff about crystals and energy, but the evidence was daunting.

Dozens of questions raced through his mind, but he tucked them away for later. "Can you walk?" he asked his friend.

Sully snorted. "No demon's gonna best me. I'm not a girl to be carried out of here on a stretcher from a puny demon attack." Then he colored deeply. "I'm sorry, sir. I didn't mean to imply..."

"Imply what, Sullivan?"

At his rough tone, Sully paled and looked at the floor. Silence descended, broken only by the tapping of Dale's foot on the floor. "Get upstairs, Sullivan."

The young SEAL sat up straight. "Yes, sir."

Once they were all back up in the kitchen, Dale went to phone for a cab, but Sully stopped him. "I'm sober now, sir. Nothing like a demon attack to chase away a good drunk. I'll see you tomorrow on base, sir."

Sir, not Curt. The formality had returned. All because Dale had once more lost his temper. Guilt pinched him, but he brushed it away.

He had demons to deal with.

Sully vanished in an eye blink. Dale pulled out a chair in the kitchen, gestured for Keira to sit by him. Interrogation time. But he had to be subtle. He shoved aside the niggling feeling of guilt. Had he his powers of telekinesis, he could have beaten the demon more easily.

"Tell me about this demon. How could it have gotten into my basement?"

"Demons are attracted to emotional darkness. It's my fault. I neglected to cleanse the basement today. It must have been lying in wait and when Sully slept, got hungry." Her lovely mouth wobbled. "I'm so sorry. I'll clean the basement now."

Dale gently clasped her wrist. "You weren't at fault. It's my house and I'm responsible for what happens here."

She looked up, her expression troubled. "I don't know if a regular cleansing with white light and crystals can help. Because there's bigger demons to worry about. And when they get here, all you can do is run screaming because they'll do worse than suck a little of your blood. They'll steal your soul and seal you screaming in hell. And no one can free you."

He gazed into her eyes, deeply concerned. What the hell had Keira Solomon run into?

"My team, the Phoenix Force, can handle demons. For now, why don't you get some sleep? It's been a long day."

"I have to cleanse the basement or more will arrive." Her eyes grew huge. "Maybe they're already down there."

Dale didn't want to return to that basement, but no way in hell was he going there alone. He followed her to her room, helping to unpack the bags of crystals and then carry them to the basement. He watched as she set several in each corner of the room and more on the steps, murmuring chants the whole time.

"If any are hiding, for now this should hold them at bay and prevent them from coming upstairs."

When they returned to the kitchen, she headed for the sink, but he stopped her.

"The dishes…"

"Told you. I have a dishwasher for that. I'll finish cleaning up. You get some rest."

And then, because he could not resist touching his lips to her soft skin, Dale brushed a gentle kiss against her knuckles. He watched as she headed toward her room, her hips gently swaying in a seductive dance. For the second time that night, he found himself wondering about Cassandra Sullivan's warning.

Her room felt icy cold. Keira lay beneath the blankets and shivered.

Although it was summer in Virginia, she could not escape the chill of knowing a demon had invaded the sanctuary of Dale's home.

After Dale had finally trudged upstairs, his heavy tread indicating his exhaustion, she'd gone down into the basement and cleaned up the mess. It had taken all her courage and strength.

She knew, more than Dale did, exactly how vulnerable this house was to dark forces.

Demons could still break through the frail barrier of white light and creep in through cracks between the windowsills, wiggle their way into the basement.

She'd dozed off for a couple of hours. Now, the blue lights of the small clock radio glowed three o'clock, the hour of demons.

The thick band around her upper arm felt reassuring and did not cut into her skin. The reminder of her tie to Dale Curtis would protect her against the Centurions. But what would protect Dale? Her crystals were drained and needed replenishing.

How much more evil was hiding below in the dark?

Keira threw back the covers and went to the dresser. Her meager possessions were in the top drawer, including the last crystal that held pure white light. Every time the demons allowed her freedom, she used her spare time to learn the healing arts of Luminaires, and used some of the money they gave her to lure fresh victims to purchase crystals.

She cupped it in her hands, relishing the purity and soothing peace, then placed it on the nightstand by the bed. As she started to drift back to sleep, something rattled in the kitchen.

Trembling, she gripped the bedcovers. Perspiration soaked the clean bed sheets. *Calm down, demons don't invade the kitchen late at night....*

But restless men tortured by them did.

Keira threw back the sheets and shrugged into her white terry-cloth robe. She slipped out of her bedroom and stood at the kitchen door.

Wearing a robe of his own, Lt. Commander Dale Curtis stood at the opened refrigerator door, staring at the contents.

Keira cleared her throat. "See anything good?"

Fork held out like a weapon, he whirled around. Dale relaxed when he saw her. "Couldn't sleep. Sorry I woke you."

"I was awake, as well." She turned on the overhead lights, dimming them.

Dale looked haggard beneath the soft illumination. She wanted to go to him, assure him all would be well and he could safely sleep again in his own house. But she knew it would be a lie.

Because nothing was safe until the Centurions were put in hell for good. The demons, once Roman soldiers in their time, were condemned to the netherworld for their cowardice, never to walk in flesh until they acquired the courage they lacked in battle.

When they'd found a way to escape hell, they found a shortcut to becoming corporeal. By torturing good, brave men, and stealing their strength, they became solid form and were able to enjoy the pleasures they had in Roman times.

They had found the bravest man of all in Dale Curtis.

He poured a glass of milk, offered her one. She shook her head. Her stomach was too queasy. Dale lifted the top of the glass cake holder and cut a slice. Her gaze wandered to the robe's hem, stopping just above his knees, showing his strong calves.

She joined him at the table.

"Amazing. Absolutely delicious."

He licked the tines of his fork, and a tingle shot through her body as she watched his tongue slowly stroke the utensil. Dale closed his eyes, long, black lashes lying against his stark cheeks. His face was all angles and planes, but his eyes, laser-sharp, were his most arresting feature.

Dale's mouth, usually pinched and compressed, now relaxed. He licked his lips and she sensed he did so on purpose. Fascinated, she watched, wondering what it would feel like to have Dale Curtis's mouth pressed over hers, his tongue tasting her with the same pleasure he now exhibited tasting her cake.

His eyes flew open and he looked at her with amusement as heat filled her cheeks.

"It's very good cake." He pushed away his barely touched slice.

"You're not having more?"

"Just a taste. I have to work back slowly to getting my strength. Too many calories and I'll go to fat." He drained the milk.

Keira swiped a finger through the frosting and licked her finger. "Indulging yourself once in a while is permitted."

"Not for me."

"Why are you so rigid?"

"I'm navy. It's part of my life. Discipline and training, that's what makes a SEAL. And endurance and strength."

"You're not a SEAL or a commander here in your home. So kick off your shoes and relax. Have a slice of cake. A whole slice." Keira sighed with renewed pleasure at the enticing taste of the chocolate. "Life is short and you never know what tomorrow brings, so enjoy every moment. That's my philosophy."

"And never letting down my guard is mine." Dale reached over and stroked a corner of her lip, wiping off frosting with a finger.

He brought it to his mouth. Keira's heart kicked hard as he licked his finger. Her body felt loose and wanting.

Dale's gray gaze burned like fire. He looked hungry, but not for food. She drew back. She couldn't risk liking this man. Or lowering her guard and trusting him.

"After we work together, you'll get to relax and sleep," she told him.

"I haven't slept through the night in a long time."

"When we start working on fine-tuning your inner frequencies, you'll have to relax and let down your guard."

Dale stiffened. "Impossible. The moment I let down my guard, look what happens. I get a damn demon in my basement attacking one of my men. I should have brought Sully up here, let him sleep in the guest room."

"It's not your fault."

"Maybe. But there is plenty of evil out there in the world and I'm not allowing it to ruin the lives of innocents."

Keira sighed. "Stop focusing on the bad guys. There will always be the bad guys out there. You have to channel positive energy to beat back the darkness inside you."

"Evil must be punished. There's no gray area about it. You saw the demon attacking Sully. You think that should be pardoned?" Dale threw out the rest of the cake, went to the sink and washed his plate.

"No. But if you consistently look for the bad, you'll find only the bad. You have to look for the good in people, as well."

He needed to heal and recover. Instead, the man held himself as rigidly as a ruler and refused to indulge in an entire slice of cake.

"Discipline and training helped me to become a SEAL and it'll help me regain my strength."

"I heard SEALs are the best of the best. But you can't focus all your time on searching for evil. There is good in the world."

Keira had to believe it, had to find the good each time the Centurions released her. The day her inner white light died, she would want to die, as well.

"That's not my job, to look for the good—it's to search out the evil and eliminate it so other Americans can sleep through the night." He traced a line on the tablecloth.

Her heart ached for the man. He risked his life so others could experience peace, but he enjoyed none himself. She

went to the refrigerator to get some juice and paused, remembering what she'd seen earlier. Tacked to the refrigerator door was a child's crayon drawing of a man next to an
American flag. There was also a photo of a little boy blowing out candles on a cake, flanked by an adoring couple.

A note was pinned to the refrigerator. She read it aloud.

"'We can't thank you enough for what you did for our
son. Because of you, Josh is celebrating his seventh birthday. You are a true hero. Josh drew this picture of you and
we thought you'd like to have it.'"

She turned and saw him quietly watching her.

"You keep this on your fridge. So you must believe in
some good in people. Helping people isn't wrong. Look
at how you saved this little boy."

Dale's mouth tightened. "For every Josh I manage to
save, or my team manages to save, there's four more the
monsters get to first. That's what keeps me up at night."

This brave man, who'd sacrificed himself to save children, had suffered greatly, still suffered. *All my fault,* she
thought, the hollow ache in her chest intensifying.

She must make amends.

Keira went into her bedroom and cupped the small
white crystal in her palms. Dale had given so much for
others. This was one small act she could do for him.

When she returned, he was standing at the sink, looking out the window, into the dark. She placed the stone
in his hands.

"Put this by your bedside, near your head. The crystal's white light will chase away bad energy and help you
sleep. I promise it. It's worked for me."

Her fingers brushed against his strong, calloused ones.
Dale's masculine scent of citrus and pine teased her nostrils.

"What about you?"

She shrugged. "Cake. And if that doesn't work, at least I'll enjoy the remedy."

Dale smiled. "Thanks. Good night."

Keira watched him walk away, the stone clutched tight in his palm.

Upstairs, Dale placed Keira's stone on his nightstand.

He cracked open a book, but could not concentrate. There was no peace at night. He would power up the laptop and surf the internet, check emails, read reports or sometimes would read one of the well-worn books he loved.

The bottles of prescription sleep aids sat untouched in his medicine chest. He refused to take them. Sinking into a deep sleep meant risking vulnerability, slowing his reaction time if he were attacked.

Always, there was a bedside lamp burning.

Some nights, he would lie down and close his eyes and breathe deeply, and drift into a peaceful sleep. And then the nightmares would begin.

They were varied, but threaded through all was a common theme. He was strapped down with heavy chains in the dark basement, listening to the sound of his blood dripping on the floor, wanting to submit to death. And then he'd heard screams, a child's screams. Little Josh, crying for his dad as the demons giggled and took him to the basement. Then a terrible silence. More footsteps and another child's screams as the demons hauled them, one by one, to the basement to die. And he struggled in the grip of the chains, helpless to stop their deaths, their shrill screams punctuating the air over and over....

And Keira wanted to practice her New Age mojo on him? He was beyond magick stones and chants, especially if it meant giving up control.

Drowsiness engulfed him, but this time he did not fight it.

Dale closed his eyes and surrendered. And dreamed.

Not of dark basements and crying, terrified children, but a white room filled with white light, and an eggshell-white bed, soft as lamb's wool.

Keira lay upon the bed, her long dark curls spread across a bank of downy pillows.

She wore a sheer white nightgown that clung to her generous curves and rode up nearly to her thigh, showing the shapely angle of her calf. Soft as the bed itself, and the pure light pulsing through the room, chasing away every single dark shadow.

No demons here.

Eyes of green sparkled with seductive promise. So sweet and pretty.

"I want you," she whispered. "I shouldn't, but I can't resist."

"Take off your gown."

He barely recognized his rough voice, harsh with command. Dale gripped the bedpost, watching as she tugged the fabric over her head and tossed it aside.

Her breasts were round and full, tipped with coral nipples. His gaze tracked down her belly to the small indent of her naval. Blood rushed to his groin, causing his slight erection to harden to stone.

Stretching out her slender arms, she beckoned to him. "Let me heal you."

His body tightened. This was a dream, but her scent of vanilla and lilies pulled at him. He did not want to awaken. Dale shrugged out of his robe. Gathering her in his arms, he kissed her deeply. She tasted like blackberry wine and sweet chocolate, like sin and innocence.

Keira tasted like all his tomorrows.

Groaning, he fisted a hand in her long hair and drew her closer, against the hardness of his body. Her softness molded against him as he kissed her hard and deep.

He felt like a teenager with his first woman. Dale mapped her body with his trembling hands, tracing each square inch of her skin. Fingertips trailed over her round, slender shoulders, caressed the knobby points of her collarbone. Her body was rounded and supple, giving and pliant. He kissed the juncture of shoulder and neck, tasting the salt of her body. A shudder coursed through her as she shifted beneath him.

He continued kissing her warm flesh, tensing his own body for better control, to keep from ruthlessly plunging into her. His mouth trailed a line to the top of one firm breast. When he encased her hardened nipple with his mouth, she gave a startled cry and arched.

But it had been too long since he'd had sex, and he could no longer wait. Dale mounted her naked body and guided his rigid penis to her soft wetness.

His heart wanted to explode when he sank into her.

Never had he felt such astounding bliss.

She was a hot, wet, silky fist around his cock. So tight and warm he wanted to die with shuddering pleasure. He thrust hard and deep and, with a strangled groan, came hard and fast, pumping his seed deep inside her. For a wild moment, knowing it was a dream, he imagined she was his wife and they were creating a child. A family of his own at last.

Coming home to Keira each night, children chattering at the dinner table, helping her clean up after dinner and then once the kids were asleep, taking her by the hand into their bedroom and making love to her long into the night.

Dazed with erotic pleasure and drunk on hope, he gazed down lovingly at the woman lying naked beneath him.

And looked straight into the face of a grinning Centurion demon.

Chapter 7

Dale avoided Keira for the next two days. Every morning, he was gone before she woke. At night, he'd return late, leaving her a polite note thanking her for the meal she'd cooked for him and left in the refrigerator.

But each night the strains of opera or classical music floated upstairs. The man did not like silence.

He was postponing their session. Dark forces were at work and Keira didn't know how long she had before the Centurions broke free and found her.

If she didn't help him to cleanse away the dark energy and become stronger, the demons would make fast work of him. Dale was her only hope for vanquishing the Centurions.

Two nights ago, his screams had awakened her. Running to his room, she'd seen him caught in the throes of a nightmare, thrashing in the damp sheets of his bed. Horrified, she picked up the crystal on the nightstand, only to realize she'd given him the wrong one.

Not a crystal for peace, but clarity.

Keira had replaced the crystal with an amethyst and run it over his perspiring forehead. She smoothed back his damp hair and watched him finally ease into a deep, dreamless sleep. Such an honorable, courageous man of great strength. A man of discipline and tremendous power, and loyalty. Something inside her had turned to restless yearning as she watched him sleep. Then finally, she'd snapped off the light and left his bedroom.

Her own sleep remained restless and edgy.

Nights brought on erotic dreams of Dale making love to her in a pure white bed, his big body moving over hers. She woke trembling, perspiration covering her skin, her heart thudding in erratic beats and her body tight with longing.

With the money he'd given her, Keira bought a massage table and new equipment. She paid extra to have the table delivered by late afternoon to an empty upstairs bedroom.

The bedroom was big, with two large windows and a western exposure to catch lots of sunlight. The walls were painted a lemon yellow, except for one mirrored wall. The mirror would reflect the white light and aid in the sessions, she decided.

The room had no furniture, which was very odd. But perhaps he'd planned to renovate.

She opened the walk-in closet and saw several boxes. Curious, she knelt down and opened one.

Baby clothes. Chest tight, she combed through them, removing an adorable little pink dress. A lump rose in her throat. Had Dale planned this room as a nursery? Had he lost a child?

With great reverence, she closed the box, then shut the door and smudged the room with sage to cleanse it of sadness.

That night when he arrived home, she was fixing dinner. The front door slammed and the sounds of opera filled the air. Like each night, as soon as he came home, he turned on the CD player in the living room.

Dale entered the kitchen, carrying a bouquet of fresh yellow daisies. Wearing a hat and a stiff-looking uniform, he looked quite handsome and very military. Even his shoes were mirror bright.

Cellophane crackled as Dale handed her the bouquet. "I've been buried in meetings with brass the past two days and it's been nice to come home to a real meal."

Keira buried her nose in the daisies to hide her smile. No one had ever given her flowers before.

"Thank you," she said.

He shrugged. "It's a small gesture to show my appreciation." He did not smile. The rigid navy commander returned.

Remnants of a price tag were still on the clear wrapping. The flowers were a gesture, a meaningless one. Keira pushed aside her small disappointment. It would not ruin her joy of the moment. She tore off the cellophane, found a vase in the cabinet and filled it with water, then put the daisies inside and placed the vase on the table. "After dinner, we'll start on your first session."

Dale shook his head. "I have a report to write. I'll eat in my study."

"The work can wait. This can't."

His brows drew together as his mouth thinned. The navy commander didn't like being ordered around. Tough.

"Unless you'd like more imps in your office, chewing on your report and your computer cables and who knows what else."

"You cleansed my house."

"But you're the conduit, the reason why they're attracted here. This—" she spread her arms wide "—is only a house."

He broached the distance between them, his eyes steely gray. "You're accusing me of being a magnet for demons."

Keira didn't back off, even as he got close enough to kiss her. "Yes."

He closed his eyes, his shoulders going rigid. Guilt

washed over her. Dale Curtis had a normal life before she'd dug her claws into him, literally. He could work all night and never have to worry about an imp tearing apart his papers.

"I'll offer you a compromise. I'll serve your dinner in your study, and you can work and then at ten, you come upstairs for your first session."

Dale's eyes flew open. "I don't compromise."

"Fine. Then I'll leave, you can be overcome by demons and you won't have to worry about paperwork anymore."

Holding her breath, she watched to see if her bluff worked. His jaw tightened so hard, she could have used it to pound nails. Finally he nodded. "I'll be in my study."

As she exhaled a shaky breath, he warned, "I don't believe in magick stones and herbs and all that feel-good stuff. This isn't going to work."

Keira gave him a serene smile. "Don't worry. I'll use some of my magick relaxing potion on you and you'll be skipping down the hall and tossing flowers everywhere. Works like a charm."

"What are you, a witch?"

"I've been called much worse."

Chapter 8

Her client was not very cooperative.

At first, he'd refused to change into more comfortable clothing. When he finally did and entered the room she'd set up for therapy, he frowned.

"Not this room. It's off-limits."

"There are no other empty rooms." She tilted her head. "Unless you wish to do this in your study?"

He looked at her as if she'd suggested painting his man-cave pink and decorating it with stuffed animals.

Scented candles burned on a table she'd lugged up the stairs. Colorful crystals were arranged around the ring of glowing candles and the slow, steady beat of a drumming circle played on the portable CD player. Keira had brought the daisies into the room as well, and turned off the harsh overhead lights.

Dale took one look at the massage table and shook his head.

"If I lie down on that, I'll fall asleep. I have to finish that report after you finish your New Age mojo crap."

Keira refused to let his gruff insult sway her. She knew he was scared, and hiding it.

"Falling asleep is good. I want you to relax. Take off your shoes and lie down."

He climbed onto the table and stretched out, stiff as a wood casket. *No, don't think of coffins and death.* She cleared her mind of negativity, thought of a field filled with sunflowers lifting their heads to the sun's caress, a cloudless blue sky and walking barefoot through a lush field of soft grass.

She glanced at her patient. Dale folded his arms across his chest.

"It smells like a flower bed in here," he grumbled.

"Lavender and rose. Aromatherapy."

He gave a derisive snort.

"Why are you so opposed to this? You're a Primary Mage. Magick runs in your veins. You need to stop and smell the roses once in a while."

"I'm a SEAL commander first. I don't stop to smell the roses because the enemy probably planted an IED in the flower bed."

"IED." She experimented with the unfamiliar word.

"Improvised explosive device. One caught one of my SEALs off guard in Afghanistan. He was killed."

Her heart wrenched again. Dale had dealt with the worst of humanity as well as demons. "The bomb blew him up."

Dale sat up, his gaze suddenly guarded. "No, a fire demon burned him to death."

And suddenly she made the connection. Dale wasn't an ordinary navy SEAL and neither was his team. They were fighting both human and paranormal enemies.

He watched her carefully. "You're not supposed to know that, but if we're going to work closely together, there is no way of avoiding it. I'll have to scrub your memories when you leave my employment."

If I live long enough, she thought.

"I'll start with a session of reflexology." She started to remove his socks and he bolted upright.

"Leave them on."

"It works better on bare feet."

"I never go barefoot."

Then she remembered. He'd been barefoot in the basement and the demons whispered to him that his feet were next—her claws would gouge his soles so deep, he'd be crippled for life.

"Forget the reflexology. We can work on that later. Let's try aligning your energy centers. Lie down. All I'm going to do is use the crystals."

Keira selected a large lavender crystal and started to wave the stone over his body, but he remained tense, his aura so dark she could barely see it flickering in the dimmed light. She set the stones back on the table. "I'm going to leave the room for a minute. I want you to remove your shirt and lie on your stomach."

Dale raised himself up on his elbows. "Why? More woo-woo crap?"

Irritation surged, but she kept her voice calm and even. "Woo-woo massages. Can't be beat for getting those stiff upper lips in the navy to relax. You'll enjoy it. Trust me."

The look on his face told her this man had not trusted anyone in a long time. She knew his scars, knew the length and depth of each one. They were all on his torso and belly and arms and legs. Not his back.

She walked out of the room, doing some deep breathing herself. Dale was one stubborn man.

When she returned, he was lying on his stomach, head cradled in his folded arms. His shirt lay folded neatly on a nearby chair.

She hesitated. The last time she'd faced this man on a table, she'd been a wolf, her sharp claws gouging out his flesh. Quivering, she stared at him.

Calm down. You're in control. Think calming, peaceful thoughts.

A field of sunflowers, lush grass against her bare feet...

She stared at the strong muscles of his back and something stirred inside her. A grass field...lying in the grass, Dale's strong, naked body covering hers as they made love...

Okay. Not so peaceful or calming. Summoning all her discipline, she focused on her task. He needed healing. She held the thought in her mind.

Keira changed the CD on the player.

Dale raised his head, his brows drawn together. "You like classical music?"

"No, but I know you do. You play it every night when you return home. This is to help you relax."

She removed a bottle of lavender lotion from her woven basket and poured a small amount into her palms, rubbing them briskly.

Hovering just above the strong muscles of his back, she hesitated. So masculine and rugged, Dale Curtis was chiseled marble. The rich scent of lavender permeated the air, slicing through the thick vanilla, cloves and cinnamon.

Dale's eyes began to close.

"Just relax," she whispered. "Don't think. Don't talk. Breathe. And relax. Let me remove all your cares."

Her fingers smoothed the lotion over his skin. The man was a little thin, but his back was ridged with muscle and sinew. Keira's hands quivered as she stroked over his back, working the lotion into his thirsty skin.

The camouflage pants hugged his taut buttocks. She worked the lotion into his skin, kneading stiffened muscles and sighing with pleasure as she touched him. He reminded her of a marble sculpture, masculine beauty at its finest. Every time she stroked over his skin, shivers of pleasure coursed through her.

Then he turned his head and opened his eyes, looking at her.

"You're all flushed," he said drowsily.

She put her hands to her burning cheeks. "It's hot in here."

His gaze dropped to her breasts, where her nipples stood out like exclamation points against the loose, flowing print dress.

This time, Keira was the one folding her arms across her chest.

Interest flared in his expression as his eyes darkened. Dale's gaze swept down the length of her dress to the hemline ending above her knee.

"You have very nice legs," he murmured.

"I think that's enough for tonight. It's getting late and I have to get up early."

"It's not late."

She thought rapidly. "I have a lot to do tomorrow. Need to get an early start, find a local greenhouse and buy pants. I mean, plants. Herbs. Rosemary, stuff like that."

"You don't need to fear me," he said softly. "Keira. Lovely name. Lovely legs."

Dale started to raise himself up, then glanced down at his torso. A dark flush covered his cheeks and he dropped back to the table.

"I'd like to be alone."

Her heart dropped to her stomach. He did not want her seeing his scars. A lump rose in her throat. *I'm sorry. I'm so sorry.*

"Tomorrow night, we'll start on the real work with the aromatherapy and crystals," she told him.

"Tomorrow night I'm busy. I don't have time for this crap."

Gone was the camaraderie and the progress she'd made. He'd turned back into himself, shutting her out.

It's your fault. Do you really think healing sessions with white light would make up for all you've done?

She closed the door gently behind her on the way out, and then went into her bedroom. All the crystals arranged in a pretty pattern on the nightstand turned dull and lifeless, reflecting her inner misery.

Chapter 9

It had been a bitch of a morning.

First, he'd awakened late and when he'd come downstairs, dressed and ready to grab a cup of Keira's excellent coffee, he found no coffee. No breakfast, and the dinner dishes still piled in the sink.

Dale hated disorganization. And in his house, his refuge, the sole place he could exert a little control in a chaotic world?

Unacceptable.

He knew she was playing hardball. Ever since the massage five days ago, he kept putting off another therapy session. Blaming the intense training sessions in the new firestorm chamber now that most of his team had returned from deployment, Dale dodged her, returning home late each night and leaving early for the base every morning. Much as he hated to admit it, he did enjoy the homey touches she'd brought into his life, from the delicious coffee to the dinners, to knowing there was someone waiting for him when he walked through the door.

Even if the someone was nagging him to do things he firmly resisted.

His housekeeper sat at the breakfast bar, reading a book. She did not glance up.

"Miss Solomon, I hired you to keep house and make coffee, not read books."

She finally glanced up. "You hired me as your personal psi therapist. When you give me an exact time for the second session, I'll start making coffee again."

Infuriated, he snatched the book from her hands and set it on the counter. "Coffee. Now. That's an order."

She plucked at her colorful skirt. "Does this look like a regulation navy uniform? Ah, think not. You're not my commanding officer."

"I am your employer. Get to work."

"Are you willing to do a second session tonight?"

"No."

"Then make it yourself."

Keira picked the book up and resumed reading.

Dumbstruck, he stared at her, feeling everything slip out of his control once more. No way was he consenting to her New Age crap, opening himself up and becoming vulnerable. Hell, every time he glanced in the mirror at his messed-up body, it was a reminder of how helpless he'd been.

He looked at his watch. Damn it, no time to argue. Today they started training with real flames and he needed his men alert and ready.

"This kitchen had better be spotless when I return. I expect dinner promptly at seven. As for your unorthodox, unregulated session…" He struggled with his temper. "You can kiss my navy-regulation trouser-covered ass."

Keira did not glance up as he slammed the door behind him.

The drive to the base took forever. He barely muttered greetings to his staff and concentrated on PT, a six-mile run with his men. Dale pushed himself for another mile, determined to prove he was back on top.

Even though he felt lower than the dirt on his running shoes.

After a quick shower, he headed for his office, snapping at several staff members who kept asking if he was all right. Would they ever leave him alone?

He *was* in a bad mood. Dreams of hot, intense sex with Keira had plagued him all night, leaving him frustrated and edgy. Then he'd woken up to find his house in complete disorder, and a battle of wills waged on the front lines of his kitchen.

Once ensconced in his office, Dale sat at his desk and stared at the stacks of paperwork. Lt. Ted Morrison, his executive officer, was on mandatory training, something he'd put off while Dale was recovering. Ted had been in charge while Dale was on medical leave.

ST 21's new firestorm chamber cost the government a chunk of change and now he had to justify it with form after form. Keegan was right. He was losing his touch with his men, and needed to get back into the field with them.

He also needed coffee.

There was a tapping sound on his door.

"Come in," he barked.

Ensign Robyn Lees entered, a mug filled with steaming coffee on a tray. "Your coffee, sir," she said.

Dale gestured to the desk. She set it down and hovered.

He took a sip and choked. "Sailor, what the hell is this sludge?"

Ensign Lees raised her brows. "I'm sorry, sir, I usually make the coffee but today Artie made it and…"

"I don't need excuses, I need a fresh cup of coffee that doesn't taste like sewer water. Now!"

"Are you all right, sir? You're not acting yourself lately." Concern etched her pretty, freckled face.

Damn it, if another person on his staff asked that question, he'd hang them out to dry. Growling low in his throat, Dale flung out a hand. A ball of dark gray energy shot out of his palm, missing the ensign by inches, and smashed into a table, shattering a vase.

Her eyes widened, and then she hissed at him and vanished.

Dale stared at his hands. Darkness. Demon darkness, just like Keira had warned.

He pushed back his chair and stood in time to see a gray tail vanish beneath the credenza.

Dale got on his knees and peered under the credenza and saw a small gray cat curled in the corner, claws extended, eyes glaring at him.

All of ST 21's support staff were paranormals. Robyn was a Halfling, a cat shifter. "Robyn, come out. Please. I'm sorry."

More hissing. The cat refused to budge.

Dale grappled for control. Great start to the day. He was losing control of his temper and had nearly hurt an ensign whose biggest sin was serving lousy coffee.

Now he had to deal with an angry cat who refused to shift back into her human form. Hell, the way he acted lately, he was lucky his entire staff didn't start using their powers for protection.

"Darling, what are you doing on the floor?"

Startled, he reared up and banged his head on the credenza. Biting back a curse, he crawled backward and stood, brushing at his trousers. A tall, slim blonde stood in the doorway. She closed the door.

"Melissa. Why are you here?"

The last thing he needed was a visit from his sometime girlfriend.

"Everyone's talking about the admiral's birthday ball next week. All the top D.C. politicians will be there. I thought I'd shop for a new gown and came to see if you needed your dress whites dry-cleaned."

Silence hung in the air.

"Of course you received an invitation," she prompted.

"Yes." It was somewhere in the pile of mail he'd tossed aside.

Relief flickered on her face. "Then you'll need a proper escort. Someone experienced in political and military protocol."

Of course. Melissa was skilled in navigating through those murky waters. She enjoyed rubbing shoulders with powerful movers and shakers.

Today she wore a dress that accented her slender figure and thin shoulders. At his silence, she sidled up to him, and ran a hand up his chest. "Darling, I haven't seen you in forever. I miss you."

"You saw me in the hospital. For about five minutes." Dale removed her hand.

She actually pouted. "And you so ill, not able to stand company. What was I to do?"

Stay with me, he thought. Keira would have. Keira, with her stubbornness, refusing to let his gruffness drive her off.

Melissa trailed her manicured hand down his chest. "I was a bad girl for running off and leaving you alone. Let me make it up to you, Dale."

Melissa liked parties and money and wearing designer dresses. Keira wore wild lime prints with pink-and-orange flowers, gauzy material that floated around her long legs. Keira didn't pin her hair up in a tight bun and fasten it with jeweled clips like Melissa, but let it flow wild and free, like a horse's mane.

A soft meow sounded beneath the credenza.

Robyn. He'd forgotten about her. Dale turned to the credenza. "Kitty, please come out. It's okay now."

Finally, Robyn, still in cat form, crawled out. Dale scooped her into his arms and she began to purr.

"You don't own a cat." Melissa looked more bewildered.

The ensign looked at her and hissed.

"Melissa, I'm busy. I'll call you later."

Then, because she was right, he did need an escort to the ball, he gave her a quick kiss on her cheek.

When Melissa left his office, he set Robyn down on the floor. "Ensign Robyn Lees, shift back now. That's an order."

When she did, clothing herself through magick, he aimed her a stern look. "Shape-shifting on the compound without permission or in nonemergency cases is expressly prohibited. I need every man and woman on this team alert and aware. We cannot allow norms to know what we are. From now on, there will be no shifting. Understood?"

"Yes, sir."

He gave a rueful smile. "And that goes for myself, as well. No displays of power. I apologize for that."

"It probably was the coffee, sir. Does taste like bilge water."

He nodded. "Call my house and tell my housekeeper to bring over the manila envelope I left on the kitchen counter. You may meet her at the gate. She doesn't have security clearance. I need those forms ASAP."

Robyn left, returning a while later with another cup of coffee. He sipped and sighed with relief. Finally.

The ensign lingered before his desk, her blue eyes sparking with mischief.

"What is it?"

"I called your house, sir, and asked your housekeeper to bring the envelope, exactly as you instructed."

Dale set the mug down on his cluttered desk. "And?"

"I'd rather not say what she told me."

"Tell me exactly what Miss Solomon said."

"She said she's not driving to the base. As for your report, you can kiss her floral-print nonregulation ass."

Leather creaked as Dale leaned back in his chair. An unfamiliar tickle began in his throat, and spread. He threw back his head and released a loud bark of laughter.

Gods, it felt so good to laugh again!

Ensign Lees smiled. "She was very nice and asked if anything happened. And I told her you got a little short-tempered."

Dale stopped laughing. Damn.

"She said you were in a bad mood and if I made the hazelnut coffee with the pinch of ginseng she sent with you a few days ago, you wouldn't be such a bear. The ginseng gives you balance. It's in the coffee she makes for you each morning. When she makes it."

Dale stopped laughing and sniffed his coffee. "I'll be damned," he murmured.

"Do you want me to drive to your house and get the envelope, sir?"

"I'll get it myself at lunch. Go round up my men. Training session at oh-eight-hundred."

As she started to leave, he saluted her with the mug. "Thank you, Ensign Lees."

Without batting an eyelash, the ensign meowed. "You're welcome, sir."

The morning training session with the portable, dry, chem-fire packs hadn't gone well. He'd pushed and pushed his SEALs, but only Sully, with his powers of teleportation, had successfully defeated the flames in the chamber. Dakota, Dallas and Renegade, all Draicon werewolves, sustained minor burns and even J.T., with his powers of telekinesis, had failed.

Greg, the new guy, had shifted into a tiger and actually charged the flames in a foolhardy show of bravado. Greg was still trying to prove himself to the team and Dale had to reel in his leash.

The half-bred demon training them had extensive knowledge of fire demons. Thad was patient. But Dale was not. He needed his men ready to deploy. All SEALs on the Phoenix Force had to become expert in defeating the flames before the other SEALs under his command could use the chamber.

After losing a SEAL to a fire demon in Afghanistan, he never wanted the team to be caught off guard. Adam was still an aching spot in his gut.

Exhausted, Dale drove home for lunch, intending to pick up his forms and then head back to base for a stale sandwich. Part of him itched to see if Keira had continued to defy him. He longed to have her banter with him, drive away the thick darkness clogging his emotions.

The house was quiet when he walked in and slammed the door behind him. Dale entered the kitchen and found Keira pulling a roast from the oven.

The savory smells of beef and wine sauce teased his nostrils. His stomach issued an approving growl.

She turned, face flushed from the heat. "Great timing. Lunch is almost ready."

Dale narrowed his eyes. "I'm only here to pick up my report."

"And why waste a good meal as long as you're here?" She gestured to a place setting on the table. "Sit down. This won't take long."

Because he was starved, and it smelled good, he sat. Dale looked around the sparkling kitchen. "You did as I asked. Good."

He was partly disappointed she'd not defied him. For some reason, he liked sparring with her. It invigorated him and he enjoyed seeing the spark in her eyes.

"Don't look in the guest bathroom." With an impish grin, she began slicing the beef.

Dale went into the guest bathroom down the hall. All seemed normal. He pushed back the shower curtain.

All the dishes from the kitchen sink were neatly piled in the bathtub.

Laughter tickled his throat. He snorted and then shut the curtain, assuming his most severe look as he returned to the kitchen and began to eat.

"Like your new bathroom decor?" Keira winked as she spooned vegetables onto his plate.

Damn, this woman was going to get the best of him yet.

He cut the meat, marveling at the luxury of having a hot lunch. It was tender and flavored with spices. Suddenly famished, he ate in a hurry. Keira brought him a cup of hot tea and joined him.

Wiping his mouth with the linen napkin, he nodded. "Thanks. I haven't had such a delicious lunch in ages."

She gestured to the white bandage on his left arm.

"What happened?"

"Small burn. Training session."

"I'd hate to see what happens when you're out of training."

He sipped his tea. "It's why we train. We're SEALs. If my men slack on their training, they become ineffective. The more training, the better they're equipped and less likely they are to die."

Her gaze grew troubled. "Have you ever lost a SEAL?"

Dale set down the teacup. "Yes. Remember I told you about this."

"I'm sorry. What was his name?"

Under the rules of ST 21, they were not to mention those who'd passed. Their team was top secret and the public could not know details. But a hollow ache settled in his chest as he thought of Adam.

Keira touched his arm gently. "You said you're going to scrub my memories when I leave your employ, so why not talk about him now?"

And so he found himself talking about Adam and the shifter's incredible bravery, his wit and how important he'd been to the team. She listened, not interrupting, and her gaze didn't wander in boredom as Melissa's would have.

He put their dirty dishes in the clean sink and washed them by hand. Keira left, returning with a first-aid kit. She gestured for him to sit at the table, took out bandages and ointment and then removed the hastily applied bandage he'd slapped on his arm.

"This is a real nasty burn."

"I've had worse." He didn't want medics fussing over him, not now, when he was trying to prove to his team he was strong.

She uncapped the tube of antibiotic ointment and spread it over the burn. "I'm guessing that your body has an increased capacity to heal, since you're a Primary Mage. But if you're undernourished and your powers aren't up to par, that will take longer, as well."

As she finished bandaging his arm, he flexed his fingers. "Thanks. I had planned to bandage it better later, when my men weren't around."

"Why didn't you want them to see you were hurt?"

"We all had a few minor burns. I'm their leader, and have to set an example."

"You should think of yourself for a change. There's nothing wrong with being a little selfish," she said.

Dale shook his head. "Self-centered people have no place in the teams. SEALs function as a team, and we're tighter than family. Brothers to the end." He paused and thought of Adam. "I would die for my men, and they'd die the same for me. I rely on them."

Keira rolled the bandages. "I believe the only person

you can really rely on is yourself. People will let you down. I've always found it better to be self-sufficient."

"You don't believe in teamwork?"

"I believe in myself and my abilities. I've seen the results of teamwork when the team isn't working to benefit anyone but themselves. Some use teamwork as an excuse to manipulate others."

Then her expression tightened, something so unusual for her, Dale wondered what caused it. Who had hurt her so badly she didn't want to get involved with anyone else?

"Who manipulated you?"

She shrugged. "Doesn't matter. I'm not into teamwork. I fly solo. I'd rather fend for myself and watch my back."

"My men watch my six, and I do the same for them. We're tighter than family."

Scowling, she packed the bandages back into the first-aid kit. "Very nice. Sounds like you're all machines in the military. I'd rather be freethinking and individualist than a cog in a wheel like you are."

Dale's temper slipped a few notches. He kept his voice even. "SEALs learn to think for themselves, adapt and survive. My team is extremely flexible. They must be, to survive in terrain from the Arctic to the jungles of South America. Rules and discipline enable us to function as a unit and work together to defeat evil."

Keira turned away, but not before he caught a glimpse of despair in her eyes. "Some evil is tougher to defeat than others. Sometimes I wonder if it can ever be defeated."

He didn't know where this was coming from. Dale touched her arm, wanting to offer reassurance and chase away her sadness. "Trust me, it can. That's why my team exists, to do all we can to protect the innocent from being hurt."

"Doesn't always work, does it? Because the innocent sometimes get hurt along with the guilty. That's life."

His guts wrenched as he thought of Adam. "That's why we have to be the best."

She pushed away from the table and began to dry the dishes in the rack. "Go back to your team. But I'm warning you, if you don't agree to the second session tonight, you're going to be the cog in the wheel that breaks them."

"I'm fine." He pushed back his chair and stood behind her at the sink. The delicate scent of her floral shampoo filled his nostrils. He glanced down at her bare feet, with the toes painted a wild blue color.

So unconventional and free-spirited.

Keira turned, her green eyes narrowed. "You're fine. So fine that your body can't heal from a burn that should have healed by now. Your aura is filled with darkness and if you care so much about your almighty team, then you'll work with me. Because the more time you spend avoiding me, and don't deny you've been doing exactly that, the less time you'll have to save yourself and them from a darkness you can't even imagine. And then who's going to save the world if you're all dead?"

Dale went still. "My team has dealt with evil before."

"Not like this." She picked up the dish towel and began to wring it in her hands, her gaze focused on the sprigs of rosemary she'd placed on a crystal dish.

His instincts went to full alert. "What are you talking about? What kind of demons have you dealt with? Who killed your family, Keira?"

"The worst kind. The kind that keep you alive when you beg to die." Then her mouth compressed and she set down the dish towel. "Tonight. After dinner. Because the longer the darkness resides in you, the weaker you'll become, and the more vulnerable."

Dale clenched his teeth and released a breath slowly. "All right."

He grabbed the manila envelope and started for the

door. Damn it, he agreed only because he never wanted to put his men in jeopardy. Keira was right. He was endangering his team.

But now he had more questions than answers because this woman with her pixie smile and troubled eyes and sparkling blue toes was turning out to be more of an enigma than he bargained for.

He would do her healing session tonight.

And then a little grilling of his own, and have one of his men investigate her.

Keira Solomon was hiding a very large secret. And he'd find out exactly what it was.

Chapter 10

Six feet four inches of pure male sat on the massage table, his body rigid as steel.

Keira lined up the crystals on the side table, centering her own energy. Not only was she dealing with a stubborn man who blocked off all positive energy, but now her own feelings also came into play. Dale Curtis was a magnificent specimen of pure masculinity. Rugged and tough, yet compassionate and courageous. Long-dead female senses sparked to life around him.

Very dangerous. Every time she got feelings for a man, the man ended up becoming demon bait. Most died.

Others had been horribly wounded, and turned into shells of themselves.

She'd learned to shut down her emotions.

Every time the Centurions released her into the world, giving her money and the means to lure new men into their trap, Keira become more despondent. They wanted her to attract strong, courageous men they would force her to torture and then they'd steal their essence and become corporeal for a few days. A few days when they would roam the earth as men once more, only men with demonic powers. They stole vast amounts of money to live a lavish

lifestyle, found women to either seduce or rape, and ate
and drank in an orgy of gluttony.

So she refused, staying alone, never even talking with
men in desperate hopes the Centurions would finally
weaken enough for her to break free of their enslavement.
Didn't work. On their own, they captured new victims for
her to torment.

Keira couldn't fight them when they triggered her wolf
to attack, but she could fight them in human form by refusing their orders. She would not lure another innocent
man into their grasp.

She learned to switch off desire like a spigot.

But now, faced with Dale Curtis, everything dormant
charged back to life, like a drought-ridden meadow after
a spring rain.

A tight black T-shirt hugged his muscular torso and
arms. Faded jeans covered his long legs. His face was chiseled granite, carved by a master artisan, the cheekbones
boasting of an aristocratic lineage, his startling gray eyes
keen and yet soulful. He even smelled delicious, clean and
outdoorsy, with a sprinkle of spices.

Dale had the sharp, intense focus that made her wonder what he'd be like, centering all that intensity on her
in bed....

Touching him... Oh, yeah, she wanted to touch him. But
she had to be professional and concentrate on her work.

"You can leave your shirt on as I do this."

She turned on the portable CD player. Soothing piano
music filled the room.

"What's that?"

"A special playlist of music I made. Guaranteed to
soothe scared dogs and cats, and scowling navy com-
manders."

"I'm not scowling."

She pointed to the mirrored wall. Dale looked at himself. "Okay, you made your point."

"You can probably play all these songs. Maybe sometime you can play the piano for me."

He folded his arms. "I haven't played in a long time."

Silently she made it a goal to coax him into opening the piano lid once more.

Keira lit a bundle of sage and smudged the room. Then she set down the sage onto a plate and picked up a crystal.

"The clear quartz crystal is ancient and sacred, and it makes the hidden transparent. Crystals have a natural vibration attuned to the earth, harmonizing with it, but also act as prisms, channeling white light from the sun's rays. Elemental energy is very powerful."

Her subject stared at the ceiling as if readying himself for more pain. Guilt squeezed her chest. She breathed in the sage and reminded herself of all the good things life had to offer and focused her energy on the pulsing clear quartz crystal.

"Once we achieve the right energy flow, I can work on pouring white light into your spirit and chase away the negative energy and vibrations."

Keira passed the crystal over his body, hovering just above his torso. His gaze tracked her as she held the clear quartz over his heart. The crystal grew black. Alarm raced through her. This had never happened. There was more darkness in him than she'd realized.

"You're filled with negative energy," she murmured, "I have to infuse you with positive energy first. Concentrate on something soothing and healing. Relax."

But he remained rigid. Keira set the stone on the windowsill.

"What do you do for fun?" she asked.

Dale looked bewildered.

She tried again. "Isn't there anything you enjoy doing that gives you a lot of pleasure?"

He raised himself up on his elbows and gave her a slow smile. "Yes. But usually it involves a bed, and getting naked."

Heat filled her cheeks. She looked away as he softly laughed.

"I didn't mean sex."

"It's how I relax and unwind. You should try it instead of playing with magick stones and energy fields."

Mischief twinkled in his gray eyes. She didn't want to think about it—Dale's strong body, naked and mounting her as they writhed together in ecstatic...

Don't go there. Be professional.

"Sex is overrated," she muttered. The demons had wanted her to lose her virginity and use sex to lure men to her side. Keira refused and even when they beat her, didn't cave in.

"Maybe you've never had the right man to show you how it's done."

Keira shook her head. "Sex without love and emotion is as pointless as fighting evil with bullets and guns."

"Bullets and guns protect people against the bad guys. You're very innocent."

The remark stung. "I'm no innocent." She'd seen things that would send strong men screaming into the night.

"Naive, then. Thinking evil can be fought with herbs and crystals." Dale lay on his side, watching her, propping up his head on one hand. "Wanting only to see the good in people."

"I hope I never lose my ability to find the good in people. Because that's what keeps me functioning from one day to the next. If someone could tell me how to find joy another way, and shove away the bad stuff, I'd sell my magick stones and follow him."

His expression softened. "No one can tell you the true way to joy and how to avoid evil. All I know is you have to stand on your feet and take in life as much as you can, and face it with courage."

For all his stubborn resistance, Dale Curtis was a good man and had a compassionate heart. He camouflaged it with gruffness, but once in a while, it peeked through.

"Thank you." Then she gave him a gentle push. "Now lie down and let me work with my magick stones."

Dale closed his eyes. She chanted sacred words as she passed the crystals over his body.

When she stopped, he sat up, alert and aware. Already she felt his aura pulsing stronger bands of red and blue.

"We're finished for now, and I'd like you to rest for a while, then we can do another session in two hours. I need time for the crystals to drain of negative energy."

"Can't we do this tomorrow night?"

"The faster we work, the better. You can take a break tomorrow night."

She needed to investigate his aura more clearly. Keira suspected the Centurion demons had implanted something in Dale, but she hadn't been able to find it yet.

He jumped off the table as she walked to the mirror.

"I've cleansed this room, but it still has very faint traces of residual energy. Not sad or negative, just hopeful. What was in here?" She paused. "I'm sorry, I don't mean to be nosy, but I've never experienced anything like it."

Dale's gaze turned haunted. "A nursery. I started painting it the day Kathy told me she was pregnant. I was overjoyed, always wanted children and we'd been trying, or so I thought. I mirrored one wall to reflect the light because I wanted our child to have a bedroom filled with sunshine. Went out and bought baby clothing. Friends gave me their baby clothing they didn't need anymore."

He gave a derisive snort. "Fool I was. The paint was barely dry when she came home and said she was leaving me. She was pregnant, but with another man's child. Her lover."

Then he touched the mirror. "I wanted to feel angry at her leaving, but realized we'd grown apart a long time ago. Never wished it to come to that. Odd, how empty I felt. As if I ached more over losing a child than losing my wife."

Keira's eyes filled with tears. She turned to hide them. So much emotional and physical pain, yet he'd remained staunch and solid.

When they left the room, she closed the door, wanting to keep the stones and herbs protected within the sanctuary. Any negative emotions Dale experienced would remain outside the room.

He glanced at her. "If we have two hours to kill, how about watching an old fifties movie? Want to join me?"

Silly of her heart to beat so fast, for that flutter of excitement to spread through her body. "Only if you let me make popcorn."

Dale grinned. "Only if you let me put extra butter on it."

"Calories."

"I'll work them off tomorrow." He stopped, braced an arm on the wall, effectively trapping her. "Some things in life are meant to be savored."

He had the most extraordinary eyes, gray as morning mist, gray that could turn hard as cold steel. Dale Curtis was a man who looked you straight in the eye and did not shy away. But his voice was deep and husky, stroking over her like the brush of warm velvet. She wanted to wrap herself in his voice to ease the constant yearning and longing for what she could not have.

They would never be lovers.

They would never be friends.

And yet this was a man of deep integrity and courage, who represented everything good and decent she wanted to see in the world.

He drew near, his warm breath feathering against her cheek. Close enough to kiss her. Close enough to coax all her dead dreams into life. Such a firm, sensual mouth, contrasting with his masculine chin and hard, lean cheeks.

Keira put a palm on his hard chest, but not to push him away.

Dale regarded her beneath his hooded gaze. Then his nostrils flared as if he'd scented something. He turned his head sharply.

Keira's heart stopped as she looked toward the stairs.

She hadn't effectively warded his house against all the demons, after all. One materialized and now stood at the stairs, cackling with glee. Dale stared.

"What the hell…"

"It's a Geldsen." Keira backed away, recoiling in disgust. "A minor demon, drawn to nobility and strength, because it lacks any of its own. It was a human woman, and traded its soul for power."

"How did it get in here?"

"I think you brought it here." This was worse than she'd thought. If Dale were a demon conduit, how many other ugly creatures would come chasing after him?

"The Geldsen is drawn to your strength and courage and honor." She breathed deep, pushing down panic. If only she had enough power and white light to ward the house, this creature could not have entered. But it was here now, and they were hard to vanquish because they had to be weakened first.

The Geldsen cackled and raked a claw down the wall, shredding the elegant gold-and-white-striped wallpaper.

Dale's expression tightened. He pushed Keira behind him in a protective move.

The Geldsen advanced, pointed spikes shooting from what were once wispy strands of red hair. With its slit of a nose, and slash of a mouth, it looked hideous, though it once was pretty, she guessed.

Stepping from behind Dale, Keira threw a crystal at the Geldsen, but the crystal cracked and shattered before touching the demon. Stunned, she reeled back, summoned a small energy ball and tossed it at the demon.

The Geldsen laughed and batted it away like a child's toy. She simply wasn't strong enough to fight demons. Then the demon ignored her and fixed its gaze on Dale.

"How the hell do we get rid of this thing?" Dale asked.

And then insight slammed into her. "Let's lure her into the therapy chamber."

The Geldsen advanced, her glittering yellow eyes fixated on Dale. "You're a handsome one," the demon cackled. "I'll eat your insides for lunch and save your man parts for dessert."

Dale grabbed Keira's hand and tugged her down the hallway. He threw open the door to the chamber. The Geldsen followed, screeching like an enraged banshee.

"In the corner by the mirror," she told him.

She prayed this would work. Hatred and envy fed the Geldsen's demon strength. Both were powerful sources. But Dale was a courageous navy SEAL and a Primary Elemental Mage.

Dale crouched in attack position as the Geldsen advanced. "Die, bitch," he snarled and threw her against the mirror.

Keira raced for the light switch. Harsh overhead lights flooded the room.

The Geldsen looked stunned for a minute. Then it snarled and reached out with red talons for Dale.

"See yourself for what you are, demon." With a hard kick, Keira sent the Geldsen reeling.

The Geldsen caught its reflection in the shiny glass and staggered back, screaming.

White light glowed in Dale's right palm, the energy ball dancing in his outstretched hand like a child's toy.

"Do it," Keira choked out. "Send her straight back to hell."

He threw the ball. It hit the Geldsen's chest, where a human heart once resided, and exploded. The banshee scream turned into a pathetic whimper as the Geldsen shattered into thousands of dust particles and then was no more.

Keira gulped down several breaths, more shaken than she wanted to let on. The Geldsen was an unwelcome surprise. She'd warded the house with as much powerful white light as she could muster, but her feeble powers weren't enough. She needed Dale stronger.

She went down the hallway and cringed at the shredded wallpaper. "Sorry about that," she told him as he joined her.

Dale's grin made him look boyish. "Never did like that wallpaper. Was planning to remodel, and that bitch just gave me a head start."

"Guess this is a good lesson." She flexed her fingers, thinking of her meager, diminishing power.

"Hoo, yeah. Don't mess with a navy SEAL." He gave another lopsided smile. "Or a pretty Luminaire. That was some kick."

"You didn't do so bad yourself, sailor."

His smiled faded and he got an intense, dangerous look. Keira sucked in a breath. This was no man to trifle with, and a powerful Mage who could fry demons even when not at full strength.

Intelligent man he was, if Dale figured out the Geldsen had not attacked her, and started asking questions why...

Let's really not go there.

"Forget the movie for now." He turned and folded his muscled arms over his chest. "Tell me why you know so much about demons. I want to know everything. Starting now."

Chapter 11

For the next two hours, Keira told Dale most of what she knew about demons, how she'd made it her business to go to libraries on her travels and consult with books.

By the time they returned to the therapy room, she felt drained and numb. Keira lit several fragrant candles and breathed in their scent, then took the largest crystal and poured all her white light into it. She placed the glowing stone gently on his chest.

Trying to keep her emotions even wasn't easy in this room filled with past pain and her own inner guilt. Keira studied the crystal and his aura and concentrated.

She needed to see the inner striations of his aura for a hidden demon signature.

Continuing with the chanting, she finally was rewarded with sparks of yellow and red that formed a pattern she knew well.

Sucking in a deep breath, she removed the now dull crystal.

Dale opened his eyes and regarded her with his usual intense focus. "What is it?"

"Demons implanted a signature pattern in your body. I

didn't see it before because it's hidden deep in your aura. The crystal has brought it into sight."

"What kind of demons?"

"Centurion demons. Basically, it acts like a homing beacon so the demons can find you, no matter where you go."

He looked stricken. "Get rid of it."

"I can't, not without your help. I need to cleanse all the darkness from you to do it."

"Terrific. I'm a walking demon target." He sat up, looking alert. "Wait. Maybe I can use this to my advantage. Lure the bastards here, including that demon wolf, and then break their necks. I've made it my goal to find that bitch."

You won't have to look that far, she thought.

Keira bit her lip and rubbed her sweating palms against her dress. "I wouldn't do that. You're the target, but the demons will use you to get to others. Maybe even your men."

Dale would use himself as a target, but refused to endanger others. "Too risky. How can I trap them for good? Tell me what you know."

Must tread carefully here. If she revealed too much, he'd get suspicious. "Centurion demons are not corporeal when they roam the earth. They're not easy to vanquish. How did your SEAL banish them?"

"He chanted a powerful Mage spell."

"Probably only strong enough to vanquish them for a little while, until they can access their bolt-hole here in this world. Once they do, they'll head straight for you."

His jaw tensed. "How do I kill them?"

She had pondered that question many times over the past twenty-three years. "Probably the only surefire way is vanquishing them and then sealing the bolt-hole they use to access this world. That way they can never return here."

"Bolt-hole. I'll get one of my men on it ASAP."

"It won't be easy to find."

She knew, because she'd sacrificed some of her free time searching for it herself.

"What would be the sig pattern of this demon bolt-hole?"

At her surprised look, he added, "I have some experience with them. My team sealed a few."

Hope filled her. If his team had sealed bolt-holes, then they had a fighting chance.

"It's not like anything you've encountered before. It has to be in the earth, connected to the earth and the elements. You won't find it in an urban environment, but it will be surrounded by an area of past violence."

He looked thoughtful. "Not Iraq or Afghanistan?"

"No. The violence isn't controllable." She struggled to explain it. "Terrorist violence is sudden, unexpected and destructive. This bolt-hole is like a rift to the underworld. It opens and shuts like a door. Enough dark energy opens it, and terrorist violence is too random to give it adequate strength to stay open long enough for the demons to use it."

She hesitated. If she gave an approximate location, it would speed up the search. But she couldn't risk Dale finding out too much about her past.

"The violence keeping it open is probably induced by the demons and not by humans. In my travels, I've come across residual dark energy from past wars, and extremely violent campaigns in Central America. Civil wars there were brutal, especially in Nicaragua. The bolt-hole may be there, in an area where villagers whisper of ghosts from the war."

He jumped off the table and headed for the door. "I've got work and I'll be in my study. Feel free to borrow any DVDs and watch a movie in the living room."

"I have work, as well." She needed to set more protective measures around the house. Keira had once felt safe and secure here, but now the house felt filled with demon land mines. She rubbed her palms against her skirt. "Tomorrow's Saturday. I need you to drive me into town with your truck to pick up some plants."

As he arched an eyebrow, she added, "Herbs and plants to ward the house. Might help."

Dale's eyes grew hard and cold. "Not as much as finding that bolt-hole. And the woman who put me in this mess in the first place. The woman in the basement who tortured me. When I find her, she won't have to worry about a bolt-hole to hell. I'll send her straight there myself."

He headed for the stairs as she sank against the wall, shivering and afraid.

Two hours later, Dale sat in his leather easy chair in the study across from a tall vampire with shoulder-length chestnut curls. Stephen was ST 21's best asset, a good friend and the best man for finding the demon bolt-hole.

The vampire had been in D.C. visiting with friends. He not only changed his plans at Dale's request, but also brought a bottle of 200-year-old French Hennessy cognac. As they drank snifters of the amber liquid, Dale filled in Stephen on the details of the demon visits and Keira's attempts to heal him with light therapy.

"A demon bolt-hole, probably in Nicaragua, surrounded by violence. Shouldn't be too difficult for me to find." Stephen sampled the cognac. "Demon sig patterns are fairly consistent, with overlays of crimson and black striations. It's how they recognize each other, even disguised as humans. They can even use the patterns as a calling card."

"The same sig Keira saw in my aura. She's trying to cleanse away the demon traces and negative energy."

The vampire looked thoughtful. "It's a time-consuming and draining process that takes a lot of power, more than a Luminaire usually has. Their methods are too fruity for me. Unconventional and feel-good. I like to kick demon ass, not bathe it in white light."

"Oh, she can kick ass all right."

Dale inhaled the cognac's fragrance of spices, flowers and nutmeg. Rich and heady, it suddenly reminded him of Keira. She seemed as delicate as oak-barrel-aged brandy, but that leg kick to the demon... He grinned and swallowed a sip.

"You're looking much better than you did in the hospital, my friend. You look alive again."

Dale roughly nodded in agreement. In the hospital, his eyes were cold and dead, blank and devoid of emotion. He'd look into the mirror and see nothing, feel nothing, except a frozen emptiness.

He wasn't a man.

He had become nothing.

When he came home, he learned to regain his life. Little things like shaving on his own with a steady hand. Sleeping with only one pistol under his pillow instead of two.

Turning off the downstairs lights when he went to bed, not leaving them blazing to chase away every shadow.

Little by little, his routine returned, with small changes. Now, instead of the basement, he kept the iron in the kitchen to press his shirts and get the crease in his pants perfect. He turned on the radio to SiriusXM's classical-music station and let the soothing tones fill the air to tune out memories of his blood dripping on the basement floor.

And then there was Keira, with her unevenness, disorganization, crystals and spontaneity, turning his ordered life upside down all over again. Keira with her shining white light and big green eyes and air of innocence amid a world-weariness he'd seen so many times in his mirror.

Keira, who was bringing light back into the dark corners of his life.

He wanted to kiss her, draw her into his arms and hold

her tightly against him. Jesus, it had been too long since he'd had sex. Melissa was often his bed partner, safe and predictable, and always combing her hair after, checking her makeup and teeth. She always seemed to worry about ruining her hair.

Orgasms, yeah, she'd had a few. Dale knew he was a good lover. Staying with Melissa had been the easy way. She never complained when his work took him overseas, never hinted about marriage or commitment. There was no real passion, no fire.

With a start he realized his relationship with Melissa was tepid as cold tea. But Keira...

Keira would probably love it if he fisted a hand in her hair and kissed her hard and deep. She wouldn't complain about getting hot and sweaty if he coaxed her to scream and beg. She'd cling to him tightly as they tangled together, two lost souls reaching for pleasure to chase away the cloying darkness....

Where the hell had that come from? He shook his head, trying to clear his mind.

"I wonder if it has to do with your new Luminaire, Keira," Stephen mused.

"She's definitely improved my life since I got out of the hospital. I'd have introduced you, but she went to bed early."

"Have you done a background check on her?"

Dale nodded and told him about the admiral's mind-meld. "She's clean, seldom stays in one place, usually takes odd jobs here and there, probably to bulk up her income. No known relationships or associations with any groups."

"Bring her to the base and have Thad check her out."

He swallowed his surprise with the brandy. "Planned to bring her to the base, but not to have my half-demon petty officer examine her. Why?"

"Most Luminaires lack sufficient power to tackle demons. Just being cautious. Especially since she's so closely connected to you. Call me a concerned friend." Stephen stretched out his fingers. "Tell me about her."

Dale did. For the next few minutes, he told Stephen how she'd invaded his life, turned it upside down. A wide grin touched his mouth as he relayed the story of the coffee.

"She sounds quite spirited." Stephen studied him. "You like her. A lot."

His shrug hid his feelings. "I like how she cleans my house."

"You like more than that, I sense it. If that's the case, don't screw it up, Curt, or you'll lose her the way you lost Kathy."

The brandy soured in his stomach. "My wife left because she cheated on me with a goddamn yoga instructor named Larry. They're probably eating macrobiotic food and living in a hut somewhere while they commune with nature."

"Your wife left because you couldn't give her an emotionally satisfying relationship. You neglected her."

"Bull. I gave her everything she wanted. There was no reason for her to leave our bed." He tossed back his drink. *When I was around to please her.* But the life of a SEAL meant deployment and down range took precedence over the home range.

Stephen leaned back and swirled the brandy in his snifter. "I'm not talking about sex. For women, it has to be more than great sex If you want a relationship to outlast the tough times. When was the last time you told Kathy she was pretty? Brought her flowers, ones you picked out yourself, not had one of your staff buy? Took a day or two off to spend in bed with her, feed her chocolate and strawberries?"

The vampire set down the glass and leaned forward,

hands braced on his knees. "Told her all your dreams and hopes? Shared your fears about the job, shared yourself?"

Dale's scowl faded. Had he been so caught up in the job that he'd neglected Kathy's needs?

"I know a thing or two about women, Curt. And I know you SEALs. You're so busy jumping out of planes and blowing things up that even when you spend time at home, your mind is still on the job."

Stephen glanced at the doorway. "That Luminaire is the first woman to make you this animated in the past ten years since Kathy left. She's the best chance you have at happiness. Don't blow it. Give her an emotionally satisfying relationship, not just the ten orgasms a night you give the other ladies who've wandered through your life."

"Twelve," he said absently. Far easier to please Keira in bed and keep her so enthralled with sex than to share himself. He couldn't risk handing over his heart because no way in hell would he risk having that particular organ sliced and diced again like his ex had done to it.

He rubbed a hand over his face. "That pretty Luminaire is my housekeeper, vamp. I have no intentions of forming any kind of relationship with her."

"Oh." Stephen ran his tongue over the tip of one fang. "Then you won't mind me indulging. I've never had a Luminaire in my bed. I bet she likes her sex with a bit of bite."

Dale grew enraged at the thought of Stephen nibbling his way down Keira's long neck, getting her naked and tumbling her into bed. He fixed a cold stare at the vampire. "She's in my house, under my protection. You touch her, and I'll snap off both your fangs and break your fingers, one by one."

A low laugh rumbled from Stephen. "A little much, Curt. See? I knew she was more than just a housekeeper and your therapist."

Then the vampire drained his brandy in a single gulp.

"Be careful, Curt. Soon as you can, bring her to the base and have Thad check her out."

"She's not a demon," Dale countered.

"Maybe not. But there is something about her you like," Stephen said darkly. "And if she's hiding something, you could be in danger, my friend."

"My heart or my life?"

"Quite possibly both."

Chapter 12

Sunrise was the best time of day.

After filling a mug with coffee, Keira opened the sliding glass doors and stepped onto the wooden deck. Pink streaked the leaden sky, chasing away the ghosts of night. Behind her, Dale stepped out, looking crisp and refreshed in dark trousers and a powder-blue polo shirt.

"You don't have to get up this early. It's Saturday," he told her.

"I like watching the sunrise and greeting the day."

Dale braced his hands on the railing. "It's just another sunrise. I've seen plenty."

"There's no such thing as just another sunrise. When you've spent a long time in darkness, you learn to appreciate every single time the sun rises, because it means a new day filled with possibilities and fresh hope."

He turned and studied her. She cradled her coffee cup, holding her hands around it protectively.

"Is that what happened to you, Keira? Is that why you travel around the country, doing your feel-good routine? Because you want to chase away the darkness? What kind of darkness are you talking about? The darkness of demons?"

How astute of him. How well he'd pegged her. But she wasn't one of the problem countries on his map. Stick a pushpin into it, categorize it and file it away. And suddenly, she needed him to know that, needed him to realize she wasn't a problem easily solved and soon forgotten.

Because for years, she had remained forgotten, a dusty pushpin tucked away in a drawer, never taken out into the light, no one ever knowing of her existence. Anyone who would have remembered her, family or friends, was dead.

Keira needed this man, who'd call her his enemy if he knew who she was. But being remembered, even as an enemy, seemed much less painful than having her life wink out into permanent darkness. Once she left Dale Curtis, that was it. She wasn't aiding the demons again. If Dale failed to vanquish the Centurions, Keira would never return to hurting others.

Even if she lost her own life.

"Everyone has demons. Some are larger than others." She sipped her coffee and lifted her face to the dawn.

"True. I have my own."

Dale crossed the distance between them, his gaze intense as he studied her. She became aware of the way the peacock-blue and green satin kimono clung to her body, how the cool morning air touched her skin and made her nipples stand erect. Oh, how she adored pretty things. They fed her soul.

But the way he gazed at her now, as if she were more lovely than the satin or the sunrise, filled her heart.

Silly heart, she thought, feeling it pound harder as he stroked a finger over her satin-covered arm. *Don't you know that hearts are made for breaking?*

Dale Curtis could steal inside hers, crush it beneath his military boots.

But she'd been lonely for so many years. Keira yearned for closeness and connection. All those horrific hours in the basement when the demons forced her into wolf form, and made her angry, pain-ridden beast rake claws over Dale's exposed body, the small part of her humanity had registered his bravery, and his sacrifice.

This was a man worth saving.

This was a man she could fall in love with.

"There's all kind of darkness. I've seen my share. It's why I cherish the light, and try to find the good in people."

Dale gave a wry smile. "I've seen my share as well, and why I try my damnedest to vanquish it."

His mouth was firm and yet looked soft, soft enough to kiss. He had a rock-hard body, and suddenly she wondered what it would feel like to hold him against her. Casual sex for once, now that she was free to make her own choices.

For a little while.

His gaze was warm and as the sun touched the horizon, his admiring look made her toes curl.

You're not good enough for him, a small voice whispered inside her. *He deserves better.*

She pushed aside the whispers, knowing they stemmed from the dark thoughts the demons had planted in her mind. Instead, Keira imagined herself looking at the monkeys at the zoo, sitting on the shore by the ocean, and eating a hot-fudge sundae in her flannel pj's while watching old movies, all the things she'd taken a little time to enjoy when the demons granted her freedom.

"You're so pretty when you smile like that," he murmured, and brushed a lock of hair away from her face.

The bare touch against her cheek sent shivers of need curling up her spine. What would it be like waking up with this man in her bed, curling her naked body against him as they greeted the dawn?

Dale didn't release her hair, but rubbed it between his fingers. "So soft," he murmured.

She slowly inched away, forcing him to release the

strand. "And it's a mess. Bedhead. Shower time. Hang out here a few and I'll make you breakfast when I'm finished."

Keeping the smile in place, she saluted him with her coffee cup and ducked back into the house.

She took a hasty shower, combed her hair and pinned it in a severe bun, then selected an old pair of jeans and a candy-cane-striped shirt. Left untucked, the tails dangling past her bottom, the loose shirt looked definitely unsexy. Then she prepared a hot breakfast of eggs and sausages.

After breakfast, she rode shotgun in his truck to a local nursery. Dale switched on the radio and the droning sounds of classical music filled the cab. Keira shook her head and gave him a mock smile.

"No wonder you're filled with negative energy. This music is boring."

He threw her a look. "It's classical."

"Dirge music."

"I suppose you'd tune in to a station that featured love songs."

"Actually I prefer rock and roll. Or bluegrass."

She punched a few buttons, brought up a satellite-radio bluegrass station and began humming the music. "Classic. Listen to that fiddle."

"I prefer violin."

"Snob. Live music is best. Always wanted to attend a big music festival, like Bonnaroo in Tennessee."

Dale shook his head. "I think sealing my eardrums with hot wax would be more pleasant."

"Expand your horizons and maybe you'll learn to like it."

She opened her purse and withdrew the checklist of what to purchase. Fennel and holly repelled evil. Burning mistletoe fended off negativity. Keira already made bay-leaf sachets, soaking the leaves in water for three days and then straining them, sprinkling the dried leaves around the house.

"Rosemary and heather, lavender against bad dreams and negative energy," she murmured. "We may not find everything at one nursery. This could take a while."

"There you go again, focusing on the negative," he teased.

"I'm not negative, just practical. This is a war. In war, don't you use every weapon in your arsenal against the enemy?"

At his nod, she continued. "My arsenal consists of plants and herbs and crystals, and what white light I can coax from elemental energy."

"Not as effective as an M16."

"No. But some demons eat M16s for dinner before gnawing on your bones as their dessert."

A long silence stretched between them. She noticed how tightly he gripped the steering wheel, his gaze haunted. "I know."

He fiddled with the radio knob, punching buttons. The lively sounds of an orchestra blared from the speakers. "Georges Bizet's opera, *Carmen*. Not melancholy or sad."

She began humming along. "This sounds like marching music."

"It is. I learned to drill in the navy to this music. Learned to take my first steps as a baby to it. Got diaper-trained to it."

Keira turned her head and saw him wink. "Tease."

As she'd expected, the first nursery they visited didn't stock all the plants she needed. They spent the morning combing through several Virginia Beach nurseries. He surprised her, this navy commander who liked classical music and teasing her. He asked several questions of the staff about landscaping and colors, and fertilizers. Like everything else he did, he did nothing by half measures.

When the truck's bed was full, Dale consulted his watch.

"Since it's Saturday, and I don't have to be at the base, let's take a leisurely ride back and stop for a late lunch."

"We should get back and start planting."

Dale took her hand and turned it over. "You've been cooking for me all this time and it's about time someone cooked for you. Let me treat you."

His calloused thumb stroked over her palm, making small circles. Keira shivered again, wondering what it would feel like to have his hands roving all over her body.

They pulled into the parking lot of an Italian restaurant surrounded by tall trees. Dale escorted her to a booth by a wide window overlooking a garden. The natural rocks and plants soothed her. Sitting across the table from him, she almost felt like they were on a date.

The slave armband around her arm was a constant reminder this man was not a potential lover, but her employer and her protector from the Centurions.

Since she'd had so few pleasures, Keira indulged her imagination. The restaurant, with its mauve leather banquettes and music softly playing in the background, was charming and romantic.

A waitress in a starched white shirt and crisp black pants took their drink orders and handed them thick menus.

Dale scanned the selections. "Lots of garlic. So no vamps here."

"Any recommendations?"

"The lasagna and the spaghetti. Food here is excellent and they have good wine."

The waitress came with a beer for Dale and a glass of ice water for Keira and took their orders. They started discussing places where they'd traveled, his favorite destinations and places she longed to visit. Enthralled, she watched him begin an animated discourse about volcano boarding in Guatemala.

The way he paid attention to her, how he kept asking her opinion and listened to her, really listened, made her feel special.

Only one other table was occupied. A man and woman on the restaurant's other side sat across from each other, accompanied by a baby in a high chair and a little boy about four years old.

Keira sipped her water. "This is a nice restaurant. Isolated, though. How did you find it?"

"My team comes here for dinner. We like it because it's hard to find for starstruck tourists wanting to see a real navy SEAL. The owners only recently started serving lunch and opening earlier. Word probably hasn't gotten out yet."

He glanced toward the restaurant's other patrons and his expression lit up. "I'll be a son of a bitch…"

Grabbing his bottle of beer, he slid out of the booth and went to the couple. "Blake the snake, how the hell are you?"

The man looked up and grinned. He jumped out of his chair and embraced Dale in a bear hug. "Curt! You bastard."

They pounded each other on the back as the woman gave an indulgent smile. Dale grabbed an empty seat and pulled it up to the table.

"Dale, this is my wife, Jessica. Jess, meet Dale Curtis. Went through BUD/S together. Ex-swim buddies until I had to drop out, wuss that I was."

"Wuss? You broke your left femur in two places." Dale stuck out his palm. "Pleased to meet you."

The woman smiled. "Hi. Honey, I'm taking Michael

over to see the fish tank while you two catch up. Keep an eye on the baby."

Dale politely stood as the woman did. Then he and Blake started talking. The waitress brought over two plates and placed them on Keira's table. She glanced over at Dale, but he seemed oblivious.

"You here alone? Want to join us?" Blake asked.

Dale shook his head. "No. I'm here with a friend."

Keira had excellent hearing, even when she wasn't in wolf form.

He didn't even glance her way. Keira drank more water, feeling invisible.

"Friend, right. Is that what you call them these days?" Blake laughed and clapped him on the shoulder.

Dale shook his head and sipped his beer. "She works for me. Nothing more. We were buying plants for landscaping."

"Speaking of nurseries, when are you going to start growing one of these?" He jerked a thumb at the cooing toddler.

Dale's expression slipped. "One day."

The baby began to cry. Blake started to get up and Dale shook his head. "I'll get her. Sit and finish your lunch before it gets cold."

His own lunch sat, untouched, across from Keira.

She watched as Dale picked up the little girl, then sat down with her, rubbing her back. He looked so peaceful and content, a lump rose in her throat.

What would it be like, to have a family? A real home and a husband and children?

Keira's throat closed up. She was Dale's employee. Nothing more. Her job was to restore his health and get him into fighting form. She inhaled the scent of her meal. Pasta wasn't her favorite, but this had a zesty, homemade smell with a bite of oregano. Food was a real pleasure.

Under the demons' enslavement, when they had a new victim for her to torture, she'd been given bread and water and only enough thin, stringy meat to keep her alive. The starvation diet made her wolf meaner, hungrier, more vicious.

As she picked up her fork, the door leading to the kitchen opened. A man in a chef's hat, dressed in a white uniform stained with spaghetti sauce, stood in the doorway.

Sloppy cook, she thought absently. The sauce had splattered over the lower half of his shirt, like a large bloodstain. She looked down at her lasagna.

The bowl filled with pasta was filled with wriggling worms swimming in sauce. Her fork clattered to the table.

Heart racing, she looked at the chef again. His face bulged and changed, the nose flattening, the eyes bulging out and yellowing, the mouth a red slash.

Demon.

Chapter 13

Keira's thoughts spun crazily in her mind as she struggled against rising panic.

My team comes here for dinner.... The owners recently started serving lunch and opening earlier....

Wildly, she signaled to Dale, who, though he had set the baby back into the high chair, was as oblivious of her as the demon chef. Of course. She was one of the few who could see through any demon's human disguise.

She had to let Dale know without alerting the demon. Keira beckoned to the waitress, who she could see now had a long, forked tongue snaking out of her thin mouth, and beady, red eyes.

"Something wrong with your meal?" she sneered.

"It's delicious. But I'm afraid my companion's lunch is getting cold. Would you mind returning it to the kitchen and reheating it?" She forced a smile. "He and his buddy got to talking. You know men when they catch up. Oh, and please bring me more garlic rolls."

The demon waitress removed Dale's plate and went into the kitchen, followed by the demon chef. That should keep them preoccupied for a few minutes.

She slid out of the booth and approached Dale, trying

to appear casual and not raise suspicion. To her relief, the food on his friend's table all looked normal.

No, the demons saved the good stuff for me, she thought. Keira squeezed Dale's muscled shoulder. "Time to leave. Don't bother with a carryout box. The meal's not all that great, after all." She looked at Blake. "Get your wife and kids out of here. Now."

Dale stared at her as if she'd grown two heads. Blake's eyes narrowed. She couldn't blurt out that the special of the day was live worms and the restaurant was run by demons. For all she knew, Blake was human, not a paranorm.

"There's a gas leak in the kitchen," she whispered. "I overheard them talking about trying to plug it."

Blake and Dale both pushed back their chairs at the same time and stood. But Dale, thank the gods, looked in the direction of the kitchen and his eyes narrowed. He knew. He saw.

His friend only looked concerned.

The woman and the little boy had finished looking at the fish tank. The brightly colored coral fish and blue-gills were all floating at the top. A sinister air fouled the restaurant, as cloying as cheap perfume. Why hadn't she noticed it before?

Because it wasn't until Blake called Dale's name, she realized. Names had power and once the demons heard the name, and saw the taint of darkness clinging to Dale's aura, they dropped the guise.

The powerful guise.

Immobilized, she watched a demon exit the kitchen and head right for the woman and the little boy. Clutched in the demon's hand was a meat cleaver.

Keira didn't wait to see if the demon planned to use it. The stones in her pocket glowed hot and fierce. She removed a crystal and called to the demon.

"The food here sucks!"

The demon turned as Dale made a strangled sound. The woman gasped and clutched her son. Damn it, still too close. She couldn't risk hurting them.

"Blake, call your wife over here. Right now," Dale ordered.

Fortunately, Dale's friend did so. Lifting the boy in her arms, the woman ran to join her husband.

"Get out of here, Blake. I'll handle this. You've got your family," Dale told him.

The man hesitated, as if he wanted to help Dale, but hustled his family out of the restaurant.

Keira threw the crystal. It hit the demon in the chest and sank deep. Gray blood splattered the clean granite counter.

Her focus centered on the dying demon, and the others now entering the dining room. Three, five... Oh, damn. Ten demons.

One she could defeat. But ten? Odds were not too good.

"Keira!"

She turned and caught the salt shaker Dale tossed to her. "Throw it on them!"

She pelted the first demon with the salt, watched its skin dissolve. The demon clawed at its chest and howled.

But they couldn't vanquish them all with salt. Dale threw another salt shaker and it landed at the demon's head. It exploded in grayish mess.

"Behind me," he growled, and removed a pistol from his back pocket. Before she had time to tell him bullets wouldn't kill these demons, the navy commander fired several shots.

Not at the demons, but at the bottles overhead on the shelves. Glass exploded, showering vinegar and pickled vegetables down on the demons, who clawed at the shards.

Dale shoved the pistol back into his jeans, grabbed her hand and they ran out of the restaurant, slamming the door behind them as the demons rushed forward. They leaned their weight against the heavy wood door as Blake stood by his SUV, his family secure in the car.

"Curt! You need my help?" the man called out.

"Stay where you are," Dale yelled back. He looked at Keira. "Cell phone, right pocket. Dial pound-three and then hold the phone up to my ear. Those are ectoplasmic demons. Shape-shifters who imitate human form. Had some acquaintance with them on a mission a few years ago by the Red Sea. What the hell are they doing here?"

Dale braced his weight against the door, fighting to hold the demons back as they scratched and pounded on the door. The frame shook.

"They didn't materialize until your friend called your name. They're after you, and everything and everyone associated with you."

She fumbled with his phone, pressed pound-three. When a male voice answered, she held the phone to Dale's mouth.

"Red zone warding, Taste of Naples restaurant ASAP! Bring all you have," Dale barked out.

She clicked off the phone and leaned against the door. Horrified, she saw a forked tongue flick between the frame and the wall, licking her ankle.

"Oh, gross," she cried out and stomped on it.

A car filled with men in navy uniforms pulled into the parking lot and the sailors climbed out. They stared at Dale and Keira.

"Sorry, restaurant's closed," Keira called out, struggling to keep the door shut. "Health-department orders. Rats inside. Big ones. Really big."

Desperate, she looked at Dale. "Use your powers. You're the only one who can dispatch them."

The door kept shaking and trembling as the demons screeched and wailed. "You'll have to hold the door."

"I can do it. Just be quick. On the count of three, when they rush outside, hurl a ball of energy at them."

"I don't have enough power for all of them. One or two, yes." Dale clenched his fists. "If only I wasn't so damn weak."

"Pull strength from the sun. Elemental energy for an Elemental Primary Mage. Hurry!"

Dale stepped away from the door and into the sun as she struggled to hold the door closed. Stretching his hands upward, he closed his eyes. Sunbeams streamed down toward him like the rays of a rainbow, pouring into his body. As he looked at her, his gray eyes glowing with fiery power, she felt her feet slip and skid.

The door opened a few inches and a claw lashed out. Biting her lip, she used all her strength to push it shut again.

"Keira, on three! One, two..."

"Three," she whispered and let go, ducking and rolling to the ground.

Dale blasted the demons with energy balls. They screamed and exploded into grayish muck, splattering the sidewalk.

Keira lay on the ground.

Gray gaze steady, Dale helped her up.

The carload of sailors stared at them, their mouths hanging open, as a shiny black SUV screeched to a halt before the restaurant. On the back of the SUV was a bumper sticker that read Orgasm Donor. Doors opened and four muscled men jumped out and raced over. She recognized Ensign Sully. The other three must be Dale's SEALs, as well. Tight-faced, they ran over to their commanding officer.

"A little late," Dale said drily. "You missed all the fun and games."

"Curt! You okay?" the tallest one asked.

He gave a rough nod. "We're fine. Need a mind cleanse on the lookie-loos over there ASAP. I'll handle Lieutenant Blake and his family. Implant the memory the restaurant was evacuated due to a propane-gas leak."

The tall SEAL grabbed a bag from the SUV and handed a penlike instrument to Dale, then took two others. The men rounded up the bystanders and used the cylinder to flash light into their faces.

Dale did the same to Blake and his family, then shook the lieutenant's hand before they headed to their car. He jogged back to her and scrutinized her face.

"You okay?"

She nodded, drawing in several deep breaths. "I had to figure out how to warn you without alerting your friend and his family. I knew what was going on as soon as the food was delivered."

His jaw tightened. "I didn't mean to ignore you. Blake and I go way back and I hadn't seen him in months."

"No prob. Not like we were on a date. Good thing, too, because if this were a date and you took me to a place where demons served bowls of worms disguised as spaghetti, I'd have to end our relationship. I prefer my worms dead and sautéed, not swimming in marinara."

He smiled and touched her hand. "Live worms and demons are deal breakers, huh? I'll remember that next time we go out."

Her insides clenched at the power of his smile, and the simple caress of his hand against hers. She didn't want this attraction, didn't want to get close to Dale.

Keira pulled away. "Not necessary. Going out to eat is overrated, anyway."

Dale gave her a speculative look as if he read her mind and knew she deliberately lowered her expectations because she didn't want to face disappointment. So much disappointment in the past.

Changing the subject, she gestured to the four men finally approaching them. "Your team?"

Dale introduced her. The tall one with the quiet air who wore a shiny gold wedding ring was Matt Parker. Dallas and J.T. were the other two, and she already knew Sully.

"Keira Solomon. She's a Luminaire psi therapist and healer, and I hired her as my housekeeper."

She kept a smile firmly in place, knowing Dale didn't want his men knowing her real purpose, though he probably wouldn't even admit it to himself.

"Luminaire psi therapist?" Matt asked.

"Yeah, but don't let that fool you. She makes a great chocolate cake and not all that wheat-germ organic stuff that other Luminaires love," Sully said.

"Luminaires. New Age hippies. Peace, love and all that bullcrap. What a waste," Dallas murmured.

He exchanged a look with J.T. Irritation gnawed at her. Why did everyone always look as if she were about to break into a chorus of "The Age of Aquarius"?

"Nice truck," she told Dallas. "Yours?"

At his proud nod, she added, "Nice bumper sticker, too. Does your mother know about it?"

The three other SEALs laughed at Dallas's red face. Keira cautioned herself. She treaded on dangerous turf. Shay, the SEAL in training, had seen her face, although he couldn't remember her name, thanks to the demon spell. But she couldn't be certain he had not told the other SEALs what little he remembered.

The best defense was a good offense. She smiled and stuck out a palm to the scowling Dallas.

"Let's start over. I'm Keira Solomon, Luminaire, psi therapist and healer, and all-around snarky woman when I've been tangling with a restaurant filled with demons. Didn't mean to poke fun at you, but when your spaghetti lunch turns into a bowl filled with worms, one does tend to get a little testy."

As he shook her hand, his eyes still narrowed, so she added, "So glad you guys did show up. We can't be certain there aren't other demons lurking inside the restaurant, demons who didn't come out." Her smile dropped as she thought of the innocents who may already have died. "Or that they killed the real owners and staff."

The scowl finally faded from Dallas's handsome face. He looked at the restaurant, his expression thoughtful. J.T. cleared his throat. "They've been opening a new restaurant in Maine. Mark and Tina took their staff with them and turned this restaurant over to their 'cousins' while they are gone."

"We didn't think any relatives would have the same home cooking as Tina makes, so most of us shunned the place." Matt gave Dale a steady look. "We were going to tell you, but it slipped our minds. You were in the hospital still."

"Right," Dale said. "Check out the rest of the restaurant. I want a full report in fifteen."

"Yes, sir. We're glad you're okay," Matt said.

"We freaked when we got your message. Not that you couldn't handle it," he added, as a scowl darkened Dale's face.

"But we worried something big was going down. After I told the others about that demon gnawing on my neck, we needed to make sure you were okay, Curt," Sully added.

J.T. and Dallas nodded.

"Don't want to lose you, Curt. After what happened to you…" Dallas stopped.

"I'm fine," Dale told him. "Now go do your job and I'll feel even better. We'll be out here."

Keira's chest felt hollow. Dale had people who cared about him.

She did not.

He escorted her over to an outdoor table while the SEALs investigated. Keira sat down, grateful to rest her shaky legs.

She drew circles on the tabletop with her forefinger. Gently, he clasped her wrist. "You sure you're all right?"

"Not really. I'm a little queasy."

"Nearly eating worms does that to you." He stroked a thumb over her thudding pulse. "Not many women could hold it together as well as you did back there. You're a strong one, Keira Solomon. Not your typical New Age hippie."

At his wink, she laughed. "Your men are like you. Very pragmatic."

"A little. But they're all individuals, each with their own talents and personalities. It's what makes the team strong, like a family."

"You're proud of them," she said, not wanting to hear more about teams and family and all the things she'd never have.

"They're good men, all of them. We've been through a lot together."

He frowned. "Why were the demons here? What did they want?"

You, she almost said.

"It's the dark energy you have inside you," she told him. "I told you, you're a demon magnet. They must have been attracted to your energy pattern, knowing you have frequented this place."

The SEALs emerged from the restaurant. Matt held up a large rice sack. "Not all of them are dead, Curt. Found this one in the freezer, trying to hide, but the temperature killed it."

Icy cold slammed into her as he set down the bag and opened it. Dread curled down her spine as she peered at the creature inside. Oh gods, oh gods. It was the size of a small woman, but with pale, hairless skin, a bald head, pointed ears, long talons and the nubs of breasts. Pointed teeth showed through its parted lips.

"Jimali," she breathed. "Oh, Jimali."

"What's a Jimali?" Dale demanded.

Not answering, Keira sagged onto the chair, trying to collect her reeling thoughts. Jimali was another Centurion slave she'd met while the woman was still human. Jimali started to enjoy tormenting men after doing it for decades, but as a result, lost all her inner white light, and eventually, her soul, becoming a shriveled, ugly shell of her former self.

This is what I'll become if I don't defeat the Centurions.

Glancing at his men, she gave a tight smile. "It's a toy for demons. Kind of like a dog toy, without the squeak. And it's not dead. The cold just paralyzed it. Keep it locked up tight because when it comes back to consciousness, it's going to be in a real bad mood."

All five men studied her with narrowed gazes. Ignoring the others, she turned to Dale. "Can I talk with you alone?"

Taking her by the elbow, he escorted her to his truck while the men continued examining the creature in the sack. Dale folded his arms across his chest. "Details. Now."

She clenched her fists and gulped down a deep breath. "I didn't want to share this in front of your men."

"What I know, they know. They're the best and most highly trained at hunting demons. Go on."

"Jimali is not a what, but a she. She's a minion, a scout sent by specific demons to find the target they're searching for. Easily sacrificed if necessary, very expendable."

"It looks almost human."

"She was human. Not anymore." Keira locked her gaze to his. "This is what I didn't want your men to know. She must have been sent by Centurion demons. They're sending out scouts to search for you, and they're narrowing in. Unless you regain your powers and eradicate the darkness inside you, they will find you, and when they do, they'll kill you."

Chapter 14

Dale didn't scare easily.

As a commander of the finest SEAL team in the U.S. Navy, he prided himself on being a levelheaded, confident leader.

Hearing that Centurion demons were on his heels didn't frighten him.

But the news sure as hell scared Keira.

Sweat trickled down her brow. He could pick up threads of her increasing heartbeat and even if his hearing wasn't ultrasensitive, the way her hands shook clearly indicated fear.

He wanted to bring on the Centurions, lead them straight to his house and he'd be waiting, not with guns and bullets, but everything he had. She was right. He needed all his powers at top performing levels.

And he needed to know why these particular demons scared her so much. The woman had calmly confronted imps, Geldsens and ectoplasmic demons, evil creatures that would send a strong man into shrieking hysterics. And now, with the news about the Centurions, she broke a sweat.

Why?

"If you eradicate the darkness tainting me, will all my powers return? What must I do to regain all my lost magick?"

Keira scrubbed her palms against her skirt. "The healing sessions will help. I'll have to ramp up the intensity and work faster, because it's usually a slow process."

"Let's do it. Right now."

Dale lay on the table in the spare bedroom, watching Keira arrange her crystals in a row. Downstairs in the basement, his men guarded Jimali, now imprisoned in a steel cage as Keira had instructed. If she succeeded in restoring Dale's powers and ridding him of the demon sig, Jimali would grow confused, like a hound that lost the fox's scent.

Right now, the creature was snarling and snapping to be free. It had Dale's scent and wanted at him, to mark him for her masters and then share in the prize of slowly torturing him to death.

He wondered if Jimali were the demon wolf he sought. Keira had been evasive when he'd asked if the demon could also be a wolf. But the thing's scent was too foul. No way in hell would he find himself attracted to it.

Unlike the demon wolf that had shifted into a lovely human woman, whose scent made his cock grow rigid even as his blood dripped to the floor.

"Like humans, paranorms have chakras, entry doors to the person's aura. But unlike humans, the more powerful the paranorm, the more protected the chakra. It's tougher to heal a paranorm than a human, and you're a Primary Elemental Mage. Your body naturally protects itself against anyone tampering with your aura and your powers."

"Then how did the Centurions strip away my powers and invade my aura?" he asked.

"They targeted specific areas by testing you to see your greatest fears and then used those fears against you, ramp-ing them to extreme levels and opening you up to being invaded. Like an enemy army striking down all a country's defenses first before taking the offense."

She gave him a serious look. "I thought couching it in military terms might help offset your suspicion of woo-woo crap. Because if this is going to work fast, you're going to have to trust me, and believe it can work."

Keira picked up a clear crystal, the glowing stone emitting a low hum. "Luminaires use a crystal infused with their own natural white light, combined with elemental energy, to divine what chakras need cleansing."

She passed the stone over his body. At his scalp, throat and heart, the crystal's serene white glow faded, becoming cloudy and pulsing weakly. "Your crown, throat and heart chakras are unbalanced, but not that weakened."

Next, she passed the stone over his solar plexus and it glowed white, the hum becoming louder and the light more strident. "Your sacral chakra is fully functional. It's tied to your creativity and sexuality." Again, the charming blush. "No problems there."

Dale agreed. He never had trouble in either of those areas, just not enough time to indulge them.

She passed the crystal over his body and hovered at his groin. Her perfume teased his senses and his cock gave an appreciative twitch. Dale tried to concentrate on something else, anything else. Baseball. Home runs. Sliding into home plate…sliding into a woman's soft, wet core. Score.

Then he imagined the Centurions, their thick, eerie giggles each time the demon wolf shredded his already raw flesh and he screamed….

Dale breathed deeply and looked down. The crystal had turned jet-black.

"Your root chakra. The sig pattern is here. This is the gateway they used. Root chakras affect fear and can be weakened from several things. Being tired, career troubles…"

He sat up. "When the demons lured me into the trap, I was exhausted, two days without sleep, worried about my men and that damn mission in Honduras. Kept thinking I should have gone with them instead of staying in the office, dealing with bureaucratic bull."

"That's it. You were restless, anxious and your guard was let down, and the demons only had to prey on your fears to slip their mark inside your aura. This is why you've been irritable and tired, and resisting any kind of change."

She went to the table and selected three vials of oils and poured them into three separate dishes. The pleasing scents of cedarwood, sandalwood and patchouli filled the air. Keira brought over a flat, round black onyx stone with runes carved into it. She placed it on his groin.

"Now for the hard part," she murmured.

"Actually, it's soft right now," he joked.

She looked sympathetic. "I know this is difficult for you, because it goes against what you're conditioned to believe. I know you're scared, too, because it is different. Trust me. Remember your origins, and remember a time when you weren't in the military, when your life was taken up more with music and creativity and you opened yourself up to other belief systems, to trusting others and yourself."

Keira picked up his hand and stroked her fingers gently across the back. "You were trained as a classical pianist and became a military man because your heart suffered to see such evil in the world. Your musical talent was set aside to focus on the physical because while your playing brought joy to others, it didn't bring you joy. Not while there were bad men out there who wanted to silence the joy for others forever."

So true. He'd traded his Steinway for a pistol.

"When we're finished, you'll be able to play again, be-

cause you'll have balance. You'll remember how to center
yourself with both work and leisure. Now close your eyes
and breathe deeply, as if you're getting ready to dive into
a deep, warm pool."

He didn't know what to say. Dale closed his eyes and
breathed deeply.

"We're going to use music to help you focus. Think of
a time when you were happiest playing the piano."

He did, remembering concertos and notes and the joy
of losing himself in the music.

The low, lyrical sound of her chanting voice drummed
a soothing vibration in his ears. Her notes corresponded
with each inhale and exhale. Harmony and melody, he
thought, concentrating on holding the image of himself
sitting at the keyboard, stroking the keys to coax the music
into life once more. Mozart's Piano Concerto No. 20. As
he imagined the final movement, working up to the final
cadenza, her chanting became louder and more urgent as
he played faster and faster.

The chords of the concerto became more frantic and
resonated with energy.

At the crescendo, a thrilling D-major finish, the music
in his mind became loud and brilliant and fierce. He heard
Keira grunt, felt something yank, hard, out of him and then
an odd but fulfilling emptiness, as if a heavy weight had
lifted from him. He felt energized and filled with vitality, stronger than he'd been in weeks. Hell, no. Months. A
low, vibrating frequency hummed in his body. His powers.

And then a loud, shrill scream split the silence. Dale
opened his eyes and sat up, staring in dumbstruck disbelief.

Keira lay on the ground, tussling with a large, white-
and-black-striped snake about seven feet long. Not a snake,
not with those segments and the blind, searching head.

A worm.

Keira screamed. "Help me! I can't fight it off any longer."

Jumping off the table, he went to seize the worm, and remembered. Dale stretched out his hands. "Let go," he commanded.

Releasing the worm, she rolled away. Using his telekinesis, he yanked the wriggling creature away from her, flinging it against the mirror. It hit the mirror with a mighty crack, shattering a glass pane, and slithered downward. Still alive. Still writhing and hissing.

Dale gave a cold smile. "Come and get it, bastard."

Gathering his powers, he sent a current of pure white light singing through the air, aimed at the worm now sliding toward Keira, who was gasping for breath as she crawled on her elbows away from the creature.

The energy ball hit the creature, sizzling along its scaly skin, and the worm screeched from its gaping mouth filled with rows of sharp teeth. Then it burst into a froth of white goo. Even as it burst, he sent another energy current toward it, burning the white gelatinous mess into ash.

Particles settled over the floor, lightly dusting the hem of Keira's dress.

He ran to her side, smoothed a hand over her sweating forehead. "You okay?"

She nodded.

He glanced at the ash-strewn floor. "That thing, that worm, it was inside me?" His guts churned at the thought.

She nodded again.

"It's what made me bad-tempered and out of balance, draining my powers," he offered.

"Worms tend to do that to people." Keira gave a shaky smile. "But it's gone now. You did it. You got rid of the demon sig. You're on your way to healing now. It will take a little while to get all your powers back, but now you're no longer blocked. And I bet you'll have better control over them, too."

"We did it. Together. We make a good team." Dale, now filled with a wild energy and joy, helped her to her feet.

Unable to resist the softness of her skin or how lovely she looked, despite her tousled curls and a smudge of ash on her cheek, he drew her into his arms and kissed her.

She stiffened and planted her palms against his chest, but then made a small whimper he knew was pleasure, as her body relaxed and her arms wound around his neck. She tasted like ripe berries and sharp wine, and her mouth was soft and warm and pliant.

His cock gave an eager jerk upward in response. Never had he been aroused this quickly or wanted a woman this badly. Even making love with Kathy hadn't been like this, searing and intense, a kiss that struck a deep chord inside him, leaving him hungering for more.

Too long the joy had vanished from his life. Dale intended to make up for lost time, and Keira would play a part. His accompanist, who had returned his life to him.

When she sighed into his mouth, and her tongue darted out to meet with his, he nibbled at her lower lip. With tremendous reluctance, he broke the kiss. Dale smiled down at her.

Such a brave, strong soul, this Keira Solomon. Never had he imagined an unorthodox Luminaire, with her unconventional magick, would cure his soul.

"Now all we need to do is find those Centurions and that damn demon wolf." He rubbed a thumb along her cheek. "And fry her to ashes, too."

Dale wanted to fry her to ashes. Keira sucked down a breath, and put a trembling finger over her kiss-swollen mouth. He was filled with energy, his powers almost fully restored.

Hers were nearly diminished. After pouring everything she had into the crystal, and then yanking away the psi worm from his spirit, she had nothing left. Vulnerable, weakened, she didn't dare say anything because in this state, she could very well spill her secret.

His sexual energy thrummed and sent vibrations of pleasure echoing in her feminine core. Drained of all energy and power, her female self responded to his pure masculine force, aching to be filled. If she didn't balance her own chakras and restore some semblance of internal harmony, she'd surrender to desire and tumble into bed with him.

Bad idea.

Dale rubbed a thumb along her lower lip. "You look like you've been kissed and kissed well. Let's take a minute before going downstairs?"

Keira tried to gather her scrambled thoughts. "Downstairs?"

"The basement. My men are there, watching Jimali. Remember?" He kissed the corner of her mouth again. "You smell like honey and fresh lavender."

"Maybe I should meditate, try to restore myself first. I'm a bit shaky."

"Meditate later. I'll even light the candles for you." Dale tugged her hand. "I don't want to spend another minute with a damn demon in my house. Right now I feel I could fry an army of them."

When they reached the basement, all four SEALs stood around an empty cage, a circle of wary, frowning men. Keira's heart pounded harder.

"Curt! It vanished. Poof!" Sully snapped his fingers.

"More like a slow fade-out," Dallas amended. "First it stopped snarling, and looked confused and then this black slit appeared in the air and Jimali was yanked inside."

"Because it lost the scent, and whoever is holding its

leash recalled it before anyone could poke and prod and discover who sent it." Keira flexed her sore fingers. Holding onto the worm that she'd pulled from Dale's aura had drained her.

He told them about the worm, and his men's faces tightened. "That thing was inside you all this time? What do you want us to do, Curt?" Dallas asked.

"I want a full search of every restaurant, bar, cathouse, doghouse, any house either I've been in, or any of you have visited in the past two months. Need a full electromagnetic scan for dark energy forces, specifically demon."

"Stephen can help us. He can scent demon blood a yard off. Vamp's a real hound dog about demons," Dallas stated.

"I've assigned Stephen to finding the bolt-hole used by the Centurions and that hellhound wolf."

"That demon wolf. When you find her, let us have at her, Curt. We'll all take turns doing to her what she did to you." Dallas growled and extended his long fingers. Claws erupted from the tips.

Draicon werewolf. Shifters who held the power of changing and other psi powers. All the SEALs nodded grimly.

Oh, gods. They'd kill her. Simply kill her. Show her no mercy. Keira pasted a smile on her face, hoping no one heard her rapidly pounding heart.

Dale paused and glanced at Sully. "We may need to bring your sister in on this."

Blood drained from the young SEAL's face as the others chuckled. "Ah, hell, Curt, don't do this to me."

"Cassandra's a pure Mystic Witch. She's got years of skill flushing out demon energy."

Dallas elbowed Sully. "Your sister's going to have a good time, looking through all those nasty places you've been to, Sul. All those skanky beds—"

"Enough," Dale interrupted. "Sully, you team with Cassandra and search all the restaurants. The family ones."

Sully looked relieved.

"The rest of you, cover the others."

But before leaving, the SEALs nodded at Keira. "Thanks, Miss Solomon, for saving our Curt's hide from that thing. We owe you one," Dallas said.

A shaky smile touched her mouth. *Remember that when you find out what I really am, okay, fellows?*

When the men left, Dale turned and lightly gripped her upper arms. "You okay? You're pale and sweating."

"I hate basements. And violence."

His thumbs slowly stroked over her bare skin, streaking the thin layer of ash left by the exploding worm. "I know. But this is a necessary violence that can save lives."

"Got it. Listen, it's been quite a day. Think I'll shower this gunk off."

Gray gaze searing into her, he stood a breath away. She wondered what it would feel like, to be subjected to his intense focus in bed, his hands stroking over her bare skin. Dale had a smoldering male sexuality she found irresistible, a promise of molten pleasure. Images flared: a naked Dale covering her, all slick, hot maleness as he pushed slowly into her untried body.

"Now you're blushing," he said softly.

Keira put her trembling hands to her face. "All these demons, zinging straight out of hell, no wonder. It's too hot. I can't stand the heat."

Dale picked up her hand and thumbed her knuckles. "There's also a good kind of heat, the type stemming from passion. The flush of a woman's skin, indicating her desire."

"Best remedy for that is a cold shower. Real cold." Keira smiled and stepped back, breaking the connection. She did not want to bond with this man, emotionally or physically.

"Don't be afraid of me, Keira. You restored me. I'm in your debt."

"I take credit cards," she said lightly.

He laughed, but as she turned and fled up the stairs, she felt the heat of his burning gaze watch every move.

She'd removed the demon sig from his aura and saved him from turning into demon prey. And now felt like a deer stalked by a hungry wolf. Not demon prey.

His prey.

Chapter 15

Sunday, Keira awoke early and donned her oldest clothing, and tackled the yard. Planting gave her great pleasure. Feeling the dirt slip between her fingers grounded her to the earth.

Her people were of the earth, and being outdoors in the fresh air and sunshine gave her fleeting peace.

Dale didn't come outside once. Keira didn't see him at all. When she took a break and went into the kitchen for a drink of water, she saw a note in his crisp, flowing handwriting.

> Went to the base for a meeting. Will be back for dinner. Save your appetite. I've got a surprise for later. My treat.

He signed it with a bold, slashing *Dale*.

When he returned home, carrying two large sacks of groceries, she was dressed in a nice dress, waiting. And deeply curious. She'd had so few surprises in life and those had not been very pleasant.

He dumped the sacks on the granite counter. "I'm cooking dinner for you."

At her crestfallen expression, Dale laughed. "Cheer up. I may not be a gourmet chef, but I make mean Maryland crab cakes."

"How mean? Do the crabs bite?"

"Very mean. Enough to tempt your palate." He playfully tapped her nose and then guided her to the high stool by the breakfast bar. "Sit, and watch the master at work."

"Should I get the first-aid kit handy, in case you slice your finger?"

He laughed, such a deep, hearty and unrestricted sound, it made her heart leap. Keira suspected this was the real Dale Curtis, the man who'd been lost inside his own soul.

As he mixed ingredients for a pie, they talked about their favorite desserts. Then he slipped the pie into the oven.

He started preparing dinner as she watched. "It's nice having someone cook for me for a change. Although this is a great kitchen to work in."

"I redid it after Kathy left. Remodeled the whole house." Dale added crab to a bowl and began to beat in eggs. "She seldom spent time in the kitchen, but I needed a fresh start."

"Who taught you to cook?"

"I did. Read books, watched television shows until I got it right. Since Kathy didn't like to cook, I learned."

She reached for the platter of cheese and fruit he'd set out and sipped the white wine he'd poured into her glass. "Cooking is like yoga. You get into the rhythm of things, it becomes like a mantra."

Dale held up the bowl and gave her a solemn look. "Ooooom."

Keira giggled.

"Not everything relates to positive and negative energy," he added. "Sometimes you have to let go, have fun for the sake of fun."

"I believe that, too. Embrace life with both hands because you never know how long you have."

Dale set the bowl down and looked at her. "What are you afraid of, Keira?"

"I'm afraid your delicious dessert is going to burn if you don't watch that oven," she said lightly.

He turned and pulled the pie from the oven. Smoke curled in the air, and instead of crisp, brown crust, the pie looked burnt.

"Ah, well. Dessert is ruined." He glanced up, his gray gaze twinkling with good humor. "But there are alternatives. Much better options."

Heat spiraled through her at the sexual suggestiveness of that look. Keira hoped he meant more fruit and cheese, because she didn't know if she could handle Dale Curtis in bed.

How could she have sex with this man? Surrender everything, engage her emotions, when they were so different?

Guilt suffused her. And what of him, and how badly she had hurt him?

He served dinner in the dining room, lighting two elegant tapers and turning off the lights. "I'm trying to be energy-efficient," he said, smiling.

The crab was excellent, served with fresh green beans, the salad crisp, and Dale put her at ease with amusing stories of growing up during a time period when "children were seen and not heard, except if they had magick powers and made their wishes known."

When he saw her glass was empty, he waved a hand, and the wine bottle rose into the air and refilled it. Keira jerked back, startled. She'd forgotten this particular power.

Dale watched her. "I'm sorry. I didn't mean to show off. Just that it's been so long since I had my powers that I want to fully experience them."

"No prob," she said lightly, sipping the wine. "As long as you don't use telekinesis to lift up my dress hem."

He grinned. "I promise if I lift up your dress hem, it will be with my hands."

His glance was warm and teasing. Keira polished off the wine, feeling more nervous than when she'd first come to his house to gain access.

Then, she'd been the one in control. But clearly he was now.

And clearly flirting with her, as well.

"You're very pretty in a dress."

Whoa, boy. "I like pants, as well."

Dale's expression turned serious. "I know I haven't been easy on you, or nice. I still don't believe in all this woo-woo crap...."

At her arched eyebrows, he sighed. "Well, not all of it. But you did something extraordinary yesterday, Keira. Thank you. Thanks for putting up with my bad moods and snarly attitude."

"I'll forgive you, if you cook dinner for me again. This was delicious." She pushed back her plate and feigned a yawn. "But it's getting late."

Now his dark brows arched as he glanced at the grand-father clock ticking in the corner. "It's nineteen-hundred."

Only seven o'clock. Too early to plead sleep. But this was dangerous, growing close to Dale.

"I've had a long weekend," she said, twisting her hands in her lap. His scent, delicious spices and wine, teased her wolf senses, awakening feelings she wanted to remain bur-ied. Dale gave her a crooked smile, and she melted.

"Watch a movie with me. I'll make the popcorn, and I promise not to burn it."

Keira hesitated. Further involvement aside from profes-sional interactions was a bad idea. But the idea of spending a cozy night, munching on popcorn and indulging in old movies, tempted her badly. She'd had so few treats.

I can resist him.

Then she looked into his gray eyes and saw the sexual chemistry flare.

"Only if you let me pick the movie."

"Deal." He stretched out a hand. "Let's shake on it."

His palm was strong, warm and calloused, the hand of a man accustomed to hard work, not pushing papers. Dale rested his hand a moment in her grip and then drew back. "Go into the den, pick out a movie and let me clean up."

She'd chosen *Breakfast at Tiffany's*. Total chick flick. Keira shook her head when he'd suggested *Lawrence of Arabia*. So he'd let her have her way. Big green eyes wide, she'd sighed happily as they settled on the sofa.

And then, halfway through, Keira fell asleep.

Dale regarded his housekeeper with tenderness. Should have been more considerate. She'd expended all her energy fighting his demons, and needed recharging, not movies and popcorn.

He'd let his libido and interest carry him away, thinking of his needs, not hers.

Removing the bowl of popcorn from her lap, he placed it on the table, switched off the flat screen. Then he lifted her into his arms, burying his nose into her hair. Fresh citrus and sunshine invaded his senses. She felt soft and warm.

Hunger hit him. Keira was wholesome and innocent, uncomplicated and assertive.

Yearning for Keira filled him. She smelled like citrus and sunshine, not old cigarette smoke and lost hopes, or money and ambition like Melissa.

Yearning for a house filled with laughter instead of silence, and munching on crisp popcorn on a Sunday night instead of a barstool and a burger.

Determination filled him. He was a navy SEAL and never quit. Not when he wanted something badly, and he wanted Keira.

Dale carried her into her room. He pulled off her shoes, tucked her between the sheets and kissed her forehead. "Sweet dreams," he whispered.

He knew what his dreams would be of, and anticipated the night when they would turn real, Keira naked in his arms, reaching out to him in trust as they made love.

For the next five nights, Dale pursued her with gentle persistence. Not overtly, always a gentleman, but his male interest remained keen.

He took her out to dinner at a restaurant his team assured him was clean of demons. He brought her fresh flowers, ones he picked up himself at a florist. And he insisted on spending every night after dinner either watching old movies or taking long walks around the neighborhood.

Keira kept him at arm's length. She brought him to the basement and they set up an exercise studio where he lifted weights and she mediated. And each night, she did a short session on him with the crystals.

The other night, he took an amethyst she'd placed on his neck and spun it lazily in the air, using his telekinesis. Delighted, she watched and clapped like a child.

"Always like doing this with my marbles when I was a kid," he'd told her, grinning.

Keira suspected he seldom showed his light, playful side to his men. The serious navy commander had a quirky sense of humor and charm.

I could fall in love with you, she'd thought, feeling despair chase away her joy.

When Saturday arrived, he apologized.

"I've got a black-tie ball to attend. I'll have to take a rain check on our movie tonight."

Keira sat on his bed, watching him adjust the tie. "I need a favor from you," he told her. "The admiral is inspecting the new firestorm chamber on Tuesday. I want you to visit the compound, meet with him and assure him I'm cured."

"It'll cost you. An entire night of watching *Doctor Zhivago*."

He shot her an inscrutable look. "How about a massage?"

"I've given you enough massages."

"I was referring to you," he murmured.

Warmth surged through her. Keira pushed aside rising desire. "You're not cured," she warned.

"I feel terrific."

In his formal dress uniform, he looked distinguished and handsome. As he turned for inspection, her heart did another little flip-flop.

"You look amazing," she told him.

His mouth curled in a wry smile. "It's the uniform. Covers all the shortcomings."

Keira went and straightened his tie. "You don't have shortcomings."

"Tell that to Melissa. She didn't think so when she saw me in the hospital." He snorted and shook his head. "Tonight, in this uniform, she'll find me acceptable."

"Is she a Mage, like you?"

"Melissa is a normal, ordinary human woman who knows nothing about the paranormal world." He gave her an apologetic look. "I'd arranged earlier to take her to the ball because I needed an escort. It's a formal obligation. Nothing more. There's nothing between us."

Cheered by this admission, she trailed her fingers over the gold buttons. "Does she know you feel this way?"

His gaze hardened. "Melissa cares about appearances. When she found out it was the premiere social event of the month, she sped over to the base to ask me. Much faster

than when she visited at the hospital. After all the nights
we spent together, I thought I meant more to her than an
invitation into military social circles."

Jealousy nipped her heels. This Melissa had known Dale
intimately, had shared his bed, his life and everything normal in it. Melissa didn't worry about demons pursuing her
or spending endless days locked in a cold, dark cage. This
Melissa never looked over her shoulder, wondering when
everything would come crashing down.

"You should probably leave soon to pick her up, if you
don't want to be late."

Dale seemed distracted. "She's arriving here in a limo
she hired for the night."

"A limo? Like the prom? Should I get out the camera
and take your photo?" she said lightly.

"Melissa insists on making a grand entrance. Appearances are important to her."

"Sounds like she uses you to climb the social ladder."

Their gazes caught in the mirror and met. Connection
flared between them. Dale cupped her cheek. Keira shivered, relishing his palm upon her skin. Strong, capable,
and yet tender.

"I'd rather stay home with you and watch *Lawrence of
Arabia,* but this is a necessary social obligation."

"Silly," she whispered. "*Lawrence of Arabia* is about
guys draped in sheets and sand. I prefer *Gone with the
Wind.*"

Warmth curled through her veins as he stroked a thumb
across her cheek. "Women in big skirts waving fans. Chick
flick."

"It's a military classic. Typical macho film. Guys smoking cigars, battles and guns."

Chuckling, he released her. "You're very persuasive
when you're trying to get your own way."

Only with you, she thought. *With you, I'd do anything*

*to get my way because then I could finally be free. Live
a normal life. Maybe even find a way for us to make this
something more.*

Dale Curtis was honorable and strong, and had all the
values she cherished. He had a playful side she found en-
dearing. But his rigid code of honor did not easily forgive.
Dale viewed life in shades of black and white, while she
clung to the gray areas, struggling to find the light amid
the darkness.

The doorbell chimed, and his expression hardened, a
reflection of the military commander with duties and ob-
ligations.

Her chest felt tight as she followed him into the hallway.

Brimming with curiosity about this mysterious Melissa,
Keira hovered at the upstairs landing, peeking through
the stairway rails like a child peering down at her parents' party.

A tall, thin woman swept inside. Blond hair pinned in
an elaborate arrangement of curls, she was pretty, with
bright red lipstick accenting a full, sensual mouth, but
beneath the glittering beauty lurked something cold, like
a hard diamond. Gold sparkled on her dress like shiny
coins. Keira squinted.

Melissa put a possessive hand on Dale's chest. "Like
my gown, darling? I bought it especially for you, to match
your uniform."

She spun around, the shiny fabric floating outward.

Dale nodded, his expression remote and shuttered. He
barely said a word. Too busy prattling about the ball and
checking out her appearance in the hall mirror, Melissa
didn't notice. Anger stabbed Keira. The man deserved a
nice night out, with good company. He deserved normalcy
and a woman who pried her attention away from herself
long enough to pay him a compliment about how handsome he looked, ask him how he was doing.

Maybe the woman needed a good reminder. Or a kick in the shins. Keira bounded down the stairs and stopped short, smiling at Melissa.

She stuck out a palm. "Hi, I'm Keira, Lieutenant Commander Curtis's housekeeper. I'm glad he's finally getting out to a party. He's been working too hard lately and deserves a nice night out."

The woman stared at her hand as if she held out a live cockroach. "It's not a party. It's a military ball. Not that a servant would understand the difference."

Unfazed, Keira regarded her shark's-tooth smile. "Sure, I get it. A ball. That's why you need such a sparkly dress. Very shiny. You match the buttons on his uniform. Wow, so bright, everyone's going to need sunglasses."

The other woman sized her up like a prizefighter studying an opponent. The briefest amusement crossed Dale's face.

"We should be going, Melissa," he murmured.

As they turned to leave, a faint, but familiar scent drifted into Keira's nostrils. Interesting. The same scent from the bar where she'd first seen Dale...

And Dale had no idea.

Then again, the cloying stench of Melissa's perfume would fool most. *Except a pure-blood wolf like me,* she thought.

"Normal, ordinary woman, huh? She never told you what she was?"

A frown touched his face as he turned. "Keira..."

The woman rolled her eyes. "Really, Dale, we don't have time for games. We'll be late."

"Sure hope they have bananas flambé at your little party. Or just plain bananas. That'll make your date hoot with glee, Dale." She gave a small, knowing smile.

Melissa's mouth pinched as she glared at Keira. "Watch

your mouth, you impudent maid. You're nothing but a lowly servant."

She got in her face. "Actually, I'm a Luminaire. And you're nothing more than a throwback to Charles Darwin's origin of species. Except you smell better. Then again, all that perfume..."

Dale's eyes widened as his nostrils flared. "Son of a..." Turning to Melissa, he narrowed his eyes. "You're a shifter."

An uneasy smile touched the woman's mouth. "I have a titch of cougar shifter. On my mother's side."

"And monkey on her father's side." Keira laced her hands around the newel post. "Chimpanzee, actually."

"You know what I am," Dale said slowly.

Melissa rolled her eyes. "Of course. You're Lieutenant Commander Dale Curtis, commander of SEAL Team 21. You're from upstate New York and your father founded Curtis Mark Industries. Your mother is known in all of New York society, all the Newport and Palm Beach social circles and all the Mage..."

The woman's mouth dropped. "I mean, Maine. I meant to say Maine."

"Mage," he corrected quietly. "Primary Elemental Mage, to be exact."

A haunted, almost sad look entered his eyes. Keira's heart twisted. Dale valued honesty and all this time his girlfriend had been living a lie, trying to use him to gain access not to military social circles, but his family's power.

Sympathy and guilt coiled in her stomach. She wanted Dale to have a good time and she'd wrecked his night. The woman had not meant Dale harm, only wanted to hide a secret from him.

How well she understood that need...

Dale checked his watch. "Forget it. Let's go."

Keira cleared her throat. "Actually, I could be wrong.

There is more cougar there than I'd thought. Good for you for concealing your shifter abilities all this time, Melissa. That takes skill, and you blend so well with human society."

But the woman didn't take the peace offering. Her gaze hardened. "I don't need compliments from you. A cheap, peace-loving hippie Luminaire who has no more power than a psi human."

She raised her brows. "Wow, you are more cougar than I'd thought. Meow much? Want to get into a catfight? No dice, sweetie. Just take Dale out and show him a good time. He deserves a nice night out."

Melissa smirked. "I plan to show him a very good time. Just like all the other nights we've spent together, when we woke to greet the dawn."

"Melissa, let's roll. Now!"

Breath caught in Keira's throat as he escorted her to the door. He was so…handsome and charming. Couldn't that twit see beyond the scars to the stunning man who bore them? Dale did deserve better. Much better than a gold-draped phony who only wanted to use him to clamber up the Mage social ladder.

Melissa scurried down the steps to the waiting limo. At the door, he turned and gave Keira a stern look. "Behave."

As he started out the door, Keira called out. "Dale!"

He turned and she made hooting sounds, scratching at her chest.

His face scrunched up into such a boyish, carefree grin, her heart leaped. Then the polite mask dropped again. "Don't wait up for me," he murmured. "And don't eat all the popcorn."

The door softly closed behind him.

Formal balls were never his forte, but he usually enjoyed the chance to socialize and mingle. And dance. Not tonight. Tonight his thoughts constantly drifted home to Keira.

Dale sat at his table, watching the tableau, as Melissa danced with the admiral. An orchestra played on a raised dais as couples swirled on the dance floor. Sparkling crystal chandeliers reflected the brilliant jewels worn by the women. Candles adorned tables holding silver fountains of the finest champagne.

The ballroom glowed like fairy lights, he thought whimsically, wondering where that thought came from.

Then he smiled. Keira. She'd turned on his imagination like a spigot.

Most of the people who knew him commented how well he looked. Even cagey old Byrne remarked he was putting on weight, looked much more relaxed and fit.

All thanks to Keira. None to Melissa.

For two years, he'd shared Melissa's life and her bed. They'd been intimate and he'd introduced her to his family. And she knew what he was, probably targeted him because he hailed from an old, established and powerful Mage family, yet never told him she was a shifter. Oh, he'd sensed something slightly different about her, but he'd dismissed it, always too much focused on other matters like work to pay attention to his private life.

Dale understood Melissa's reasons for never telling him. Wishing to discreetly blend into the human world, many paranorms hid their identities, even from other paranorms.

He could forgive the omission.

But he couldn't ever trust her again.

Honesty was a value Dale cherished with those in his life, because as a SEAL and a paranorm, lies were necessary to protect lives.

Those under his command knew his strict rules about honesty. *Be honest with me. If you mess up, admit it.* Bet-

ter an admission than trying to cover up the truth because
he would find out and the consequences were not pleasant.

He needed a woman in his life who held those same
values. A woman without secrets, a woman who told him
the truth and left nothing hidden.

Suddenly he grew weary of duplicity and false smiles
and social climbing. Dale longed for home, his sweatpants
and faded T-shirt and beer, not champagne and starched
uniforms.

He made his apologies to the admiral and other digni-
taries. Melissa was stiff as he kissed her cheek good-night,
but upon leaving he saw her flirting openly with an atten-
tive, politically influential lieutenant.

A very human lieutenant.

Dale watched them, an amused smile quirking his
mouth. "Good luck, buddy," he murmured.

Thoughts of Keira's monkey sounds kept the smile on
his face.

It was past midnight when the cab pulled in front of his
house. Light shone from the den halfway down the hall.

Curled up on the leather sofa, Keira ate popcorn, a
dreamy expression on her face.

Dale tugged his tie loose and dropped beside her. She
glanced up. "Home so early? You okay? They didn't wear
you out, did they?"

"Never been one for stiff, formal events. Besides the
company's much better at home."

She gave a shy smile.

"I told you not to eat all the popcorn."

"And when did I ever listen to you?"

Dale shrugged out of the jacket, tossing it over a chair.
Keira raised an eyebrow.

"What's this? Mr. Starched Shirt Meticulous, actually
throwing his clothing around? Hope you don't expect me

o hang it up for you. What do you think I am, the housekeeper?"

Grinning, he kicked off the polished dress shoes. He slid close, grabbed a fistful from the bowl. She looked startled, but did not move away.

"What's this?" He pointed to the screen.

"Black Swan."

He gave her an incredulous look. "You like romance movies and chick flicks. This is a dark drama about a ballerina who takes on the role of Odile from *Swan Lake* and how it twists her mind. It makes *Psycho* look like a comedy."

"It's a musical. Has music in it."

Giving an amused look, he munched on the popcorn.

Keira was fun and carefree. She made him feel comfortable, relaxed and, hell, he was enjoying himself for the first time in months. Then she gave a small sigh as the strains of *Swan Lake* played. "What was the ball like? Was there lots of dancing?"

Dale ate another kernel. "I didn't dance much."

"Afraid to show your two left feet in their very polished, shiny shoes?"

"Actually, I'm a good dancer with the right partner." He finished his handful of popcorn. "Didn't see one there tonight."

She sighed again. "I love watching dancers. Just wish I had…"

Keira fell silent

He wiped his fingers on a paper towel. "Tell me."

"It's stupid."

"Try me."

Glancing up through her long, dark lashes, she set down the bowl and wiped her hands. "No one ever taught me to dance. Not the formal, elegant dances like the waltz. Always imagined what it would feel like to sweep across the floor. I thought it must feel like flying."

She looked so dreamy and wistful, his heart gave an unexpected tug. Dale stood, pushed back the coffee table and chairs, clearing a space. Then he pulled her to her feet. "Come."

At her puzzled look, he added, "I'm going to teach you to dance."

She felt good in his arms. A perfect height, the top of her head reaching his nose. Scents of citrus and sunshine filled his senses, chasing away memories of Melissa's heavy perfume.

Keira gazed upward, uncertainty in her eyes.

He gave his first real smile of the night. "Trust me."

Slowly, he showed her the steps. She matched his pace and they swept around the den. Laughing, she followed his lead, matching his stride perfectly. As the music ended, she gazed upward in sheer adoration.

Dale stood still, amusement shifting to a stronger, deeper emotion.

"You're staring at my mouth," she breathed.

"Because I keep wondering what you'll taste like. I've been wanting to do this for some time now." He cupped the back of her head with a strong hand. "Slow and easy. Relax, sweetheart. I'll take it slow and easy."

Lowering his head, he kissed her. His mouth gently covered hers. Keira's lips felt soft and warm beneath the pressure of his own. Slowly he teased her mouth to open to his, toying and nibbling with her lower lip until she finally yielded.

She stiffened against him, her breathing ragged, her heartbeat erratic and pulsing as he pulled her closer. Then she sighed beneath his mouth and wound her arms around his neck. She felt warm and soft in his arms, her mouth pliant beneath his. She tasted like sweet raspberries and buttery popcorn, and her mouth was hot silk. Dale deepened the kiss, his erection pulsing. Never had he been this swiftly attracted to a woman, never had he felt such exhilarating bliss in a mere kiss.

He wanted more, needed more, his body aching and demanding. But he sensed her innocence and confusion twining with blossoming desire. When she pulled back a little, he abruptly released her.

Hunger washed through him as he studied her mouth, swollen from his possessive kisses.

He wanted her badly and, judging from her delicate flush of passion and darkened pupils, she wanted him, as well.

"I think I'll call it a night," she whispered, eyes huge in her heart-shaped face.

Dale tapped her pert nose. "Sweet dreams, Luminaire."

As she left, he collapsed on the sofa, rubbing a hand across his face, filled with desire and dismay. He was falling fast for Keira Solomon, the most unlikely woman he'd ever met.

And he still knew little about her.

But soon, he'd find out. Because the rules had changed. He'd let Melissa onto the base, never dreaming she was a shifter. The woman held more interest in his family's power than the team. But what if she did want something much more dangerous?

What if Melissa had been a snake, lying in wait to prey upon his staff, his SEALs, hoping to destroy them by using Dale to gain close access?

He couldn't endanger his team. Dale fished his cell from his trouser pocket and dialed Stephen, who answered on the first ring.

"Report, vamp. And don't tell me it's past your bedtime or you're too busy having breakfast in bed with a blonde."

"Actually, I was dining on a blonde in bed," the vampire deadpanned. Then he drew in a deep breath. "I have intel for you."

"Report."

"Not over the phone. This needs to be delivered in person. Tomorrow morning. I'm in New Orleans, but I'll catch the red-eye. Be at your house around noon. Long as you don't have any demons lurking in the corners. Had my fill here in Naw'leans." The vamp's Southern accent came across strong and thick.

Stephen hated demons and had tangled with a few nasty ones.

Dale smiled. "No. No demons here. Not a hint of one."

Chapter 16

Keira could not sleep, thinking about that kiss.

Tender and yet passionate, it cranked all her hormones into overdrive. Temptation had called her to fist her hands in his dress shirt, pull him closer and then see where the night led them. Worldly when it came to life's evils, she was totally innocent in bed. She wanted Dale, wanted to finally taste passion.

But she couldn't make love to this man she'd nearly killed.

Not until he knew the truth. Keira had dealt with too many lies and too much deception to save her skin. If she were finally to be intimate with a man, she wanted Dale. And she wanted nothing but honesty between them.

Somehow, she had to tell him who she really was....

Finally she drifted off. And dreamed.

Vermilion. The color of death was vermilion, sharp and biting. Vermilion, dripping from a platform in the room's center, cold and dank.

She put a hand against the wall to steady herself, but the room kept swaying.

"Admit it. You ripped him open."

"Not me. I did not..."

"You—"

"I am innocent…."

"Are you saying you did not torture those young men? You have done worse, much worse, with your claws." Behind Dale, the demon giggled and clapped.

"Please…"

"You let them bleed to death. You watched them scream and writhe in pain. You did it. You tore them open. The demons were bystanders. You did it all." His voice became deadly calm. "You tortured me. You left me to die in the dark, alone. In agony."

"Never kill. Never. I care, I care about you, Dale." Her voice dropped to a bare whisper.

He said nothing, only studied her with his cold, dead gaze. Members of his team formed a horseshoe around him, a tight little group. All the SEALs were clad in battle gear, their expressions hard and cruel.

They wanted a pound of her flesh for the torment she'd inflicted on their beloved leader.

Dakota, the Draicon werewolf with the deep blue eyes, spoke in a loud, booming voice. "Keira Solomon, I find you guilty of the deaths of all your past victims. Guilty of attempted murder of a U.S. Navy lieutenant commander."

"Guilty," each SEAL echoed.

"Sentence?" Dale asked them. He looked at Keira, his full, sensual mouth turning hard with resolve. "There can be only one sentence for such evil. Death."

Keira stared into the mirror as she combed through her damp hair. Showering failed to rinse away lingering wisps of last night's horrible nightmares.

She still felt slick with sweat, a film of guilt coating her. Maybe today, she'd work up the courage to somehow tell Dale and have nothing stand between them.

Nothing to prohibit them from becoming lovers.

The comb stopped halfway through her hair.

How could she tell him? Dale needed her to find the demons and needed her guidance in vanquishing them. Telling him the truth risked expulsion from his life, or worse.

Male voices sounded in the kitchen. They sounded serious, official. Deeply worried, she twisted her long, damp hair into a bun. She dressed in a pair of black trousers, strappy sandals and a long-sleeved blue shirt.

In the kitchen, she saw that Dale stood near the sink, gazing out the window, a mug in his hand. The delicious scent of hazelnut coffee filled her nostrils. Amusement mingled with apprehension. Finally, he knew how to make his own coffee and make it right.

He turned and offered a warm smile. "Good morning."

Then she noticed a man sitting at the breakfast bar, a glass of clear liquid before him. Chestnut curls tumbled down to his slim shoulders. He wore a rumpled gray shirt and dark circles were under his intense green eyes, as if he'd gone without a night's sleep.

Mingling with the strong smell of coffee, and Dale's delicious scent of fresh air and pine, was the new smell. The bite of whiskey, the burn of hot passion and a metallic scent she instantly recognized.

Keira stiffened.

Blood.

Vampire.

The man also went still, his gaze tracking her like a predator. Dale, oblivious to the sudden tension, waved at the stranger. "Keira, this is Stephen. He works with my team. Came over the other night, but you were already asleep. Stephen, this is Keira, Luminaire extraordinaire, and my housekeeper. She cleansed the house of demons. And she makes a damn fine cup of coffee."

Warmth filled his gaze, but she felt icy cold. Vampire.

She'd encountered a group of them while imprisoned by the Centurions.

Heard them tearing into the victim she'd refused to torture, and he'd died a horrible death, his shrieks stabbing her ears like icy spikes.

After the vampires, she never fought the demons' compulsion again. Instead, she'd devised a new method of trying to save their victims.

"Hello." Stephen's gaze narrowed. "You're the Luminaire."

His nostrils twitched. Fear rolled through her. Vampires had exquisitely sensitive olfactory senses. They could smell a wounded person more than one hundred yards away. Some could even detect the slightest defect in a person's...

Blood.

Perspiration beaded her temples, trickled down her back. Panic rose in her throat, sharp and biting. She started to back away. Too late. The vampire stood and rounded the breakfast counter. Sharp white fangs flashed as he hissed.

"Stephen," Dale snapped. "Watch it."

"She's no Luminaire. Get her out of my sight." The vampire's talons elongated, along with his fangs. His eyes turned bloodred.

Keira turned and ran into her room, slamming the door shut. She flung herself on the bed and buried her head beneath a pillow, trying to shut out the sounds.

Shrill screams of agony, sounds of tearing, wet flesh, cackling laughter.

Sobs wrenched her shoulders as she cried. Would she ever find redemption?

Dale stared after his housekeeper and then turned to his friend and colleague. "You bastard, what the hell did you do to her?"

Ashen, the vampire collapsed back on the stool. "Demon

blood. She has demon blood, Mage. I can smell it a mile away. The stench…it turns my stomach, burns my nostrils."

He picked up the glass of water and gulped it down, wiping his mouth.

Dread shot through Dale. He set down his mug very carefully. "You're wrong."

"Not about this. Ever. You know how much I loathe demons. Ever since that San Fran episode…"

"She can't be a demon. She killed an imp in my house, fought demons with me…." Dale staggered back against the counter, leaning against it for support.

Stephen stared at the hallway where Keira had fled. "I'm not saying she's a demon. But she has the blood. Maybe she's a hybrid."

Mind spinning, Dale grappled for explanations. "Like Thad, the petty officer who's been training my SEALs in the firestorm chamber."

"And you know how I can't stand to be near him, either." Stephen's mouth thinned. "But this one, your Luminaire, she's hiding something big. And the blood inside her, it's powerful. Dark and evil. Thad's a puppy dog compared to her. Keira, she's much worse, a…wolf."

Demon wolf.

The words flashed through his mind. Pain pulsed in his skull, behind his eyelids. Dale pressed a hand to his head. Damn headaches.

Frustration tensed his muscles. He'd acknowledged the feeling, dealt with it. Sexually, he found Keira desirable, wanted her in his bed. She'd aided him and helped him recover. But his position as ST 21's commander put him at risk for infiltration by enemies, both human and non-human.

Keira couldn't remain in his life until he knew exactly what she was….

"What are you going to do?" the vampire asked.

"Bring her to base. And have her thoroughly examined."

After she heard Stephen leave, Dale knocked softly on her door. Keira hastily splashed cold water on her face, dabbed a wet washcloth over her puffy eyelids.

"Let's talk," he said quietly and she followed him to the kitchen.

He poured a fresh mug of coffee and handed it to her. "Black, right?"

Keira nodded and leaned against the counter.

"First, let me apologize for my friend. Stephen's not very social in the morning. He's more of a night owl." His expression shuttered. She couldn't tell what he thought.

He could want to kiss her again.

Or kill her.

Acid churned in her throat at the suspense. She set the mug down. "Spill it, Dale. What did he tell you?"

"He says you have demon blood inside you. A strong strain of evil demon blood."

Oh, damn, this was worse than she'd thought. Everything inside her screamed to tell him the truth. But the cold look on his face and her fears kept her from doing so. She couldn't face his rejection or worse if he knew the truth now.

I'll level with him. Just not now, she thought.

"I must ask you some questions." He walked over to the kitchen table, pulled out a chair. "Please sit."

Keira sought refuge in a defensive attitude. "Interrogation time? After everything I've done, you've decided to treat me like a suspect? Or are you simply going to assume I'm guilty?" Bristling, she sat, fisting her hands beneath the table to hide their trembling.

Dale sat across from her, his expression neutral, but his

posture commanding and powerful. "I don't assume. But I want honest answers."

Warily, she looked at him. "Go on."

"Are you demon?"

"No."

"Was either your father or your mother a demon?"

"No."

"Have you ever been possessed by a demon?"

"No."

"Have you ever held an evil thought about killing another and acted upon it?"

She considered. "I wanted to kill that ass who ran me off the road when I was driving to Virginia."

"I'm serious."

"So am I. You should have seen how I nearly wrecked my bike."

"Keira, do you have demon blood inside you?"

Sharp, concise and commanding, Dale had turned from friend to a powerful military commander. The scrutiny made her squirm, lashed her with guilt and despair. Not now, she thought. Please, not now.

The best defense was offense, she remembered him saying while they'd watched a war movie the other night. Keira sprang to her feet and slapped the table, making the vase with fresh roses rattle.

"Damn it, Dale! I told you my parents were killed by demons and I've been hunting demons all this time, risking my hide to eradicate them. That vampire smelled demon blood, of course he'd smell it, after all the contact I've had with them!"

He didn't flinch. Didn't move a muscle. Dale remained still, his gaze penetrating and assessing. No emotion. The Mage was rock-solid.

While she was rapidly turning into an emotional mess.

"I want you to take a blood test." He drew in a deep breath. Okay, maybe not such a rock. Hope filled her.

"A complex blood test that analyzes your paranormal abilities and determines exactly what you are."

Keira stilled. "A test that will tell you if those abilities include demonic powers."

"Yes."

"No." She shook her head, strands of hair tumbling down from her loosely pinned bun. "You talked of trust with your men, trusting them and how you created this bond. And you won't share that trust with me, after we've worked together, fought together! Is your loyalty only to your team because they're SEALs?"

"My loyalty is to the men and women under my command," he said quietly, but a shadow crossed his expression.

"And I'm not on the team, not good enough to claim your loyalty and trust. Just good enough for making you dinner, a few fun nights out and movies shared with popcorn. That's all."

"Keira..."

The roses he'd presented to her with such a flourish seemed to mock her with their bright crimson and sweet fragrance. Crimson like blood...

With a strangled cry, she swept the vase off the table, sending it crashing to the floor.

Dale sprang up and ran to her, placed a hand gently on her shoulder. "Did you cut yourself?"

Why? Hoping to get a blood sample to analyze?

But she shook her head and wrapped her arms around her chest. "I'm going to my room now. Please, leave me alone," she said dully.

He did not respond as she sped down the hallway.

* * *

She couldn't hide forever.

Nor could she avoid him.

An hour later, she headed into the backyard. Picking up her spade, she dug in a frenzy and planted the remainder of the hydrangea bushes. Keira touched a leaf. Living things, those would ward off demon magick.

If only they could ward off other things, like distrust and suspicion.

He had a right to be suspicious, she reminded herself.

The sliding doors opened. Dale climbed down the deck steps and knelt beside her.

"I'm sorry I upset you," he told her. "Allow me to make up for it with lunch?"

Suspicion filled her. Dale Curtis was a single-minded man.

"Why? Are you dining at a blood bank?"

"No. I do wish you'd level with me, though."

"I leveled with you as best as I could." True enough. "And now you want to take me to lunch?"

"I'd like to get to know you better." Gray gaze steady, he studied her.

"More interrogation? As a navy SEAL commander questions a suspect?"

Dale sighed. "I want honesty from you and I'll be honest with you in return. I like you, Keira. A lot. I like spending time with you, as a man does with a woman. It's my day off. Let's abandon our roles. No more SEAL commander, no more Luminaire."

Understanding filled her. "And if I am a demon, the more time you spend with me, the more you'll be able to tell what I am."

"I know you don't like worms in your food, so that's a good start." He smiled, then sobered. "No talk of blood, tests or demons. It's Sunday, my day off, and it's a beautiful day. I'd like to spend the afternoon with you. Thought we'd eat out and then bike ride at the beach."

Tempting. She sighed. "I never learned to ride a bike."

"You ride a motorcycle. Not much difference. I'll teach you. You can learn this afternoon."

"How hard is it?"

Impish light glinted his eyes. "They say it's like sex. Once you do it, you never forget how."

Chuckling at her blush, he touched her hand. "Come on. When you're finished, have lunch with me. Let's spend the afternoon having fun."

"As long as there's no demons in the restaurant."

Dale chose a crowded diner by the beach. The diner's other patrons were mostly navy personnel, some uniformed, crammed into the mulberry-colored booths near the window, or sitting on stools at the counter. The air was warm, and smelled of grease and fried food.

In a forest-green polo shirt that hugged his wide shoulders and khaki shorts that displayed long, muscled legs, Dale looked handsome and athletic. Every hormone within her sat up and saluted.

"It's safe here. Nothing to worry about except clogging your arteries," he assured her. "My men checked it out. Just burgers and sandwiches, though."

Keira dipped a French fry into a lake of ketchup. "Good. I've lost my appetite for Italian. I'll take a heart attack any day over meeting another demon."

She wanted to tell him the truth. Maybe here, in the open where he couldn't risk a meltdown. Or take out his gun and shoot her.

Two sailors perched on stools at the counter kept glancing at them and whispering. Dale's jaw tightened. She caught the words *commander* and *injured badly* and *back on duty*.

Anger stirred inside her. Couldn't he enjoy an outing without everyone looking at him as if he were a specimen on display?

Keira pivoted and fixed a cold stare on the sailors. "Yo, Popeye and Bluto, want to quit ogling me? I know I'm cute, but this obsession of yours has to stop. I'm with this guy. Go chase Olive Oyl."

Red-faced, they turned back to their meals. Dale gave her a brief smile. "You don't let much faze you."

"Just demon worms in my meal. Forget them. Tell me about being a SEAL. What kind of training does it require?"

He told her about BUD/S, the intense program all recruits entered to qualify as SEALs.

"Drown-proofing," she murmured. "Sounds difficult."

"It's actually a good skill to learn for anyone who lives near water."

"Do you dive a lot with your team?"

Dale's expression shuttered. "Not me. I'm a commander, and I usually don't accompany my men on missions."

"Your missions require a lot from you."

"Honor is our code. Death before dishonor, like many military branches. We believe it and live it."

Keira gulped down her iced tea. "It also sounds very rigid and unforgiving. Mistakes are made. Can you ever forgive a big mistake?"

Dale looked surprised. "Of course. Mistakes are how we learn."

"What about from someone who isn't a team member? Could you forgive a betrayal from your family?"

"My team is my family."

"Someone not your family, a friend perhaps."

His mouth compressed into a firm slash. "Doubtful."

Her own resolve wavered. She couldn't tell him the

truth, not now. Later, she promised herself. Dale would know the full truth.

They left the restaurant, drove to a public beach and parked. Dale retrieved the two shiny bikes he'd placed in the truck's bed. After walking their bikes to the sand, they stopped at the shoreline.

"The sand, not the boardwalk?" she asked.

"Too crowded. You need space. These are mountain bikes, with wide tires. They'll suffice."

Keira looked down at the bright blue bicycle he'd borrowed from a neighbor and made a moue of distaste. "I don't know about this...."

"The only way to learn is to get on. And if you fall, you fall on sand. Less injury." Dale held out a hand. "Just like I showed you back home. You can do it."

Keira depressed the ringer on the silver bell adorning the handlebars. Dale lifted his dark brows.

"Stop stalling."

"I'm not stalling. Bells keep demons away."

"You expect them to come racing along and knock you off your bike?"

"Nope. Figure I can do that all on my own."

"Get on and start pedaling. I'll be right beside you."

Dale rode nice and slow, although he itched to speed down the beach at breakneck speed. Beside him, Keira wobbled precariously. Suddenly she hit a patch of loose sand and toppled over, crashing onto the sand. He stopped, concerned. Churning waves washed over her legs. "You okay?"

Sitting on the wet sand, she grinned. "I wanted to fall. Because I needed to know what it feels like."

His heart kicked up a notch. Damn, she was so cute. His gaze dropped to those terrific legs, the sexy curve of calf and thigh. He wondered what it would feel like hav-

ng those legs wrapped around his hips as he thrust deep
and hard inside her....

Then she splashed the waves curling around her body.
"Wow, this is great. Forget the bike ride. Let's swim!"

After unfastening her sandals, she ran into the ocean
and dived straight in.

Retrieving her bike, he parked it. Transfixed, he watched
her frolic in the ocean as if this, too, were a new experience. Never had he met such a fascinating woman who embraced life and didn't shy away from the unknown. Keira
had a sense of adventure that refreshed his jaded soul.

Desire pumped through his blood as he watched her
splash in the ocean, chortling with delight. Such energy
and passion. Would she be like this in bed, tumbling with
him in unbridled sensuality? Melissa had been cold and
stiff, lukewarm at best.

With Keira, it would not be screwing, but making love.
Slow and tender, and other times, hot and abandoned.

His hands tightened on the bike's handlebars. And
then he realized she had dived into the waves and had
not emerged.

Panic clawed at him. Dale kicked off his shoes and ran
into the water. He dived down, ignoring the stinging salt
in his eyes, searching for her with all his senses. Then he
spotted her hovering on the bottom. He wrapped an arm
around her waist, and tugged her to the surface. The current turned wicked, wanting to drag them out, but he used
all his strength, swimming parallel for a while, then aim-
ing for shore in deep, strong strokes. When he hit bottom,
he stood, righting her.

Like a mermaid, Keira twisted her long, dark hair and
wrung out seawater. She looked as insouciant as if she'd
emerged from a bathtub.

All the water made the white shirt transparent. He could

see the outline of her breasts and the darkness of her nipples through the fabric.

Sexual frustration and anger bit him. He put his palms on her slender shoulders, feeling fragile bones beneath her skin. "What the hell were you doing down there?"

Wide green eyes stared at him. "Drown-proofing. You said it was a good idea for everyone who gets near water."

His mouth dropped open, and then he began to laugh. Dale cupped the back of her head and lowered his forehead to hers. "You nutcase. You'll be the death of me, scaring me like that."

He lifted his head and studied her. Droplets clung to her long, dark eyelashes. Her emerald eyes glimmered like wet jewels. So sweet, and oddly naive and yet savvy, Keira was food for his jaded appetite. He couldn't resist that mouth, warm, soft and glistening.

Dale kissed her, losing himself in the sensations, not caring that he was a navy commander on a public beach. Not caring that she'd waltzed into his life and spun him out of control.

Not caring about anything except the sweetness of her mouth, the hesitant flicks of her tongue against his, the richness of her fragrance.

Not caring about the demon blood surging through her veins...

Damn it. Breaking the kiss, he drew in a deep breath, noting the flush of passion tinting her cheeks, the confusion and desire shading her eyes. "Let's get back to riding."

This time, he remained behind her as she pedaled, her movements assured and confident now, her wet hair trailing behind her in the breeze. Dale concentrated on shoving aside burgeoning feelings for this pretty Luminaire. He was a navy commander first. His duty to his team came before romance and relationships.

But deep inside pinged a familiar ache. He was falling hard and fast for this woman.

And if she were a demon, he didn't know if he could stand it....

He would find a way to test her blood. Somehow.

Chapter 17

Tuesday dawned sharp and clear. Keira rolled out of bed and jumped into the shower. Dale had already left for work. But when she came into the kitchen to grab coffee and a croissant, she spotted his neat, crisp handwriting.

Be at the base at 1100. The admiral will be finished with his tour by then and I'll arrange a personal meeting.

He signed it *Dale*. And added a small smiley face.
The smiley face eased her nervousness.
In the mirror, she studied her appearance. The sleeveless floral dress was light and breezy, and the green and yellow contrasted well with her dark hair. A matching green sweater made her look more presentable for a visit to the navy base.
Dale left the keys to his Jag sitting on the breakfast nook. She adored driving the car, listening to its smooth purr as she accelerated. Heart beating hard, she drove to the base and at the gate, presented her ID.
The base was huge, intimidating, with hulking buildings that screamed military power. Keira tried to calm

her racing pulse. She followed the directions Dale gave her and pulled up to the fenced compound housing ST 21. The sentry checked her ID, glanced at her with curiosity and waved her through.

After she parked, Keira left the Jag, keys jangling in her hand. The weight of several eyes rested upon her.

Electronic eyes. Cameras were posted around the compound's entrance.

A concrete walkway, flanked by bushes, wound up to a steel-door entryway. Keira took a closer glance at the bushes and saw more cameras planted in the middle.

She waved at one.

At the door, a uniformed guard opened it before she could press the buzzer. Keira glanced at her watch. "You're late. I expected someone to come out the moment I left the car."

The man grinned, looking less severe and more boyish. "Sorry, miss. Would have, but the commander gave express orders to meet you at the door and not strong-arm you."

"I'll bet he did," she murmured as he escorted her inside.

They passed through three locked doors and a series of security checks, including a metal detector. As the sailor escorted her down a hallway to yet another steel door, she joked, "Didn't think you needed a metal detector here, with all the X-ray eyes under Dale's command."

The sailor flashed another grin. "The stuff up front is all show-and-tell for brass. Don't need it."

After they cleared the last steel doorway, they met with Dallas, one of Dale's SEALs. Dressed in green battle fatigues, he looked harder and more lethal than the good-natured man who'd helped trap a demon inside the Italian restaurant.

Her escort bid her goodbye.

"Commander Curtis asked me to take you on a tour of the compound," Dallas said.

"He's not joining us? Too busy trying to make coffee?" she teased.

"Commander Curtis is on a conference call with brass in D.C., ma'am."

Ma'am. Not Keira. The SEAL did not crack a smile. The man who'd jested in Dale's basement had vanished, replaced with a military-erect professional. Keira swallowed hard. So different from the casual, friendly jesting she'd experienced.

Down a long hallway they walked as Dallas explained about the compound's importance to the team.

"We train daily, on-site and off, when we're not deployed. Air, close-quarters combat, diving, marksmanship and more. Training is essential to our survival."

At the hallway's end, he opened a door and they walked outside into the sunshine. The yard resembled a bizarre jungle gym, with rope climbs, towers and equipment. A few men were fighting in hand-to-hand combat.

"Over there is the shoot house where we conduct live-fire training."

She walked over to the monkey bars. Dallas gently clasped her wrist as she went to touch it.

"It's electrified. Oh, not enough to kill," he added, seeing her stunned expression. "Just enough to give you a good jolt."

"You train with live current?"

"Every SEAL on ST 21 has to be prepared to encounter the unexpected. Both paranormal and normal human traps. Training with live-current conditions us to become impervious to it, but we have SEALs who can absorb the current into their bodies and use it to maximize their powers."

Fascinating. In the distance, gunfire cracked and popped, making her jump. Dallas gestured to a target range. "Today we're using regular ammo. Tomorrow is when we train with the heavy stuff."

She didn't want to ask about his idea of heavy.

They walked to a small concrete building. Dallas punched a few numbers on a keypad and opened the door.

There was a small area, like a holding cell, and a large door. Dallas flicked on a switch and opened the door to a large, concrete-lined room.

"Our new firestorm chamber." Pride was evident in the junior lieutenant's voice.

"May I?"

Keira walked inside the room. Senses tingling, she looked around. The walls were thick concrete, with blackened marks scorching the sides. She placed a palm on one wall and shuddered.

She turned to Dallas, who was standing with his hands folded behind his back.

"You use real fire?"

Admiration filled his voice. "Curt insists. He says just like we train with live ammo because the enemy won't use blanks, we need to use real flames because demons won't use stimulated ones."

A shudder raced down her spine. "What kind of demons fight with flames?"

"Mostly pyrokinetic demons." A shadow crossed his face. "But we sealed all of them in the netherworld. Bastards won't be coming out anytime soon. Biggest threats are from minor demons or hybrids. Worst are the Igninus demons. They shift into inanimate objects, furniture, tables, even photos on your wall, and then attack when your back is turned."

They continued the tour. In a gymnasium, men fought with various weapons. Dallas showed her the weapons the SEALs trained with. Not only regular navy issue, but also strange objects like pentagrams, throwing stars, spears and even a whip tipped with tiny sharp triangles.

"Looks like a torture chamber." She laughed lightly.

Dallas picked up the whip. "We confiscated this from a rogue wizard using it to torture his apprentice."

Keira touched one of the triangles, shuddering as she imagined the inflicted damage. Muscles knotted in her back as she thought of the pain the young apprentice suffered.

Seeing her expression, he added, "The boy suffered more emotional trauma than injury. The wizard would crack it behind his back as a threat."

"So cruel."

Dallas's face tightened. "We've witnessed much worse."

He nodded at a nearby dummy holding out a silver wand. He flicked his wrist and cracked the whip, slicing the wand in half.

"The wizard invented the whip to destroy his enemies, good magicians who threatened to expose him. We turned it into a weapon to disarm him without causing injury."

"Works good if your target is standing still," she murmured.

He gave her an amused look. "The dummy is for practice shots. We train on each other as active targets. It's necessary because any rogue wizard holding the wand will be moving against us. And probably tossing energy bolts at us, as well."

Revulsion coiled low in her stomach. "What if you miss?"

"We don't, because we're working as a team and we always watch each others' sixes."

Must be nice. She never had anyone working with her, or watching her back.

"What if one of you is having a bad day?" She thought of how nasty the Centurions could be, and when they got impatient, poured on the pressure, making her life even more hellish.

At his blank look, she explained. "What if you're working with someone you dislike, or someone who has a problem with you? How can you trust him not to miss and hit your face?"

"We're SEALs first, ma'am. We have to trust each other in training and down range."

"Down range?"

"Deployment. I don't get along with all the men on this team, but I sure do rely on them to do their job, and they rely on me to do mine." He set the weapon neatly back on its peg.

"Gives a whole new meaning to whipping you guys into shape."

Dallas did not smile. "Curt insists on our regular training as SEALs, and extra training as paranorms. Double duty, but we do it gladly because we know what we're up against. The Phoenix Force is often a last resort, protection for civilians against the darkest evil."

She felt deep awe at what these men did. And Dale commanded them all. Keira wistfully wondered what it would feel like to have the respect and devotion of a team that worked closely to protect others, instead of forming alliances to hurt them.

They concluded the tour at a small cafeteria with long tables and folding chairs. Dallas nodded. "I'll leave you here, ma'am. Ensign Robyn Lees will be here soon to escort you to your next meeting. May I fetch you coffee?"

"Only if it's hazelnut."

The barest smile touched his mouth. "I do enjoy your special coffee, ma'am. We're fresh out. But we do have regular."

"I'll make sure to send more over. Thanks, but I'm fine."

She went to the counter and brushed a finger against

it. So much responsibility and so many lives under Dale's command. Keira began to understand his rigid need for order and discipline.

If he blinked wrong, or made a bad decision, not only did he put his men in jeopardy, but lives could also be lost. Many lives.

She thought of the blood spilled by the Centurions and imagined it multiplied by several hundred...no, several thousand.

Keira shuddered.

"Good morning, Miss Solomon."

She startled and whirled to see a petite, freckle-faced woman clad in the standard khaki, short-sleeved uniform. "Whoa. I didn't hear you come in. You're quiet as a cat."

"You could say. I'm Ensign Robyn Lees, here to escort you. Commander Curtis asked me to relay to you his wishes that you report to the infirmary before meeting with the admiral. He requests you take a blood test."

"He does?" Anger spiked. "Still hasn't given up on that one. You can tell him to kiss my...never mind. I'll tell him myself."

The ensign's blue eyes twinkled. "Thought you'd say that. If you refuse, I'm requested to escort you to the conference room."

They went back into the hallway. At the end, the ensign opened the door to a narrow room with a long, polished table and leather chairs. A large-screen television was at one end.

"Please wait here, ma'am."

Catching her unique scent Keira smiled. "You're the ensign who spoke to me on the phone the other day. Cat shifter."

The ensign grinned. "Your recipe for coffee's real good. Although I prefer milk to get started at oh-five-hundred."

Keira laughed as the woman closed the door behind

her. She sat at the elegant, polished conference table, tapping her fingers.

This was too easy. Dale was not the type to give up. *Don't want to take a blood test? No prob, just go to the conference room and await the admiral.*

When the door opened, she half expected Dale to storm inside, a scowl on his face, demanding she hold out her arm.

Instead, a short, stocky man entered. Like the others, he wore a khaki uniform, but instead of close-cropped hair, his fell below his collar.

Keira stood and pushed back her chair. "Where's Dale? And the admiral?"

"Commander Curtis will be here soon." The man smiled, but it didn't meet his dark eyes. "I'm Petty Officer Thad Lennox."

The scent of darkness and rich crimson slammed into her. "You're a demon," she said, backing up against the table.

He pushed back a lock of hair, exposing pointed ears. "Half demon and half Fae. But the good half of me is committed to serving my country, and fighting people like my father. He was a real piece of work." Thad picked up a small, cylindrical object. It looked like a wand.

Or a probe.

Keira's frantic gaze darted to the conference table. It had elongated, turning into a narrow metal slab, covered with disposable paper. Suddenly she realized shelves lined the walls, holding a variety of instruments and equipment.

Illusion. They used illusion to lure me inside, fooling me into thinking this was a meeting room.

Thad politely gestured to the exam table. "If you'll please sit, this will only take a moment. It won't hurt, I promise. But I must run some scans and examine you."

"Why are you doing this to me?" she cried out.

"Just relax," he murmured. "All I'm going to do is touch you, right here on the forehead...."

Panic surged, bright and hot. He'd know. And Dale would know, and in this compound, surrounded by paranormals trained to kill, she'd be dead in seconds. Self-preservation kicked in. Keira's claws emerged and a snarl ripped from her throat. Lashing out, she caught the petty officer by surprise. Cloth tore and blood bubbled up from the furrows she'd carved into his upper right arm.

He didn't even cry out, or glance at the wound, only stalked toward her with a determined look. Dimly she heard a door behind her open.

"Sir," Thad said quietly. "Do it."

Something stung her buttocks, sharp and piercing. Keira staggered, and looked back.

Dale stood behind her, pity tightening his expression. He plucked free the dart and tossed it aside.

Gray clouded the edges of her vision. She started to collapse and fell into his strong arms.

The last thing she saw before losing consciousness was his handsome face, and the coldness of his gray eyes.

Chapter 18

Thwock. Thwock.

The tennis ball banged against the far wall. Dale caught it in one hand.

At the hospital, they showed him tricks to cool down his anger and deal with frustration and strengthen the left hand, which had been weakened during the attack. Squeeze the tennis ball.

Instead, he'd tossed it at the wall and practiced catching it left-handed. The mindless routine soothed him.

Not today.

The ball landed in his sweating palm as a knock sounded on the door. "Come," he said.

Thad entered, bearing several sheets of paper. He placed them in front of Dale and perched in a chair before his desk.

"She's not a demon. But she has demon blood inside her."

Thwock. The ball burst in Dale's grip. He tossed it aside. "How?"

"I don't know. It's very dark and powerful. But it's muted, as if she's struggled to contain it." Thad's faced tightened. "Whoever she is, Curt, she's not evil. But she's tangled with some nasty creatures. My guess is they used her, and injected her with their blood to bend her to their will."

"I don't need guesses, Petty Officer. I need facts. Deal in facts." Dale pushed aside the report and rubbed his face. "Is she a Luminaire?"

"Oh, hell, yeah. But Luminaires, anyone can claim to be one. A Luminaire is more a title than a species. Mostly Fae. They're into white light and chanting and healing with crystals. But their magick is weak and usually ineffective unless combined with others. This one…"

"Her name is Keira."

"Keira, she's putting out powerful vibes. And claws." He ruefully examined three jagged tears in his shirtsleeve. "Caught me by surprise. She could have gone for my throat, but I sensed she deliberately avoided it because she only wanted to defend herself. Animal instinct."

Claws. Animal instinct.

Wolf.

Another memory pinged, sending a searing ache through his head. If only those damn Centurions hadn't put a memory spell on him. Every time he thought he was getting close to answers, the memories became like mist. He needed to focus on the present and stay sharp.

"Answer my question, Petty Officer. To the best of your knowledge, what is she?"

"I honestly don't know. But she's very strong and there's a deep well of courage running through her. Whatever she's endured, she's fought it hard and long and it hasn't overtaken her." A small smile touched his thin mouth. "Make a hell of a SEAL, sir."

"How is Keira?"

"Still unconscious, but resting comfortably in the infirmary. Do you want to see her?"

Dale shook his head. "When she wakes, have her escorted to my office by Ensign Sully."

Surprise flared on the half demon's face. "Yes, sir."

When the man left, Dale leaned back in his leather chair. Had to handle this with the utmost sensitivity and diplomacy. Rushing to sick bay to offer comfort would put him on the defensive, and weaken his position before his men. Here on base, he must maintain command.

The man in him wanted to comfort her with assurances and seek understanding.

The military commander knew he must maintain a rigid posture to keep his people protected.

He'd done the unforgivable. Broken her trust.

Dale rubbed a hand over his face. He hoped she would understand, and eventually forgive him.

But even if she did, he knew it would be a long time before he forgave himself.

Cold and darkness surrounded her. Keira moaned, thrusting out with her hands to survey her surroundings. The cell was damp and noxious, filled with the stench of dried blood. A pencil-thin shaft of sunshine speared the gloom, falling on the concrete floor. Crab-crawling over to it, she huddled in the tiny beam, desperate for light, for warmth. And then she saw her hands and realized the stench came from her—her hands were covered in someone else's blood.

A startled scream tore from her throat. She bolted upright.

Only to find herself lying on a narrow, but comfortable bed, a warm blanket covering her. A counter filled with instruments and a small sink was across from the bed.

She put a hand to her pounding skull. A sick room.

The door opened and cheerful, impulsive Sully walked

in. But no wide grin touched his face. He looked as rigid and stiff as his teammate, Dallas.

"Are you all right, ma'am?" Sully had morphed into a stranger. Ensign Sully, whose loyalty came first to his commanding officer.

His rat-bastard, sneaky commanding officer.

Grief clogged her throat. Keira tossed aside the blanket and stood on wobbly legs, pushing aside his hand as he sprang to help. "I'm fantastic. Get me the hell out of here."

The barest emotion flicked in his eyes, then vanished. "I apologize, ma'am, but Commander Curtis has requested your presence in his office."

"Oh?" She smoothed down her floral skirt with a trembling hand. "You can tell your Commander Curtis he can go to hell. I'll give him a first-class ticket."

Now his lips did quirk. "Can't do that, ma'am. Please, come with me."

No prob. She knew her way out.

As they entered the hallway, she bolted, running for the thick steel door standing between her and freedom. She didn't want Dale's explanations or having him poke her with needles or probes.

The door was in sight, so close, the handle near.

Two strong hands pulled her back. Whipping her head around, she saw Dallas on one side, Sully on the other.

"Miss Solomon, please come with us," Dallas said tersely.

Screw this. Summoning all her wolf strength, she flung them off and ran for the door. The handle was in her grasp. Keira jiggled it. It did not move. Panic surged, bright and hot. She was trapped, caught in an endless nightmare where they'd force her to do nasty things, force her to their will....

Two hands caught her upper arms and started to pull

ier back. Keira screamed and held on to the door handle. Solid steel splintered, and snapped off.

"Stop it, you morons."

The men let go. Keira whirled, holding the door handle like a weapon.

Ensign Robyn Lees stood in the hallway, scowling at the SEALs. "Is this any way to treat the commander's guest?"

"He ordered us to bring her to his office ASAP. And not let her escape." But Sully looked shamefaced.

"She broke the door handle. The goddamn door handle." Wonder and respect flared on Dallas's face, turning him from a military robot into something human.

"And you're lucky she didn't break your neck or claw you like she did Thad, the way you two have been man-handling her. Have you ever heard of finesse? No, you're too busy blowing stuff up and jumping out of planes. Stand down, both of you."

As Dallas and Sully stepped back, Ensign Lees held out a freckled hand. "Miss Solomon? Please, will you come with me? It's okay. I promise you'll be fine."

The warm assurance in the woman's voice eased Keira's fears. Swallowing hard, she took the ensign's hand.

The woman removed the door handle from Keira's death grip and slapped it into Dallas's hand. "Get maintenance here ASAP to fix that door."

As they walked down the hallway, the ensign squeezed her hand. "Don't mind them. They're good men, just over-bearing at times when Commander Curtis issues a strict order."

"They listen to you."

"Have to. I'm the team's communications expert. When they're down range, I coordinate getting all the supplies the team needs to do their job."

The officer glanced at Keira's right arm, where the

sweater had ridden up, exposing her upper arm. "That's a slave armband."

Keira's guts squeezed. "How did you know, Ensign?"

"Call me Robyn. My sister had one. She was enslaved in Egypt, but I freed her."

"Recently?" Maybe this woman could help her.

"About 2,500 years ago. Slave to a cruel Egyptian noble." At Keira's startled look, she grinned. "I'm much older than I look."

"How did you free her?"

"I used my influence. Cats were worshipped by the Egyptians so I had a little chat with the pharaoh. He freed her."

No pharaohs could free Keira from her demons. Despair set in as they reached a closed door with a shiny brass nameplate that read Lieutenant Commander Dale Curtis.

Robyn squeezed her hand again. "Go on. He can be a bear at times, but he does things for the right reasons. He's a good, honorable leader. We need him back the way he was. I've seen the changes in him because of you. Help him."

A tremendous balloon of anger and resentment deflated. This wasn't merely about her and how he'd mistreated her.

Mouth wobbling, she nodded. "Thanks."

Keira went inside and shut the door behind her.

The office was large, with a conference table and ten chairs to her left, and an enormous hand-carved wood desk to her right. A matching credenza lined with papers, books and a few photos sat beneath a window behind the desk.

A long leather sofa and two matching chairs made up a sitting area in the back, with a polished table in front of the furniture. Behind the sitting area was a door.

Dale was perched on the sofa, a silver tea service and two delicate china cups before him. He stood. "Keira, please join me."

So civilized for a brutal beast, she thought. Arms wrapped around her waist, she sat at the sofa's head, watching him through narrowed eyes.

"Are you all right?" he quietly asked.

Nodding, she watched him pour amber liquid into a china cup. Dale handed her a saucer. "Chamomile tea laced with honey. Nothing else, I promise."

Keira took it and sipped, feeling the warmth slide down her throat. Silence hung between them for a moment. Gradually the tension squeezing her chest eased.

He set down his teacup. Legs spread wide, Dale braced his hands on his knees and looked at her straight in the eye.

"I owe you an explanation."

She tensed, and the armband around her biceps gently squeezed, a reminder of her predicament. *Can't leave, as much as I want to. I put myself in this man's hands and until he releases me from our agreement, I'm trapped, just as I was with the Centurions. Except they didn't break my heart....*

She glanced at his face and the brief sorrow in his eyes gave her pause.

"I did not mean for you to get hurt, but what was done was necessary, and I take full blame."

"Go on."

He picked up his cup and took a sip. "I have nearly two hundred men and women under me, and I'm responsible for their welfare and protection on this base. If one so much as sneezes, I know. It's my duty as commander to protect the safety of the men and women on this compound."

"You thought I was a demon and wanted my blood."

"I didn't know what you were, and that unknown factor risked the lives of my staff." He set down the cup, his gaze serious. "I felt myself drawing close to you. You're an integral part of my life and a potential threat to this team because of that relationship."

A shadow drew over his expression. "When you pointed out Melissa's true origins, I realized what kind of threat existed. Melissa was thoroughly checked out because of my position, but not for...dangerous paranormal powers."

"She's a chimp, not a demon."

"A moot point. I failed to thoroughly investigate her background and vowed never to fail again. That's why I brought you here for an examination."

"Thanks a lot. Had a real swell time. It was better than a day at Disney."

Unsmiling, he regarded her. "If you were a demon, and gained access to this base because of me, you held the power to destroy lives and relay secrets."

She rubbed the armband. "Your goons would have stopped me."

"SEALs," he corrected. "They were under my orders to keep you guarded, and prevent you from leaving. I apologize if they acted rough."

"I've had worse."

"So I understand." Sympathy filled his gaze. Tensing, she wondered what the hell he'd discovered.

I'm still sitting here, in one piece so he can't know I'm the demon wolf he wants....

"Thad informed me you have traces of powerful demon blood in your system, but you have an equally strong will and have been fighting it. He informed me you attacked him, in self-defense and could have easily killed him. I understand you've suffered greatly."

The atmosphere grew thick with tension. Keira shrugged to diffuse it.

"I believe you were infused with this demon blood by the same ones who killed your parents."

A huge knot unwound in her stomach. True enough. She nodded.

"It takes a strong woman to survive a demon attack,"

he said softly. "I remember, I met such a female…once… long ago…."

He pressed fingers to his temple. "Never mind. What I am telling you, Keira, is that I know my actions were hurtful to you. I am sorry for upsetting you, but I won't apologize for doing it because the safety and welfare of my team will always come first. No matter how important a woman is to me."

Dale stared at a small, burnt hole in the wall behind the sofa. "Because of you, I've begun to heal. I can't thank you enough. I've broken the trust you put in me, but hope to regain it."

Jaw set like granite, he looked as if he'd been carved from ice. Suddenly she realized there was a bigger issue here. Much bigger, one he refused to share.

"Dale, what aren't you telling me?"

He rubbed a hand over his face.

"You say you want to regain my trust. Then tell me what's really wrong."

His big shoulders turned rigid and he shook his head. "I'm fine."

"You're not fine. I'm not one of your staff. You don't have to pretend or keep up appearances with me. Damn it, I helped you heal, saw the darkness inside you." Keira struggled with a tangle of emotions. "I would never betray your confidence. I want to help."

Silence hovered in the air a moment. She waited.

When he spoke his voice dropped to a bare whisper. "I'm losing control."

"No…"

"Yes." The shuttered look dropped from his expression and he looked stark and haunted. "I've had doubts about leading my team. Doubts that haven't left, doubts I never had until my captivity in the basement. I've been a SEAL for years. Learned to push past the pain and endure, but the torture in the basement… It left me a damnable, whimpering mess, a shell of a man."

Ice coated her veins. She waited.

"My greatest concern isn't me, it's my men and my ability to lead them. Every morning I push my physical limits to show them I'm strong, while inside, I still feel like an empty shell. Weak and ineffective. They know it, too."

He glanced at the hole in the wall. "That damage is from my powers. I lost my temper with Ensign Lees and nearly hit her with an energy bolt."

Stunned, she looked at the neat, round hole. "Well, you didn't. And after meeting her in person, I daresay she can take care of herself."

"Yes. But my staff continues treating me as if I'm the battered, beaten man Shay and Kelly found in the basement. When they get overly solicitous, it's frustrating. You're the only one who doesn't treat me like a helpless victim, as if I'll fall apart any moment." He paused. "Until I find the damn demons who imprisoned me, I'll never fully be able to move forward and be the man I once was, the commander they respected and need to guide them."

Breath caught in her throat. Dale was strong, but it took an even stronger man to admit to vulnerability.

Maybe she healed the darkness in his soul, but he still needed to heal from the trauma in the basement.

All along, she'd been selfish, only calculating how she could wrench free from the Centurions and finally gain freedom. Bigger issues were at stake.

She'd been so imprisoned by her own pain that she'd failed to see the bigger picture. Dale wasn't self-centered. He worried because everything he did directly impacted others under his command. The man could not even have a relationship without wondering if the woman was going to turn into a chimp…or a demon wolf, and endanger his men.

Keira chose her words with care. "You're a good and honorable man, even if your methods are questionable. I don't like what you did, but I do understand your motives. You're doing this for your team."

Maybe the concept of teamwork had benefits. She'd only seen the negatives.

She looked him straight in the eye. "You're not weak. Far from it. You're enormously strong and courageous. An ordinary man would have surrendered and let the demon darkness defeat him. You didn't." She took a deep breath. "I'll help you continue to recover."

Dale did not speak for a moment, only continued to study her. Finally his shoulders eased slightly. "Thank you."

"It will cost you." The ghost of a smile touched her mouth. "More sessions with the crystals and two entire nights of watching any chick flick I want."

"Deal. I'm a SEAL. I can take such torment." He smiled and walked over to her, dropping beside her on the sofa.

The tantalizing scent of him wound around her senses. So close. She leaned away.

"Don't be afraid of me, Keira. I won't harm you."

I'm not afraid of what you'll do. More scared of what I'll do.

"I've begun to care for you, Keira. Not as a patient for a healer, but as a man cares for a woman." He took her hand. "You're beginning to mean a great deal to me. That's one reason why I needed you thoroughly checked out by Thad."

He stroked a thumb over the tips of her fingers. "You had claws."

Her stomach roiled. "They come out when I feel threatened. I shift sometimes."

Dale frowned. "Into a wolf?"

She looked at him and shrugged, hoping he couldn't

hear her pounding heart. "Not a wolf like you think. I'll tell you more later."

He frowned and pressed a finger to his temple.

"You okay?"

"Damn headaches. I get them when a memory starts to return."

"Then don't think about the past," she told him, clutching his hand. "You're strong. We will find those Centurions and you'll be able to move on."

A tremor raced down her spine as he slowly stroked a thumb across her knuckles. Erudite Dale enjoyed classical music, but also commanded an equally powerful military force. Never had she encountered such strength.

She'd wanted to siphon that strength and use it to break the chains of her captivity. How utterly selfish. Keira thought of the shining hope in Robyn's eyes, the solemn pride of Dale's SEALs and the trust they put in him.

You will heal from the trauma, she silently promised. *If it takes the last ounce of my white light, you'll become the man your team needs.*

"Oh, he thoroughly checked me out," she added when she remembered what he'd said earlier. "Must admit, when he came toward me with that probe thingie, I thought I was being abducted by aliens for secret experiments. But then you hit me in the butt with that needle and everything turned nice and dark and forgetful."

A rueful look crossed his face. "It was a regrettable choice. I've been wanting close contact with your pretty little bottom for a while, but not with a dart gun."

Flushing at the implication she lowered her gaze. Dale tipped her chin up with a finger. "Look at me, Keira. From now on, no more secrets between us. Nothing but honesty."

So close. His full mouth hovered near hers. Slowly, she closed her eyes and felt his lips soft upon hers. Such a gentle, sweet kiss. Her mouth parted and he pressed closer, not pressuring, a subtle invitation to a closer dance.

So patient. SEALs were quite patient, she remembered reading. And persistent.

Dale waited for a cue.

She needed to touch him, needed this connection, a physical touch to anchor her to a future filled with possibilities instead of a bleak past. Keira's tongue darted out and traced his lower lip.

Groaning, he cupped the back of her head and drew her closer. His mouth moved over hers, teasing and coaxing. Oh, she never guessed the sweet power of a kiss, how it could turn her into a melting puddle of sheer want.

When they pulled apart, her ragged pants filled the air. His pupils darkened, nearly overcoming the slate-gray irises. His hot, hungry look equaled the frantic racing of her heart.

That look promised they would be lovers....

"We'd better stop before the admiral gets here and accuses me of testing out a new kind of therapy."

Keira touched her flushed cheeks. "Oh, damn. Is there a way I can cool down? Have a bucket of ice handy, or a walk-in freezer?"

Dale looked amused. "The bathroom's through that door. Go freshen up."

As she started off the sofa, he pulled her down for another, lingering kiss. But this time, his hand reached around and gave a gentle squeeze to her bottom.

She playfully slapped his hand away. "Not so fast, sailor."

"Just checking to make sure I didn't hurt you too badly with the dart gun." His sheepish grin melted her all over again, making him look adorably contrite, like a boy caught stealing cookies from the jar.

"I barely felt it," she told him, and then went into the bathroom, closing the door behind her.

But as she splashed her face with cold water and then stared at the mirror, she had the sinking feeling Dale could hurt her much worse if he accidentally discovered the truth.

She would tell him tonight.

No matter what.

Chapter 19

All during dinner, Keira wrestled with one burning question. How could she confess her secret to this man?

The lamb chops were tender and succulent, the vegetables tasty and crisp. With his help, she'd prepared a perfect meal. They'd laughed and talked about everything that didn't matter, from reality television shows to her weakness for chocolate.

They'd talked about everything except her origins and his torture.

Together, they cleared the table and loaded the dishwasher. Then Keira glanced into the dark backyard.

"Let's go outside. I need to tell you something."

An inscrutable look crossed his face. "I need to show you something."

A cool breeze caressed her neck and teased her dress hem as they stood on the deck. Keira looked up at the cloudless night sky studded with tiny stars. Fairy lights, she thought dimly, and a pang of sharp sorrow pierced her.

Gripping the railing she stared at the grassy yard, the forest stretching beyond the wood fence protecting his property. "You asked about my origins. I'm a Celestial Hunter. A wolf."

She felt him join her, felt his intense focus upon her. "I've never heard of that type of wolf."

"My people are…" *Extinct.* "Quite rare. We live in packs that rove from country to country, seeking privacy so we can shift and run wild."

"Why didn't you tell me before, sweetheart?"

Gentleness laced his voice, the endearment causing her throat to clog with emotion. "Because I am a wolf, but not any wolf."

Hands clammy, she rubbed them against her skirt. Sweat beaded her forehead, trickled down her back, gathering in the waistband of the pretty mint-green panties she'd chosen out of pure desperation, a feminine defense for this night.

The night when he'd surely take his revenge.

Images flashed before her… Dale, chained to the platform, begging her to stop, screaming at her to stop. But she could not, her claws gouging into flesh, cutting deep into muscle and sinew…the stench of his blood making her beast grow wilder and more feral….

Keira squeezed her eyes shut and dug her nails into her palms. "I'm the woman who hurt you so badly."

A heartbeat of silence. Another. *Breathe, just breathe.*

She opened her eyes, only to see confusion clouding his eyes. He winced, and pressed a hand to his forehead. "Damn. Another headache. Where the hell are these coming from?"

From the mind spell the Centurions implanted deep inside your brain. Somehow, she must cajole him into pushing past the pain and remembering.

"When you were tortured by a demon wolf who shifted into a woman…" She choked back a sob. "That woman was me."

Would he remember and react? Or was the memory too deeply buried? Torn between wanting his memory to return and keeping her secret, she reached out and ran her nails down his strong left biceps.

The biceps she'd carved into ribbons...

But he didn't even flinch. Dale simply kept studying her, as if she were a long-lost acquaintance he couldn't quite place.

Frowning, he pressed his fingers to his head. "There was a woman, a tall blonde woman, thin, she wore bright red lipstick." Dale's mouth flattened. "That's the woman who tortured me."

Stricken, she stared. He'd just described Melissa, his ex-girlfriend. The memory spell planted in his mind by the Centurions was extrapolating the image of his girlfriend and substituting it for whatever memories Dale had of Keira in the basement.

For nearly three weeks she'd worked up the courage for this moment. And it proved fruitless.

The only way he'd remember was the Celestial pendant. Back in the basement when she'd been in human form after torturing him as a wolf, when the demons left Dale alone to regain consciousness, she had sewn it into his flesh as protection, the sacred pendant among her people being the only item capable of avoiding her killing bite.

Once Dale touched the pendant, it would trigger all lost memories, demon spell or not.

"You're not the demon wolf who hurt me, Keira. You're the woman who saved me," he said quietly.

She opened her mouth to protest, but he pressed a finger against her lips. "Please. Let me speak now. I have something to show you. And damn, it's taking all my nerve to do this."

Lights flooded the yard and the pool as he flipped a switch on the wall. Then he stepped back, and before her eyes, the tall, handsome Mage with the scars and the serious air seemed to melt into the air.

In his place was a muscled, gray timber wolf. The wolf raised its head to the moon and howled, then bounded down the steps and raced through the yard.

Throat dry, she watched, her own wolf longing to join him and run free. Every cell pulsed with yearning, the beast inside clawing to get out, but unable to be free. Her female responding to the strong male wolf now running through the yard, leaping over the serene rock arrangement by the garden she'd planted.

Mesmerized, she descended the steps, watching from the pool's concrete deck, her hand resting on a lounge chair.

The wolf trotted over to the bushes and sniffed. Eyes gleaming like gray flashlights, he lifted a back leg and marked one she'd planted.

Marking his territory.

She recognized the primal gesture. To warn other males away, and a promise to her to later claim her in the flesh and make her his own.

Female hormones stirred and arousal pulsed. He loped toward the pool. The wolf leaped in, water splashing over the deck, baptizing her in a cascade of droplets.

A wolf had jumped into the pool.

A naked man emerged from it.

He rose from the water like Poseidon, lacking only a trident and beard. Water cascaded down his sleek flanks, his muscular, scarred abdomen.

Powerful thigh muscles rippled beneath his skin as he mounted the steps.

Keira took a step back. Another, as he left the pool and advanced, his black hair slick and wet. Her gaze traveled from the twist and tangle of scar tissue marking his chest and torso, to his strong, powerful thighs and the curve of muscle of calves, back to the apex of his legs and the water beading in the thick, dark hair of his groin.

His thick, long phallus. At rest, it was impressive.

She looked up into his face, tense with anticipation.

"You see what I am," he said quietly. He spread out his arms, reminding her of Darwin's celestial man. "What happened to me. This is me, Keira."

Deep, jagged scars lined his torso and chest, silvery gouges bisecting every plane of muscle and sinew. More scars flared on his thick thighs, ending just above his knees.

She'd gone for the thickest muscles to do the least damage.

He waited quietly, watching her face. Melissa had not seen him naked, only the bandages covering the injuries. But her horrified gasp and avoidance afterward had been enough warning.

The SEALs on his team knew his injuries, saw them each day when he swam laps with them. But no woman had seen him naked since a wolf had carved his torso like a roast.

Exposing himself like this was a gamble, but necessary. Dale had sworn to be honest with her after the exam at the base.

He would not keep secrets from her any longer.

No pity etched her expression. He saw a flicker of wonder and, as she glanced downward, frank female appreciation.

His sex stirred.

"So strong. Such a strong, courageous male to take such a brutal torture."

A dim memory flickered. Soft voice and sweet scent winding around his body like velvet ropes, a lick of passion teasing his groin, desire and pain mingling together until he wanted to scream and never stop....

Spikes of pain slammed into his temples. Dale pressed
a hand to his aching head.

"Are you okay?" she asked.

He nodded, struggling more with pride than pain.
Damn, getting naked in front of a woman usually meant
pleasure.

Now it meant possible rejection. Gathering all his
strength, he plunged ahead.

"I'm beginning to care for you, Keira. And I want no
secrets between us. Especially…this." He pointed to his
maimed torso.

Dale watched her reaction, his heart beating fast. Never
had he felt this vulnerable and exposed. Not even when
he'd been tied to the platform in the basement, helpless
against the wolf's claws. He'd fought the chains, resisted
the compulsion to scream with his last breath, until the
pain became a hot, living agony scraping over bone and
flesh. Even then, the hoarse cries torn from his throat were
shrieks of rage and promises of revenge.

Now, all he faced was silence, and Keira. Waiting for
judgment.

Or redemption.

Melissa had not wanted to see him naked. On the way
to the ball, she'd whispered how they could spend the night
together. When he'd informed her, with overt sarcasm, it
would require him to remove his clothing, she'd only replied, "Darling, we can always turn off the lights."

Tonight, Dale had flooded the backyard with lights,
flipping on every lamppost, the pool lights, hell, even the
motion-detector lights.

Leaving nothing to Keira's imagination, letting her see
every single ugly groove and hollow marking him.

Her lovely mouth wobbled as her large eyes grew luminous. Then she stepped forward, and placed her hand

on his chest, over his heart. Her palm was soft and warm against his chilled flesh.

"They couldn't scar this. Your heart. No matter what they did to you, they could never take away the courageous, noble man who stepped forward to save a child's life. Your scars are medals, a testament to your honor."

Tears shimmered in her eyes. "You are the bravest man I've had the privilege to know. Thank you for sharing this with me."

Something inside him eased. Dale cupped her cheek, thumbing aside a tear.

"Don't cry, sweetheart."

"It hurts to know how you suffered," she whimpered. "How you were in so much pain. I wish...oh, how I wish I could have stopped it."

Distressed, he bent his head and kissed the corner of her mouth. "It doesn't hurt. Not anymore."

A cry tore from her throat, a wrenching sob. She wrapped her arms around his neck and kissed him. He tasted her, and the salty tears running down her cheeks. Dale deepened the kiss, joy tumbling through him. She moaned beneath his mouth, and drew closer. His sex stirred fully, eager for more.

Dale nipped at her lower lip and broke the kiss. He gazed down at her, all thoughts of vulnerability gone, wanting only one thing.

"Make love with me."

He needed to be a man again, needed to feel whole. He needed her in his arms, her soothing touch stroking over bare flesh, healing him.

Keira slid a palm up to caress his jaw. "Yes," she whispered. "Tonight."

"Now."

He swung her into his arms and she gave a startled, but happy yelp. Legs dangling over his arms, Keira hooked her hands around his neck. "You don't do anything by half measure, do you, Commander."

"Never." His grin faded. "Not when it comes to you. I'm not a romantic, Keira. Just a man who's been to hell and back and needs you, desperately."

He hooked a strand of hair behind her ear. "I want you so much, I'm trembling inside."

Dale leaned his forehead against hers, needing to touch her, hold her, keep her close. "I want to wrap myself around you like a vine, entwining myself so deeply we become one. I want to make love to you until we become so close, we flow into each other like water. Push myself so deep into you that I become an unquenchable fire, burning you with passion. Give yourself to me, Keira, and I promise you I'll give you pleasure to remember for a thousand nights."

And then she pulled away, her gaze soft and shining, and touched his cheek, her soft hand a redeeming caress. "Yes. A thousand times, yes."

As Dale kissed her she wrapped her arms around him, losing herself in sensation.

For years, her heart had been guarded by walls as thick as her cell, encaged in a protective layer. Never had she wanted to share herself, give her heart away to a man and hand him the power to hurt her.

For the first time since those awful days in the Nicaraguan jungle when the Centurions killed everyone she loved, Keira wanted to open her heart. Dale could hurt her, badly. But she'd lived too long in the darkness.

Only the light would suffice.

Warmth suffused her as he kept kissing her, his wet body pressed close, the hardness of his erection digging into her lower belly. Keira moaned, wanting to sink into him, wrap herself around him and forget the world. Draw in his inner light and blend it with hers, bond with him in the flesh as their spirits would surely entwine.

Let him chase away the emptiness for a while longer.

Dale kept inching backward, toward the deep end. Oh, she was going off the deep end, losing herself in the sharp sweetness of his mouth....

He stepped back and they fell into the water together. Coldness washed over her. Keira emerged, sputtering, as he laughed and playfully splashed her.

"My dress!"

"Take it off and let it dry out."

She swam until she could stand, and wrung out her long hair. Fierce hunger glinted his gray gaze as he approached, eyes level with the water, like an alligator. Keira looked at the burning lights. He had the courage to get naked before her.

The dress clung to her like shrink wrap, but she wriggled out of it. Dale's warm gaze caressed her as she reached for the clasps of her bra and finally set it aside, then pulled down the matching green panties and tossed them onto the pool deck. Shyly she stood before him, feeling suddenly vulnerable.

He framed her face with his warm, strong hands. "You're so beautiful."

He kissed his way down her neck, while palming her breasts. Each stroke of her turgid nipples brought flaming warmth, oh, such lovely warmth it felt like she'd never be cold again. Squirming, she kissed him back, rubbing against him, not knowing exactly what to do, but eager to explore.

Dale nuzzled her neck and spread a palm over her belly, then slid his hand lower, between her legs. Fresh heat flared as he slid a finger between her slick, wet cleft. "Oh, man, I want you so much, so much..." he muttered against her neck. "Sweetheart, if we continue this, we're in trouble because we need to get upstairs…."

Deftly he slid a finger into her tight channel. Keira winced slightly. "Upstairs where the condoms…"

He stopped and raised his head with an expression of shock. "You're a virgin."

"Uh-huh." A little embarrassed, she ducked her head.

"Look at me, sweetheart."

Finally she did.

"You're thirty years old?"

"Thirty-four."

"And never had sex."

"I never met a man I wanted," she whispered, suddenly embarrassed and feeling awkward. "Not until you. Are you sorry?"

He gave her such a tender look, her heart melted. "Never. We'll just take things nice and slow."

Upstairs, he pulled her into his bedroom, tore off the covers with one hand and tumbled her backward to the mattress, droplets of water from their bodies dampening the sheets. She explored his body, every scar, each curve of muscle. Tattooed on his right biceps was the small insignia of an eagle with outstretched wings behind an anchor, a trident and a pistol gripped in its claws. Keira leaned on an elbow and examined it.

"Budweiser, what they call the SEAL pendant," he told her.

"It means a lot to you, being a SEAL."

He nodded. "Toughest, and best, life I've ever had."

"So much you marked yourself with it."

"Not the first mark. When you become a SEAL, they give you the pendant, place it over your chest and pound the pin into your skin." Dale grinned at her stunned look.

"That's barbaric."

"It's brotherhood."

"Macho, overrated, he-man ritual…"

He kissed her, and the warmth of his mouth made her forget her next thought. He'd seduced her with pleasure and promises of more, stroking her skin and baring her to his hungry gaze.

His hands slowly caressed her hips, then he left her mouth and nuzzled her neck, gave it a slow lick. Pain, sharp and brief, laced her as he nipped her skin. His tongue caressed the wound, replacing pain with erotic pleasure.

Dale cupped her hips and kissed his way down her quivering torso. Then he slipped his hands between her legs, drew them apart and put his mouth on her. Shocked pleasure shot through her.

He suckled her intimate feminine flesh, his wicked tongue stroking and teasing. Stretched out like a sacrifice, Keira released a frustrated whimper as the pleasured tension built higher and higher. Then, with his tongue he stroked the one place aching for his touch. Quick, powerful flicks that drew her taut, made her moan as she clutched at his silky hair, gasping until she threatened to fall apart, building the pleasure higher and higher.

With a shrill shriek, she climaxed, crying out his name. Tremors spilled through her, leaving her in a sensual haze. Dale stayed with her, tenderly kissing her intimate flesh as he cupped her bare bottom.

He sat back, his heavy phallus bobbing from the apex of his muscled thighs, and slid a hand across his wet mouth.

He moved his palm over one breast and gently squeezed, then lowered his mouth to sample her rigid nipple. Dale pushed a sleek thigh between her legs, rubbing against her sensitive, quivering flesh. She squirmed, then fisted a hand in his hair as he tasted and suckled her breast.

This Mage possessed a dark magick and turned her into a slave, shuddering with need. She would do anything he asked.

As she arched upward to the stroke of his thigh and the flick of his tongue, Keira shattered again in an explosion of hot, wet heat. Moisture gushed between her legs, bathing his strong thigh.

Her chest rising and falling with each ragged breath she stared into his darkened gray eyes, watching the steely coldness turn to tender warmth.

He smiled. "We're not quite done yet. Not for a long while."

She thirsted to see his control shatter, his passion shatter as she had shattered in his arms. Sexual pleasure washed through her, the little aftershocks of orgasm rippling along every nerve.

Keira sat up, and with a strength that surprised her, pushed him backward. Dale looked surprised, then amused, and she began exploring his body. She kissed a narrow hip, ran a hand over his taut belly and traced the groves and indentations her wolf had carved into his flesh. She felt a pang of pure sorrow, then focused on bringing him pleasure, delighting as his muscles quivered beneath her touch. Keira kissed his collarbone, then traced a line over his broad shoulder with her mouth. She licked smooth skin stretched over hard muscle and sinew, tasting the slight salt of his skin. Awe spilled through her at the vast differences between male and female. His was a warrior's body, thick with muscle, while her body was softer and pliant.

"Turn over," she ordered.

"Aye, aye, sir," he murmured with a twinkle in his gray gaze.

Dale turned onto his stomach as she straddled his thick, muscled thighs and ran her palms over the silky hair on his legs, marveling at the strength in his limbs. She slid her hands up to the smooth tautness of his bottom and squeezed, smiling as he groaned with pleasure.

Keira trailed hot, wet kisses up from his bottom, along the smooth muscles bisecting his back, to his nape, loving the groans she culled from him. Then as easily as she'd pushed him back, he slid from beneath her and flipped her onto her back. Dale reached into the nightstand and removed a foil packet, tore it open and sheathed his erection.

Intensity radiated in his gaze as he settled his muscled body between her opened legs. Bracing himself on his hands, he stared down at her. She felt his rigid length probe at her wet, tight opening. Keira stiffened in real alarm.

"Shhh." He stroked her hair. "It's all right, Keira. Don't resist me. Relax."

It wasn't going to work. She was too tense and too small. But she wanted this.

Dale laced his fingers through hers, locking their hands together. He pushed forward, his penis like a thick steel bar invading her softness. She gritted her teeth. As the burning pressure turned into real pain, Keira gripped his fingers as if he were an anchor amid a stormy sea. His heavy weight pinned her to the mattress.

"Mine," he whispered. "All mine."

He pushed hard and deep inside her. Caught by the sudden shock of pain, she cried out, but Dale caught her cry with his mouth, kissing her deeply. As he raised his head, a single tear trickled down her cheek. He tore his mouth from hers, chased it away with his tongue.

"I'm sorry for hurting you," he said quietly.

I'm sorry I hurt you, she longed to say. Instead, she pulled him down for another deep kiss.

Locked deep inside her, Dale remained still. The burning pressure between her legs eased, replaced with a curious, delightful friction. He began moving, as her inner muscles clasped the male intruder eagerly, caressing him. Dale tensed and groaned. A bead of sweat rolled off his forehead and spilled onto her breasts like a teardrop. Tentatively, he began to move, groaning as he threw his head back and closed his eyes.

"So good, you feel so good," he muttered.

Emotions raged through her, a maelstrom of joy and intimacy so intense, she could barely stand it. She, who had delivered nothing but pain and suffering to this man, was now giving him this intense pleasure.

His face alight with fierce desire, Dale spread her legs open wide. Keira braced herself as he thrust deeply, their bodies, slick with sweat, rubbing over each other. He stiffened, then his body shook as he shouted her name. Stroking his damp hair, Keira welcomed his heavy weight as he collapsed atop her, his head pillowed beside hers. After a minute, he slid off, disposed of the condom. Then he joined her in bed and gathered her tightly against him.

"You okay?" he asked softly, stroking her hair.

Tenderness shone in his eyes as she nodded. She felt complete and satisfied and filled with awed wonder. Something had happened, and more than making love. Something wonderful, and frightening. Her heart, Keira realized with dismay. She'd done more than give her body to his powerful Mage. She had opened her heart to him.

They lay in drowsy contentment as Keira curled against him, her head pillowed on his broad shoulder. Her fingers slid through the damp hairs on his chest, tracing the scars she'd placed there, wondering when Dale would remember she was the demon wolf he hated.

Wondering what he'd do when he finally remembered...

She had made love with this man, let him into her body, bared her emotions before him. They'd tangled together in hot passion last night. Dale was an excellent lover, tender and considerate.

Now, in the soft light of dawn, he looked official and commanding, a stranger capable of breaking her arm.

Or her heart.

She watched him dress in his navy blue double-breasted jacket with the thin gold stripes on the sleeves. Layers of medals decorated his left breast, along with a shiny gold pin, an exact duplicate of his inked arm.

So handsome and distinguished.

She jumped up and helped him adjust the navy blue tie around his crisply ironed dress shirt. Her fingers rested on the navy SEAL pin, a symbol of his dedication and honor.

"Fancy duds, sailor. Got a date?"

"With brass in D.C. I'll be back late."

Gray eyes twinkling, he caressed her cheek. "I've never had a naked woman help me dress."

Glancing down, she blushed and covered herself. Dale pulled her hands away. "Don't. You're such a beautiful sight in the morning. You make my blood race."

He kissed her, making *her* blood race. Dale leaned his forehead against hers. "If I stay here, all your hard work will go to hell because I'm going to rip off all my clothing and get naked with you in bed."

With a final kiss, he donned his white hat and left the room.

Keira sat on the bed, hugging herself. They were closer than ever, and nothing seemed to threaten her bliss. No Centurions banging on her door, invading the house. Keira touched the slave armband on her biceps.

Under Dale's protection. As long as he never renounced their agreement verbally, she remained safe.

But for how long?

Chapter 20

Her first dinner party ever. Keira felt more nervous than a new bride entertaining her husband's business partners.

Dale wanted to fully incorporate her into his life. All the Phoenix Force SEALs and their wives and girlfriends were invited. And, at Keira's insistence, Ensign Lees. She needed a familiar face, female company who could set her at ease.

Because being around Dale's team at an intimate dinner party scared the hell out of her. What if one of them had been in the basement along with Shay? What if she were recognized?

And Shay himself, his presence was left as a question mark. He might make it. Probably not.

Leaving Dale to finish preparations, Keira went onto the back deck and stared at the sun sinking behind the trees. Pink streaked the sky. Dale had family. He had his team, who would die for him.

She had no one.

Suddenly she felt unbearably lonely, missing her people, though it had been years. She thought of her little brother, his bravery and kindness.

How the Centurions, too, had brutally slaughtered him.

A sob rose in her throat.

The sliding glass door slid open. Two warm arms encircled her waist. "Sweetheart, what's wrong?" He pressed a soft kiss to her nape as she gathered her composure.

"I'm worried about dinner. All those big bad SEALs and we're serving a wussy fondue to start. Can't imagine them eating fondue."

Dale turned her around. "Honesty, Keira. Remember?"

I remember, but you don't.

"I was missing my family," she admitted. "Missing them, oh, so much. You have parents, two sisters and nieces and nephews. And your team, who are your brothers in blood. I have…no one."

He kissed the corner of her mouth.

"You have me."

Dale kept kissing her mouth, little brushes of his firm lips. "And once the guys really get to know you, they'll adore you. They'll have to, because if they don't, I'll assign them to deploy to the nearest ice cap to target-shoot penguins."

Horrified, she drew back. "Penguins?"

He grinned, the gesture impish and boyish. "Well, maybe just the ice floes."

A steady beat of gnawing trepidation pounded through her veins. "I made enough for the entire navy. You're not expecting anyone else to drop by?"

"Ensign Lees and her boyfriend. Shay's on the road. Won't be joining us."

Relief flooded her. She grasped his shoulders to steady herself. "Okay. Let's do it."

Ensign "Call me Robyn" Lees brought her boyfriend, a hybrid wolf shifter. "We fight like cats and dogs," she'd told Keira, with a teasing but adoring look at the tall, lanky man.

The men immediately gathered in the dining room,

where the cheese fondue was set up on a side table. They
began animated discussions while their wives and girlfriends shook their heads.

"Boys and their toys." Sienna, Lt. Parker's wife, shook
her head. "I swear if Matt isn't blowing something up or
shooting something or running as a wolf, he gets so restless."

Keira smiled stiffly. "You mean running with his wolf."

Six sets of eyes gazed at her.

"She doesn't know," Robyn told them.

"We're all paranorms. I'm a Fae," Sienna explained.
"No need to watch yourself. Just worry about a sudden
surge of magick or someone accidentally releasing a power
bolt."

"Or Sully materializing in the bathroom when you're
taking a bubble bath." This from Leona, a pretty blonde
witch, who blushed when she realized what she'd revealed.

The women laughed and started talking about male
faults.

Tightness in her muscles gradually faded as she listened. These women were ordinary, despite their origins.

Maybe I can fit in with Dale's world.

Leona sighed. "I get so tired of the guys all congregat-
ing together, and then we sit around and gab. For once, can
we all get together? Any ideas, Keira?"

Inspiration seized her. "A few."

She went to the untouched Steinway and opened the lid,
lovingly skimming a few keys. Dale had not played for her.
But she sensed the music inside him, sensed his love for
his art had been set aside, and had not died.

Keira sat at the bench and began banging on the keys.
The women laughed and held their ears. But Dale entered
the living room, dismay on his face.

"Sweetheart, I'm allergic to bad playing. Must you?"

"Only if you take my place."

Abandoning the piano bench, she looked at him. All attention riveted to Dale, who stared at the piano with the same avid longing he'd centered on her last night.

You can do it, she mouthed to him.

The cocky smile he flashed assured her he could.

Dale sat at the bench. The SEALs exchanged amused glances. "Cover your ears, wolf," Dallas joked to Dakota.

He began to play, fingers rippling over the keys, coaxing the music out with each skilled and swift stroke. Keira closed her eyes and enjoyed the music, her spirit singing with each note.

When he finished, a crashing crescendo, there was silence. Then Dakota clapped. Everyone else followed, the applause like thunder.

Gaze soft, Dale turned to her.

"Thank you, for giving me my music back."

He reached up, cupped her nape and kissed her. Keira closed her eyes, not caring they had an audience, not caring about anything.

She wanted to hold this moment in her hands, and cherish it forever.

"You'll thank me more if I don't burn dinner," she whispered, and kissed him again.

Scurrying into the kitchen, she focused on setting out the dishes. The other women drifted inside, helping, their chatter making her feel accepted and normal.

Now she was not a wolf held captive by demons all these years, but a woman with a man who cared deeply for her.

Maybe even loved her

Like I love him.

The potato masher stopped in midair. Stricken she stared into the half-beaten potatoes. Love Dale? She couldn't love him, couldn't give her heart to a man accustomed to strict military procedure, who readily admitted his team meant more than any relationship.

A man grateful for her "woo-woo" methods, but who would never eagerly embrace her ideals of trying to find the good in people. Because he was too busy searching for the bad.

Keira ignored the bitter feeling as she continued preparing the meal.

Tonight would be a good night. No matter what. No demons, negative thoughts or sadness would dash her hopes for a successful dinner.

Keira pulled the dish of green beans from the oven as the doorbell rang.

Voices sounded in the hallway. A deep, assured male voice and a woman's voice that sent a chill rushing down her spine as she froze, holding the casserole dish.

"Sweetheart, look who's here!"

Turning, she peeped through the kitchen down the hallway.

And dropped the platter of green beans. It shattered on the floor, vegetables splashing at her feet, the walls.

Oh, please, no, not now, not now...

In through the door walked a fair-headed woman with a gentle smile and a tall, rugged SEAL. Chief Petty Officer Sam "Shay" Shaymore and his new bride, Kelly.

The only living people who could reveal her true identity.

Panic clogged her throat. Keira staggered back against the counter, staring from the kitchen at the happy reunion taking place in the hallway.

"We didn't know what to bring, so we brought it all. White, red and the bubbly stuff." Shay thrust three wine bottles at Dale.

"Champagne, Sam." Kelly kissed his cheek. "So good to see you again, Curt. You look well. Much better. There's color in your cheeks."

"All thanks to my girlfriend. Come on in, make yourselves comfortable. Need to get into the kitchen. I believe there's a crisis with green beans."

Crisis? More like a full-fledged emergency. *Break out the life vests, boys, I'm sinking.*

The other women fussed and helped her clean up the mess, efficient and effective, as she dropped to her knees. She focused on picking up the shards of broken dish.

Like the shards of her broken life.

Dale rushed into the kitchen and dropped beside her. "You okay?"

"The green beans jumped out of the oven and to the floor," she said lightly.

Concern etched his handsome face. "Forget it. I'm more worried about you."

A lump rose in her throat. *Soon, you won't be.* "I'm fine. Get everyone seated. Dinner's almost ready. I have more than enough veggies to make up for the dead green beans."

As the others gathered in the dining room, she bowed her head, fighting for control.

Shay would see her. And tell his commander. She expected nothing less. She was caught. Maybe she could plead a headache, go upstairs before Shay saw her…

If she bowed out now, she'd bring more attention to herself. Suddenly she just wanted the ruse to be over with, for Dale to know the truth.

He'd heard it from her, but did not believe her.

Maybe hearing it from someone else would convince him.

In the meantime, she'd do her damnedest to ensure everyone had a good time.

Dale deserved a nice night with his men and their significant others.

Pasting a wide smile on her face, she carried the first course into the dining room.

* * *

The man stared at her through dinner. Sweat poured down her back as she ducked behind the tall arrangement of fresh roses Dale had brought her. But there wasn't any escaping the scrutiny of Chief Petty Officer Shaymore.

Every dish was met with praise. Talk flowed easily, the women steering the conversation as surely as a captain guiding a destroyer out to sea, avoiding shoptalk. It was a lovely evening, or would have been, if not for the young SEAL studying her as if she were an enemy in their midst.

But I am.

When dessert was finished, she stood to clear the table. Shay stood, as well, and glanced at Dale. "Sir, I need to talk to you."

"Sounds official. This is a dinner party. Can't business wait until tomorrow?" he asked.

"Honey, he's right. Let's relax. No shoptalk," Kelly told her husband.

Shay sat, his narrowed gaze focused on her like a wolf's. Ignoring the panic curling in her stomach, she began to clear the table.

The others helped. She shooed the men from the kitchen.

"Dale, why don't you play some more? Entertain everyone. Try something modern that doesn't sound like a dirge."

He shot her an amused look. "Beethoven is not dirge music."

As everyone filed down the hallway to the living room, Kelly remained in the kitchen. "Keira."

Here it comes...

But the woman's voice was soft and her eyes were kind. "It's you, isn't it? The woman from the basement."

She started to deny it. Shoulders sagging she nodded.

"Sam and I didn't remember your name, some kind of memory block. But your face, I'll never forget it."

Hugging herself, she stared at the floor. "And you remember what I did to Dale."

"I remember how terrified you were, how you begged the demons not to make you hurt him anymore. You were forced against your will." Kelly glanced at the open doorway, where laughter drifted down the hallway, followed by the piano playing. "Have you told Curt?"

"I tried to tell him. He doesn't remember."

"A memory-blocking spell. Or perhaps he doesn't want to. You have to trigger his recollection of what happened."

"Don't ask that of me," she whispered. "I'd rather die."

"No one will blame you for what happened. You were a victim, as well."

Bitter laughter choked her throat. "Oh, right. Tell that to them...." She jerked a thumb at the hallway. Paul and Robyn had already left with excuses. Only the SEALs remained, a close-knit gathering of men who'd die for their leader.

Or kill anyone who hurt him...

The woman clasped an odd silver pendant hanging from a chain around her neck. She rested a hand on her arm. "Then let me help you. Close your eyes."

Trusting this woman, trusting anyone who knew what she was, proved difficult. Keira shook her head.

"Please. I want to help."

Finally, she closed her eyes, relaxed. A warm tingle raced through her veins, and she felt a rush of connection, entwined with pure love. The love shook her to the core. Tears trickled from her eyes.

Then the warmth faded, and Kelly removed her hand.

She opened her eyes, wiping them with the corner of the frilly white apron. "What did you do?"

Kelly pointed to the pendant. "I used my triskele to link us. A slim link, but a psychic one. It will deflect Sam's

fury because if he tries to hurt you, he'll sense me and all
the love I have for him."

"Such a powerful love," she whispered. "You're blessed."

A sad smile touched Kelly's mouth. "I love him with all
my heart, but he has faults, too. And one is struggling to
forgive someone who's hurt him, or anyone close to him.
Curt is more than his commanding officer. He worships
him like an older brother and would do anything for him."

"I'll remember that."

When the last bottle of wine was polished off, their
guests left. She joined Dale in the bedroom, collapsing
onto the pretty window seat.

"You were terrific. Thanks." He kissed her, his mouth
warm and firm. A tingle raced down her spine.

Dale started to tug his shirt over his head. Keira reached
for the lamp.

"Leave it on." He stood before her, scars crisscross-
ing his muscled chest. "I want to make love to you in the
light. "

Keira undressed and dived under the covers. Dale aimed
her his crooked smile and tugged the covers back. Then
he jumped onto the bed and pulled her to him, kissing her.
His tongue traced the tight seam of her mouth. He tasted
like cherries, wine and chocolate. Beneath the gentle, yet
authoritative pressure of his mouth, she moaned for more.

He rolled over, opened the nightstand drawer and retrieved a condom. Dale ripped open the foil package and
sheathed his erection. Then he applied a liberal amount of
lubricant over his shaft.

"I'm sorry. I can't wait."

He mounted her and pushed his penis deep inside, past
her tight muscles. Keira clutched at his wide shoulders, her
fingers digging into the scars her claws had created. He

began to move, his fierce gaze capturing hers. It proved too intense and she closed her eyes.

"Look at me, Keira. I want you to see who's making love with you," he told her.

He nuzzled her neck, blew into her ear. She shivered delicately, her nipples hardening into tight buds.

With exquisite smoothness, he pushed into her. Keira writhed a little, trying to find some ease as his thickness penetrated her fully. She sucked in a breath, and relaxed, opening to him. He pulled back, and began to stroke inside her, his penis rubbing against her sensitive tissues, the friction creating a delicious heat. His muscles contracted as he thrust, powerful shoulders flexing.

Slowly, he moved, giving her time to become accustomed to him. Tenderness shone in his darkened gaze. Something inside her eased, the demon blood receding to the furthest corners of her mind. Keira felt only pure goodness, and joy, none of the guilt always dogging her heels. It felt as if Dale's courage and goodness pushed away the evil darkness inside her with gentle, healing light, the strength the demons tried to steal from him now flowing freely into her as they joined their bodies. Silky chest hair rubbed against her aching breasts, his hard torso sliding against her soft abdomen. She arched to meet his rhythm.

Wonder came over her face as she watched him. His mouth parted on a gasp, lips trembling. The bed beneath her was as soft as down, the male pressing her backward onto it solid muscle. It felt as if he locked her spirit in his, a closeness she'd never experienced until now.

His thrusts became more urgent, harder, until his flesh slapped against hers. Wrapping her legs around his pistoning hips, she reached for it, the tension growing until she felt ready to explode.

Screaming his name on her lips, she climaxed, her core squeezing him as she shattered, her back arching.

He growled in satisfaction, gave one last thrust and threw his head back with a hoarse shout. Dale collapsed atop her, his face pillowed beside her, his breathing ragged. She bore his weight, welcoming it, but then he eased out of her and rolled over, pulling her into his arms.

She lay in his arms, listening to his pounding heart, her fingers tracing the horrid scars lining his pectorals, the ridged muscles of his abdomen. But for once, she felt no guilt over them.

"Do you find my body repulsive?"

Startled, she raised her head. "No. Why are you asking?"

"I asked Dakota tonight for the name of a top plastic surgeon he knows. Man's an expert at removing scars."

"Why now?"

His expression shuttered. "Just thinking about options. My shirtsleeve rode up tonight. Leona, Sully's girlfriend, noticed my left arm. She cringed and turned away. A natural reaction. I'm used to it."

"A natural reaction for a woman whose worst day consists of a bad manicure, not tangling with demons. She's superficial. I'm not."

He smiled, but doubt remained in his eyes. *Fine. I'll show you....*

Keira leaned over and kissed his scars, one by one.

"These are badges of courage and sacrifice. You sacrificed yourself to save innocent children."

A sudden memory struck. "They can be removed by the one who placed them there, through a tremendous act of sacrifice and courage."

Such sacrifice was beyond her. *I'm a coward,* she thought, grief tightening her throat. *Can't do it.*

Because doing so would mean surrendering her life back to the Centurions. Only this imprisonment called for worse than a dark cell, and infrequent beatings and the terrible price her victims paid.

What the Centurions would do to her would make Dale's torture seem like a slap and a tickle....

Keira closed her eyes, resting her palm on Dale's chest. He pulled her down for a kiss. "No more talk of scars. I want to love you tonight, Keira. All night."

After, she lay cuddled against him. Soft and warm, sleeping like a contented puppy.

Dale stared at the ceiling, unable to sleep.

Sex had been explosive, exquisite and powerful. Filled with feelings he'd denied himself for years, he relished making love to this woman.

Keira had cracked open the cold shell and touched his heart.

He wanted to cherish her, protect her as a man did for a woman he intended to hold and keep. Keep her so awash in pleasure she'd never seek another's bed.

Not like Kathy. At that thought, the familiar ache returned, but this time, it was a distant throb instead of the wrenching pain from the past.

How could she fit into his world, with her unconventional gypsy lifestyle? The free-spirited attitude of a world outside the naval base called to her like a siren song.

Keira might remain content for now. But for how long? Would she pack up and move on like his ex, seeking a less structured life, filled with people like her who wanted to see only the good in others, instead of seeking out the bad?

Maybe she's right. There is a point to finding the good in others.

The thought startled him. With a rueful smile, he realized he had dropped his rigid black-and-white views and embraced the gray.

Just like she did.

"You're a witch," he whispered into her ear, kissing her cheek.

But one troubled thought remained, chasing away elusive sleep.

He'd opened his heart to this woman, shared his deepest emotions. Yet as sweet and open as she'd been, whispering her hopes and dreams to him in bed, Keira still held something back from him. And if it turned out to be something big, a betrayal as shattering as Kathy's, he must excise her from his life.

Dale couldn't forgive such deception from a woman again.

Ever.

Chapter 21

A steady rain fell the next morning as Keira trudged down the stairs, rubbing her eyes. In a crisp khaki uniform, Dale sat at the kitchen table, reading a thick report, an empty coffee cup before him. She opened the cabinet, took out a cup and poured herself coffee, added the creamer Dale had bought just for her, and then refilled his cup. They had settled into a routine of two people who intimately knew each other's needs.

When she set it before him, he glanced up, warmth in his gaze. "Thanks."

She leaned against the counter, sipping, feeling alive and happy for the first time in...when? Couldn't remember ever feeling like this, all the joy pushing back the darkness, making the past blur completely. He was dedicated to his job, focused on keeping the men and women of ST 21 safe. Little by little, she peeled back his layers, finding more of the man beneath.

The more she discovered about Dale Curtis, the more she liked. A tentative friendship had deepened to something more, her feelings growing stronger each day until Keira knew she cared deeply about this Mage. And yet beneath the effervescent joy and serenity, was a tiny blipping light. A lighthouse beacon winking through all the sparkling giddiness.

He's going to find out who you truly are. And then what?

Keira refused to consider. *I just want to be happy for once. I'll take whatever he's willing to give and worry about the consequences later.*

Still reading his report, he pushed back his chair and got up, sipping his coffee. His concentration remained absolute until he reached the counter, and set the cup and paper down.

Curiosity overcame her. "What are you reading? It looks utterly fascinating."

He spun around, grabbed her by the waist, papers spilling to the floor. "Not as fascinating as you."

He buried his face in her throat, delivering hot, nipping kisses. Squealing with laughter, she pushed at his chest. "Dale! I'm hungry."

"So am I," he muttered, sliding his hands down to her butt and squeezing. "I'm craving a Keira breakfast special. You, naked against the counter."

Pulling back, he looked at her, tenderness in his eyes. "Or are you too sore for this? I want you to feel nothing but pleasure this time."

A furious flush heated her cheeks at the intimate reminder of last night. In response, she pulled him down and kissed him, desperate to feel him close against her, keep the magic alive and dancing for a while longer.

Absorbed in his mouth nibbling at hers, his hands stroking the small of her back, she dimly realized they were being watched. Dale pulled away, his eyes narrowing as he turned around.

Dressed in camouflage rain gear as if prepared for attack, Chief Petty Officer Samuel Shaymore stood on the deck outside. Even in the pouring rain, he could not disguise his cold fury.

Wriggling free of Dale's grip, she became uncomfortably aware of the thin cotton sleep shirt riding up her thighs, her nipples standing in hard points against the fabric. Far worse was the fear snaking down her spine like the stroke of a cold finger

She knew why Shay was here....

She went to dart away, but Dale shook his head.

"I'm not letting one of my men chase you away." He tapped her nose, his gaze soft. "Stay here."

Dale slid the door open. "Shay. You've got lousy timing."

The SEAL's gaze slid to Keira. "Sorry, sir. I have to talk to you. Alone. It's very important."

Panic squeezed her chest. Keira fisted her trembling hands.

"Whatever you have to say can wait for my office. Fifteen minutes..." He glanced down at his watch, then over to Keira, his expression intent. "Make it thirty-five."

But Shay stepped into the door, rain dripping off his cloak onto the floor as Dale started to close it. "I'm sorry, sir, but this can't wait. It's personal." He glanced at Keira again with that glacial look. "Not about me, but you."

Dale's jaw tightened. He flexed his hands, then nodded. "My study."

The young SEAL pushed past, not looking at Keira. Dale sighed and dropped a kiss on her lips, his mouth warm and firm. He looked at her with such a devoted expression, she felt tears rise in her throat.

Knowing after hearing what Shay said, he'd never look at her like this again.

"This won't take long. Don't go away."

He playfully touched her nose and went down the hall. The study door closed behind him.

For a moment she stood still, looking around the cheerful kitchen, memorizing every detail of Dale sitting at the table. A memory to tide her through the upcoming lonely nights.

Keira hurried down the hallway to gather her things.

"Spill it, Shay. I am a little busy."

Dale watched the SEAL pace back and forth in front of the fireplace. In all the years he'd known the Mage, he'd never acted this agitated.

Finally he turned and looked him straight in the eye.

"Your relationship with Keira... You're getting quite close to her."

Dale narrowed his gaze. "And what concern of it is yours? It's my private life."

"She's not who she pretends to be."

He frowned, then relaxed. "You're a little late. I found out exactly who she is."

Shock slackened Shay's jaw. "You know?"

Dale steepled his fingertips, rested them against his mouth. "At the base before you arrived, I had Thad check her out. She's a Celestial Hunter wolf with demon blood, not only a Luminaire. She saved Sully's life from a demon in my basement."

"Maybe her motivation wasn't so altruistic."

He went absolutely still. "Say what you mean, damn it, and make your point."

Shay hesitated. "I don't trust her, sir. And I don't want to see you in a position where she can hurt you. Again."

Now this conversation had taken a peculiar twist. "I'm a big boy, chief. I can take care of myself."

An odd shadow of grief crossed the Mage's face. "Do

you remember anything about that time in the basement, Curt? When Kelly and I rescued you?"

Dale's mind raced. Memories still fogged, only a shrill screech of pain, talons over his flesh. And deep, deep sorrowful sounds of someone weeping. Him?

As time passed, the memories became more clouded. Thankfully. But pulsing beneath was a blinking red light, a warning he knew he should not ignore.

But hell, it had been so long since he'd felt this peaceful, this damn happy. Why spoil a good thing with trying to recall a horrific nightmare?

"Keira is the wolf who hurt you in the basement. Kelly thinks she was forced into it, but I had to tell you to watch your six."

A horrific pain slammed into his skull. Dale held his head and bit back a moan. "The woman who tortured me had blond hair."

Shay stared. "Curt, she did not…"

"She did. I know she did." Dale stood. "If that's all, I'll see you on base. I don't want to discuss this any more with you or anyone else."

Shay nodded. But as he went to leave, Shay grabbed his arm. "Mage to Mage, Curt, I'm here for you. If you ever need me, no matter what, or when, call me. You're more than my commander, and more to Kelly, too. If we didn't care, I wouldn't be so worried."

Dale smiled briefly, touched the other Mage's finger, watching their auras spark pure gold. "You're a good man, Shay."

"You, too, Curt." Emotion pulled his face tight. "That's why I'd hate to lose you. Watch your six, Commander. Never let your guard down. Not even for a woman who loves you. Or one who pretends to."

He slipped down the hallway, leaving Dale to puzzle over his cryptic warning.

* * *

Fleeing to the garage, Keira found her bike, kick-started it and roared away.

Driving endlessly, tears streaming down her face, not caring where she headed, just running, running. Running from her pain, from reality.

Rain fell into her eyes, mingling with the salty tears. Little traffic on this side street this early. A black pickup truck approached from behind, the driver blaring the horn.

Dale.

Keira pulled over and stopped the bike and dismounted, barely able to see through her tears and the rain. The truck pulled up behind her, the motor shutting off. Dale jumped out, leaving the door open. He ran to her and clasped her arms.

"You okay?" he asked.

When she nodded, he cursed low and pulled her roughly into his arms. "Don't ever do that to me again. You scared the hell out of me, racing away like that in this rain where you could take a bad spill. Damn, Keira, if I hadn't seen you take off, and followed… Why did you do it?"

Her mouth wobbled. "Shay didn't tell you? What I am?"

Dale lowered his forehead to hers. "Shay warned me against you. I told him I know about your demon blood and I can take care of myself."

"Dale…" she began.

And then he kissed her, cutting off her next sentence, his mouth warm against her frozen lips, his arms solid and sure, anchoring her to him.

When they both broke apart, gasping for breath, Dale lifted her into his arms. He jogged to the truck and lifted her into the shotgun seat. He climbed in beside her and closed the door, chafing her hands. And then he stopped, made another low sound and pulled her into his arms again, his fingers fumbling with her leather jacket. She managed to remove it and his hands slid upward, cupping her wet, unbound breasts. He squeezed and kneaded, so warm, so good. Keira gasped for breath and hitched up her skirt. With a rough grunt, he ripped her panties, tossing the shreds aside as she fumbled with the zipper on his jeans. His penis sprang out, hard and ready.

"Condom. Glove box," he gasped.

She found it, ripped off the foil wrapping and he rolled it over his erection. Dale lifted her up and she slid down, half-afraid he wouldn't fit; she was too dry, but her body was ready for him, and they slid together like all her dreams, as if they truly belonged. He groaned and lifted her hips as she gripped his wide shoulders and began moving up and down, his thrusts becoming wilder and faster. "Come on, sweetheart, come with me," he urged and as he threw back his head and stiffened, she orgasmed.

Dale shouted her name in the truck, the symphony of the rain drumming against the truck, as the cymbals of thunder crashed around them. Keira clung limply to him as he finally slowed and held her against him, her wet body shaking with bliss now, the cold chased away by his heat.

She never wanted to leave.

She must leave, for she didn't belong with him.

He buried his face against her shoulder and gave a low curse again, kissing her throat. Slowly he lifted her, disengaging them, and then he ripped off the condom and tossed it onto the floor. Her breathing ragged, her heart knocking against her chest, she looked at him.

"And here I thought you never let anyone litter in your truck."

He kissed her again, his mouth tender and gentle this time. "Except with you. You throw all the rules out the window."

Dale zipped up his jeans as she put herself to rights, the space between her legs aching and pulsing and wet.

He pulled his cell phone from his jacket pocket and dialed a number.

"Sully? Favor. Pick up Dallas. I need Dallas to drive Keira's bike back to my house. It's at…" He glanced at the street sign and gave the intersection. "Thanks."

He thumbed off the phone and started up the truck.

At his house, he hustled her into the shower, turned on the twin knobs to hot and undressed her. As she stood beneath the spray, shivering again, he soaped her body.

After, he toweled her off, helped her shrug into a terry-cloth robe. Dale lifted her into his arms and placed her gently on the bed. For a moment she lay in silence. And then she turned to him, unable to bear the quiet anymore as she watched him stand at the window.

"You'll be late for work," she whispered.

"They can do without me for one morning." Lightning cracked, spearing the air with brilliant light. "Storm's getting worse."

"I used to be afraid of lightning, until my mother taught me it was a natural element of the earth, one that some Mages can harness for power." Keira slid out of the bed and joined him at the window, flattening her palm against the glass.

"I can," he said quietly. "But I haven't in a long time."

Keira clasped her robe tightly. He needed the power now. If he were to engage any more demons, he needed to draw his strength from the earth.

"Maybe it's time you recharged. It's the perfect opportunity." She clasped his hand. "Come with me, outside now."

Dale's brows wrinkled, but he followed her down the steps.

The rain slowed to a gentle patter, but lightning still crackled in the air. They went outside to the backyard to a clearing away from the trees. Wiping rain from her forehead, Keira took a deep breath.

"Stretch out your hands and focus all your powers as a Mage. You're going to be a lightning rod and pull power from the storm. You're more than 400 years old and you've done this before. You can do it and it's not going to be a direct hit. I'll help you."

Closing her eyes, Keira began the chant, coaxing the lightning to him. Dale extended his arms. His total trust in her squeezed her heart hard.

Creating a small ball of energy, she tossed it into the air. "Now, Dale! When the lightning hits the bolt, yank all the power into you!"

The bolt zigged and zagged across the sky and crashed into the energy bolt. Dale closed his eyes and yanked hard. Energy crackled and sang as it surrounded him in a white glowing light. He kept pulling and pulling, like a sailor towing a rope.

And then the skies grew quiet and the storm abated.

Dale opened his eyes. They were burning white, sizzling with power.

A little afraid, Keira stepped back. Never had she been close to this much power. Little sparks leaped off his body, crackling in the air.

Finally, the white glow died down and his eyes resumed their normal gray shade.

But Dale was not normal. She sensed it, knew it. He had gone from a strong, but frail Primary into a force of nature, a force equal to defeating the Centurions.

"You did it," she whispered.

He looked at her and his expression shifted, becoming hungry and intense. "I need…"

Dale took her hand and tugged her into the house, upstairs to the bedroom. Without words, he lifted her onto the bed, kissing her deeply.

Then he unzipped his trousers, his penis thick and straining toward her, and reached for a condom, then sheathed himself. Dale opened her thighs wide, his hands cupping her bottom, pressing his penis at her soaked cleft. He thrust deep.

Oh, gods, it was too much, too intense. Sensations overwhelmed her, his power singing to her, surrounding her, creating a friction between her legs, her breasts.

"I'm a demon," she gasped.

"You're a damn witch," he countered, thrusting harder.

They came together, shattering, their bodies shuddering, her shrill cries mingling with his hoarse shouts. After, trembling, she rested against his broad shoulder. "I have something to confess. I am the one who hurt you in the dark."

Dale kissed her temple. "Shhh. It's all right. Nothing you can do would hurt me."

"They made me do it. The Centurions…"

He kept kissing her, his mouth trailing kisses down her neck. "I'll defeat those bastards. I could defeat ten thousand demons. They won't lay a hand on you."

Why wouldn't he listen to her? Keira moaned as he fastened his mouth on her breast and began to suckle her.

Tomorrow, maybe, when he wasn't so drunk on power and love.

Then he kissed her and began making love to her again and she forgot about being the demon who had tortured him, forgot everything except the erotic bliss he coaxed out of her with every powerful push of his hips.

Her man was headed down range.

Dale gathered a team together for an operation that would take him away for a week, maybe longer. And he put himself on the team, as well.

Standing on the tarmac with the other SEAL families, Keira placed her palm flat on Dale's chest, feeling his beating heart. Clutched in her left hand was her Celestial amulet. The amulet would help keep him safe.

But she risked his memories returning if he touched it, for it had been sewn into his flesh as protection against her wolf fangs.

"Can't tell you where we're headed. Hang tight, get together with the other wives and girlfriends."

Dale kissed her.

Thinking of the love Kelly held for Sam, she clung to hope. Dale was her lover, and he cared for her, had begun sharing his heart. Surely reason would overcome anger if he discovered her deception.

She tucked the amulet into the deep chest pocket of his shirt. "For good luck. It will keep you safe."

He kissed her, his gaze warm and tender. "Miss you. Don't worry, I'm going to kick ass. And don't stay up all night, eating all the popcorn when you watch your sentimental chick flicks."

She wrapped her arms around his lean waist, the rough fabric of his BDUs abrading her cheek, and hugged him tight.

Then she pasted on a brave smile and waved as he walked onto the tarmac toward the plane, trailed by the other soldiers. Always out front. Always the leader.

The briefing took place at a U.S. naval base in Kuwait. Adrenaline pumped through Dale's veins. He itched for action, but centered his breathing, as Keira taught, and listened to the platoon leader. He'd spent the past two weeks honing his training with VBSS: visit, board, search and seizure.

This was a night op, floating out to the enemy craft, sneaking the team on board before the bad guys could crack open an eyelid and say, "Huh?"

Night op with a twist. Interdiction of noncompliant vessel, a merchant ship intel said carried a shitload of weapons. Including chemical weaponry. Sarin gas, used to kill innocent children in their sleep in countries torn asunder by civil war.

The op began flawlessly, speeding out to the international shipping lane on a Mark V boat with his team on board.

Then, in a rigid-hulled inflatable, they pulled alongside the vessel, against the hull.

Dressed in black, wearing black balaclavas and masks showing only their eyes, they silently aligned their boat with the craft, the choppy waves bouncing them like rubber dolls, hooked on and boarded, climbing up the narrow ladder and over the ship's rails, quiet as mist.

Accuracy and stealth.

Dakota, the point man, signaled on his radio. Deck was deserted.

They fanned out, slipping open doors, tossing flashbangs inside each cabin, then seizing stunned prisoners. Pow, pow, pow, precision and accuracy.

Dakota approached, sweat streaking the black greasepaint on his face.

"Report," Dale ordered.

"All clear. Shitload of illegal weapons in the cargo hold. Including enough dynamite to blow this bastard to hell."

A chill raced down his spine. "Get the prisoners to the aft deck and load them ASAP. I'm going for one last recheck."

"Curt."

"Do it."

Something about that last cabin niggled at him. They'd cleared all the cabins, but in the last one, something tinged his nostrils.

Weapon trained on the door, Dale entered the cabin.

Empty. Bunk beds, a small desk, cramped quarters. Closet cleared, nothing in the head.

But his Mage senses tingled. He poked at the lower bunk with the barrel of his weapon, and flung it back. Nothing.

The tingle grew stronger.

Senses on high alert, Dale backed away, his gaze trained on the bunk. Never turn your back, he'd always drilled into his men. Not even when a room's cleared of ordinary human threats, because when the average terrorist was hauled away, something nasty and paranormal could remain....

The sheets on the lower bunk rustled and began to rise into the air. Shaping itself into the form of a six-foot-tall creature, with red, beady eyes, a slit of a mouth and gray, jellied skin. The stench of kerosene filled the room.

Hell!

Rolling away, he fired at the creature. Bullets pierced the gray jellied hide, and grayish goo leaked out.

Igninus demon. Not as powerful as the pyrokinetic demons that took down Adam, but lethal.

The demon advanced, holding out its hands. Bastard packed not bullets, but a different arsenal.

Demon fire.

It sprayed from the creature's hands, sweeping over the deck. An arc of fire shot toward Dale and missed. Tongues of flame danced closer, heat licking Dale's face. Needed more room to maneuver.

He darted for the door, rolled, dodging flames shooting his way, his mind keenly assessing the threat. If that fire reached the hold...

Dale slammed the door shut, feeling the heat pour through the steel frame. In moments, the demon would be freed and fry his ass.

Worse, fry his team and blow the ship.

Training in the firestorm chamber smoothly kicked in. *Hit 'em hard, at their weak point, and extinguish the fires. Can't fight the flames, can't carry enough CO_2. Find the enemy's soft spots and attack.*

His mind raced over options. Igninus demons' true forms were comprised of a thickening gel acting as an incendiary device, like napalm. If he tossed an energy bolt, the demon would simply explode like napalm, spreading the fire. Bullets proved useless.

Fire was fire. Triangle of fire, heat, fuel, oxygen.

Remove the heat.

Evil versus good. Cold versus heat.

All this flowed through his mind in seconds, like a fast-moving film. Dale took a deep breath, summoned all his energy directed by Keira into him through the lightning storm.

"One, two…three!"

Flinging open the door, he dive-rolled, sending streams of ice-cold white energy directly into the stream of fire. The Igninus roared and staggered back. Dale kept up the power surge, fighting the flames, surrounding the demon with white, cold energy.

Footsteps sounded, running fast. The demon began to solidify into ice, its glowing red body turning frosty.

Dropping his hands, he turned. Dakota, Dallas and Sully stood in the doorway, staring at the twisted lump of ice.

"Find all the foam fire extinguishers you can and hose down every single cabin. More could be lurking inside," he ordered, slumping against the doorway, suddenly weary, his powers diminished.

On the transport back to the States, he sat with his men. Good op. They'd not only taken down a vessel filled with weapons destined for terrorist use, but a cargo of demons, as well. Dakota and Dallas, using their Draicon wolf senses, flushed out two more Igninus demons hiding in the hold, ready to torch the dynamite, sending a foul cloud of sarin gas into the atmosphere.

Inside the C-130, it was noisy as hell, the vibration making his jaw shake. Dale leaned forward on the webbed bench.

"Those shit-kickers waited until the ship was close to NATO waters," Dakota said suddenly. "With the wind shifting, that gas would have hit our ships."

"They failed." Dale rubbed a hand over his face.

"Good job, Curt. You froze its ass. Glad to have you back with us." A grin stretched over Dallas's face, sweat smearing the black greasepaint. "Knew that firestorm chamber training would come in handy."

"Except how do you explain it to D.C. brass?" Sully affected a high-pitched tone. "Excuse me, Senator, I know you're whining about budget expenses, but we need this chamber to protect civilians like you. Curt will do a little demo on your bony ass now with a blowtorch."

"Hooyah, Curt," J.T. called out. "That was some fine blow job you did."

"Frosty the blowman," Renegade added. "Kicking demon ass to the Artic. You're a mean son of a bitch, Curt."

Weary, but exhilarated, he grinned. Back on top again. Keegan was right. He needed time in the field with his men, needed to bond with them again. And this op proved it.

"Can't wait to get back to Kelly and some nice home cooking." Shay leaned back with a tired smile.

"You mean some home loving." Renegade poked him in the side. "Like Curt here. He's got a very pretty lady waiting for him. She even gave him a magick juju pendant for luck."

"More like protection." He wondered about that. At the

least, the demon fire should have burned him. Not even his eyebrows were singed.

Keira had tucked the amulet into his pocket. He'd totally forgotten it....

Reaching into his pocket, he pulled out the small pendant. Two crescent moons interlaced. It felt warm in his palm.

Dale went still, staring at the amulet.

Flashes of memory surged, rolling through him like a slide show.

Panic squeezed his guts. Arms stretched above him, legs spread, sounds of whispering in the inky darkness. A slow stroke of a claw across his feet. Fighting, writhing, screaming in his mind, the delicate scent of flowers wrapping around his body, lacing through him, making his blood surge thick and hot, his cock stand stiff...

Blood, warm and viscous, seeping down his body, dripping on the concrete floor...

Drip, drip, drip...

Anguish surged, bright and hot as the white-hot agony of claws gouging out his flesh.

"Keira," he whispered, cupping the amulet.

"Curt? You okay? You're looking a little pale." Shay climbed over the men and knelt down, removing the amulet from his shaking hands. "Hey, buddy, take it easy...."

Power exploded from him like a geyser, energy beams shooting from his outstretched palms, pinging off the airplane's interior. Men cried out, ducked down to avoid the bolts. The airplane tilted wildly. And then he was on the floor, strong arms holding him down, deep voices telling him to hold on, it would be fine, everything would be fine.

A long, deep scream sounded, an inhuman cry of pain....

Dimly he wondered where it came from and realized

it was him. The arms holding him down belonged to his SEALs.

"It's cool, Curt," Shay soothed. "It's all right. Everything's going to be all right."

Dale closed his eyes. Shay lied.

Nothing would ever be all right again.

Keira finished arranging roses in a crystal vase and set them upon the polished Steinway. Her man was headed home and everything had to be perfect.

Checking her appearance in the hall mirror, she smoothed down the pink-and-blue-flowered dress. Dale had teased that it made her look like a garden. A soft smile touched her mouth as she remembered how eager he'd been to remove it from her....

A truck pulled into the driveway. Bursting with anticipation, she ran to the windows and stepped back in confusion.

Not one truck. Four.

Men clad in green battle dress uniforms stepped out. Dale's SEALs. Dread twisted her stomach. Oh, gods, something had happened and they were here to tell her....

And then a tall, rugged man stepped out of the back-seat of the last truck and stood. Dale. Weak with relief, she leaned against the window.

Relief turned to real fear as the SEALs marched up to the doorway, their faces grim. Her pulse spiked as she began to tremble. *He knows.*

The front door opened. Waiting in the living room, she watched the men file inside. Weapons holstered at their sides, they formed a deadly phalanx, stiff and solemn, refusing to meet her gaze.

At last Dale walked inside and quietly shut the door behind him. Heavy combat boots trudged over the wood floor. He came into the living room, face ashen and drawn, gray eyes hard as bullets.

"It was you," he said in a low voice.

Keira wrapped her arms around her waist. His expression seemed dead and empty. "I told you, but your memories... They put a block on your mind." Quivering, she bit her lip. "Please, let me explain...."

"Nothing to explain. You're the damn wolf who tortured me, turned me into a shredded mess. Keira."

Dale looked shattered. "Keira, the Luminaire who believes good can be found in people. The woman who heals those who are broken...after her wolf claws break them. How many other men have you done this to?"

She could not answer, only wrapped her arms around her waist.

"All this time I talked to you of fighting evil, of battling dark forces, and you...did...that?"

Her heart squeezed tight. She managed a brief nod. "I never wanted to hurt you. I was forced."

His voice dropped to a bare whisper. "How could you make me believe in your goodness, in light and hope? What kind of sick game is this?"

"The Centurions forced me to torture you!" she cried out.

Please believe me.

"Did they force you to come here and destroy my trust in you?" He spoke in a whisper, as if every word wrung from him was too painful to voice aloud.

His voice became louder, more strident. "Break my heart all over again after I started to care for you, believe that we had a chance together? You betrayed me. I placed my life in your hands, my spirit! In the hands of the demon wolf responsible for this!"

He tore open his shirt and lifted the sweat-stained T-shirt

below it, exposing the network of jagged scars bisecting his muscled torso.

Shay swore quietly and glared at her. Sully muttered under his breath.

"Dale, please. I'd take back every single one of them if I could. Don't let what I did in the past destroy what you have now." Tears blurred her vision. She wiped them away. "You care for me...I care for you. Reach beyond the pain and see what we have together. Just trust me a little...."

"Trust you?"

"I've shared with you my devotion. My heart. Give me a chance...trust me again and I promise I'll do anything for you."

Her voice dropped to a broken whisper. "Anything."

"The only trust and loyalty I'll give is to my team." He glanced at the SEALs. "They never caused me to question their loyalty. Not like you."

He took a deep breath, closed his eyes. "Keira Solomon, I renounce you. I renounce our agreement."

"No," she cried out.

The slave armband popped off her biceps, tumbling to the floor. Through her tears she saw the brilliant sapphire wink at her, as if mocking her protests.

Emotions in a lather, she felt her wolf give a rumbling growl. Without the protection of the armband, Dale was now vulnerable to attack. Keira squeezed her fists, desperate to control the beast. Must not turn on him, must not...

She looked up at Dale's face and saw the anguish shadowing his eyes, saw the tightened jaw and the grief. And felt a dim flare of hope.

"Keira," he said thickly. "Why did you do it? Why did you torture me in the dark? You've done nothing but help me since you got here."

Sensing his utter confusion and torment, she took a tentative step forward. "Because I was forced. They forced my wolf…"

A derisive snort from Shay. "Right. Don't listen to her B.S., Curt. Get this demon out of your life. I swear, after I saw what she did to you in the basement, how could you let her stay here?"

The wolf inside her snapped. Without the armband's protection, she found herself surrendering to the beast's emotions. Bones lengthened and fur rippled along her arms. Keira shape-shifted.

And faced Dale, emotions a red haze in her wolf mind, only wanting to get rid of this insidious pain, find relief with her claws. Growling, she advanced, stalking toward him. Face paling, he backed up, as his men withdrew their weapons.

"No," he said sharply. "Don't hurt her."

Dale dived for the carpet and picked up the Celestial amulet, holding it out like a weapon. Then he tossed it at her. The amulet hit her nose. Soon as contact was made, she shifted back into human form. Naked, trembling and vulnerable, she clothed herself by magick and stood.

"Told you, Curt," Shay said in a low voice. "How the hell can you trust her when she can turn on you in a heart-beat?"

I'm sorry, she wanted to say, but could not find her voice. It didn't matter. She saw the condemnation in his eyes, in the eyes of his men.

His team, the only ones he trusted.

"Get out," he said tightly. "Out of my house and out of my life. Sully, go upstairs, help her pack her things. I want you gone in twenty minutes. I've given you enough cash to tide you over a while."

Biting her lip to suppress her tears, she started to leave and saw him throw the slave armband at the piano. It hit the vase of roses, sending them spilling to the carpet. Water poured over the pristine, polished cabinet of the Steinway, dripping to the carpet. Like his blood had dripped in the basement.

Sullivan accompanied her to the bedroom where Dale moved her belongings. Packing didn't take long. She took the saddlebags and trudged downstairs, the ache in her chest turning into a stabbing agony.

Sullivan held the door open. She went through it.

She did not look back.

Money presented a slight problem. She had left the 3,000 dollars in cash Dale had given her on his dresser. She had enough cash to select a nice hotel on the beach for two weeks, but Keira didn't worry about conserving her funds.

Without the armband's protection, it would not take long for demons to capture her.

For two days, she took a towel and chair to the beach, sitting on the sand, staring at the lacy waves crashing upon the shore.

Remembering how Dale rescued her from the churning surf.

Remembering how they'd made love.

And then the memories became so thick and rich with grief, she wanted to bat them away, but did not. Soon enough, they'd become wisps, cobwebs torn in the wind.

All she had to sustain her through the long nights were memories of Dale.

On the second night, Keira walked outside into the warm Virginia Beach air. A restaurant a short walk away promised good seafood and an oceanfront view while dining.

Sandals dangling from one hand, she strolled along the sand, shuffling her feet in the warm grains, avoiding the crush of pedestrians on the boardwalk. A short set of steps led to the boardwalk and the restaurant. Keira trudged up the stairs and gazed at the diners eating outside, separated from the boardwalk by a low wall. It looked like a fun place, crowded, with lots of laughter and good times.

Perhaps here, she would not feel quite so alone.

A strong, masculine scent filtered through the briny air, drawing her short. Lifting her nose like a wolf to the wind, she gazed around. Pedestrians squeezed past, talking and laughing. She saw no handsome navy commander with piercing gray eyes.

But the spicy scent of his cologne, twined with the richness of his scent of crisp pine and cold snow, tantalized her senses like steak to a starving man. Keira stopped, panic and longing crashing together.

At a corner outdoor booth, Shay and Kelly sat with Dale and a blonde woman she did not recognize. The blonde's hair was long and luxurious, and the tight black sheath she wore, along with a slim string of pearls, hinted of money.

Dale said something and the blonde laughed, squeezing his hand and leaning close to whisper into his ear.

A date, she thought, stricken. *I haven't been out of his life more than two days and he's dating.*

Keira swallowed hard. Yearning filled her, to draw close one more time, feel the warmth of his wide mouth pressed against hers, the strength in his arms entwined around her waist, sheltering her. Hear his whisper that nothing would tear them apart.

But it did.

She did not deserve happiness for her crimes. But this honorable Mage had done nothing wrong, except finally believe she was not evil.

He deserved joy, to find someone special who would cherish him.

As I did.

A sob wrenched from her throat. Two men in sailor uniforms glanced her way. Keira turned and scurried back to the hotel, her appetite gone.

They caught her the next day.

Keira struggled hard as the demon minions grabbed her arms in her hotel room. She tossed a white energy bolt at one, killing him. But then more materialized, dozens of them holding her down.

Flat nostrils twitching, they clapped a restraining collar around her neck.

They materialized inside a large, empty warehouse. The stench of old blood and death tinged her nostrils.

Seated at a card table was Antony, the oldest Centurion. Ghostly specters floated around him, the others still unable to take form, but freed from the bolt-hole. The minions threw her down to the cold concrete floor. The collar bit into her throat, making her gag.

"Nice to see you again, Antony. I see you're still a glutton. Ever think about a diet and exercise?"

"Leave us," Antony ordered. He thumbed a small device, the size of a cell phone.

When the minions dematerialized, he depressed a button on the device. Muscles spasming, she jerked and twisted on the floor. When the convulsions ended, she got to her knees and glared at the demon.

"I expected you to find me sooner. What's wrong? Your GPS malfunction?"

"A slight delay in Nicaragua, opening the bolt-hole to allow my brothers to escape." He studied his fingernails. "We had to wait until the armies under our control widened the doorway."

If only she'd found the bolt-hole and the book of ancient spells that originally summoned the Centurions from hell. But Keira did not know where it was hidden.

Antony, the only Centurion to keep form since the demons were summoned by the soldiers fighting in the Contra war, hid the book well and kept moving it.

He gave a cold smile as she rubbed her neck. "Unfortunately, your new restraint does not work as effectively as the armband, but it will suffice. The Tasers Jimali stole for us make a poor substitute for controlling you."

Hope surged. Without the armband and the proper spell to compel her to shift into wolf, Antony couldn't force her to torture more victims.

"I can take whatever you dish out. I won't torture any more men for you, no matter what you do to me. Go to hell," she snapped.

"We know where your brave navy SEAL commander is. Tonight, I will take him captive."

"He'll fight you. He's no longer defenseless, and no longer able to be lured into a trap. All his powers have been restored."

He turned to a ghostly specter hovering nearby. "He will fight us. The base is secure. We cannot enter, even with Thad's identification card."

Panic tightened her chest. He'd already tested accessing the base. "Where is Thad?"

"He escaped when Jimali captured him. Unfortunately." Antony seemed confident. "But we have the means to take out your navy SEAL commander. We know his weakness for his men, and will lure him into a trap once more."

Antony seemed overly confident. He leaned forward, his belly spilling over the studded belt.

"Dale can't be touched. He's far too powerful."

Antony gave a mocking grin. "Yes. And with his death, I shall live forever, and seize his team for my brothers to torture."

Horror pulsed through her. "I won't torment him anymore. You have no power to force me to do so. You'll have to torture him yourself."

"Ah, but my methods are so inconsequential compared to the lure of your demon wolf, who can make him scream with pain and pant with lust. You are the reason why I have remained alive these past decades."

She was why the demon lived as a human. He had killed the one who summoned him twenty-three years ago, seized the Book of Spells used in the summoning and then tore through the fighting armies like a buzz saw, stealing the bravery they used to fight. But the energy infusion never lasted more than a few days. And then Antony had chanced upon her pack, and realized the riches of having someone else do his dirty work.

All those men she'd been forced to torment. Keira's heart clenched. She must atone for her misdeeds.

"Only you can save your navy commander. What will you do to save him?" Antony asked. "Will you die for him?"

Keira squeezed her eyes closed. His men were strong and might rescue Dale, but until they did, he would suffer more torment, and the haunted, empty look would return to his eyes. She wanted him to live, be happy....

There was a slim chance Dale and his team would track the demons. Thad was alive and the team would find the Centurions before other innocent men died. But they would probably not be in time to save her....

Fierce resolve filled her. She opened her eyes.

"I will. Spare him, and take me in his place. Leave him alone."

"Such a rich prize, freely offered." His thin, wispy laugh sounded like teeth chewing on tin foil. "Who needs a navy SEAL when we have you, Keira?"

Antony stood and reached into a small bag, withdraw-

ing something. Horror pulsed through her as she spotte
what he held.

The spiked whip from Dale's compound.

"A lovely little decoration. I had the pleasure of removing it from Thad when he used it against Jimali as she attacked him. Unfortunately, I was too late to save her."

He shrugged. "A pity. She served us well. But the whip
is a good exchange for her life. How I have longed to test
it on bare flesh."

Don't think of what will happen, she told herself. *Think
of Dale, his courage, his wide smile as he played the piano.*

His happiness.

At the first strike upon her back, she arched and did not
cry out, holding fast to the image of a brave navy SEAL
commander.

You will not scream.

But a while later, she did…

Chapter 22

To try to cheer him up, Shay and Kelly held a small dinner party that week. Most of the SEALs from the Phoenix Force crowded around the table with their wives and girlfriends.

Kelly cooked a delicious repast, tender London broil with new potatoes and a delicate tomato basil soup.

Every bite of steak congealed like old grease in Dale's stomach. No fault of Shay's bride. Hell, a gourmet meal or an MRE tasted the same.

Ever since Keira had left, he found little enjoyment.

Shay had dragged him to a blind date with an acquaintance of Kelly's, a pretty blonde from her aerobics class. Deidre was fun, he supposed. Her loud, horsey laugh grated on his nerves and the thick, cloying perfume made him gag.

Unfortunately, he'd told a small white lie, assuring her he'd had a great time.... Yeah, swell. And Kelly insisted Deidre join them tonight at their dinner party.

Seated around the long dining table, members of his team ate and laughed. No laughter rose in Dale's throat.

I've lost her. For good.

Once again, his impulsive temper kicked in. His damnable, rigid code of honor had booted her straight out of his life. The same code of honor that refused to listen to his wife when she'd pleaded for him to listen for explanations about why she left.

I can never forgive such betrayal.

But had Keira betrayed him? The woman risked all to heal him, and opened her heart to him.

What hurts more, he thought. *My pride at being a gullible fool, allowing myself to be lured into a demon trap, or my heart?*

Bitterness rose in his throat like acid. But pride and stubbornness made for bad companions.

"You look so lost in thought. Anything I can do?" Deidre tossed her hair like a mane, and preened, displaying ample cleavage.

He thought about palming Keira's much smaller breasts, her tiny, excited cries as he'd suckled her nipples and made her explode with pleasure. Unabashed and unrestrained, honest in every sensual reaction. He thought about the warmth of her smile, and how she'd trembled with passion in his arms, and how damn good she'd made him feel, how he wanted nothing more than to return the passion.

Hell, he thought. *I have to find her.* He thought of her alone, lost, wandering the world with demons searching for her.

Dale threw down his napkin and pushed back his chair and stood. "I screwed up, badly. I'm going after Keira, going to find her and bring her back. It's not safe out there for her. Who's with me?"

His men looked at him steadily, and one by one, they stood. Then Kelly whispered into Shay's ear and, scowling, he stood, as well. The depths of their loyalty squeezed his heart. They'd follow him to hell and back.

Kelly smiled and touched her husband's hand and Dale knew she'd talked Shay into it.

Suddenly her smile faded. A horrified look came over her. She arched, pushed back from the table and screamed.

Shay pushed back his chair so fast, it toppled backward. "Kel! What is it?"

But she kept screaming, horrible, anguished sobs of such pain, his heart dropped to his stomach. A person made those terrible sounds only for one reason.

He'd made such sounds in the dark, as his blood dripped off the platform in the basement....

Turning, Kelly stiffened, head thrown back, fingers digging into the table.

Streaks of blood dampened the back of her lemon-yellow blouse.

Bile rose in his throat. Shay's desperate gaze snapped to him. "Curt, please, you're a Primary, do something!"

Running to the screaming Kelly, he saw the silver triskele pendant around her neck glow with white light. Dale yanked the chain, pulling the triskele free. The pendant sizzled in his palm. Yelping, he dropped it.

And then a horrific pain lashed his back, a thousand burning knives sinking into his skin.

Just as quickly, the pain faded. Deeply shaken, he looked at Kelly slumped in her seat, chest heaving with each ragged breath.

The blood vanished from her blouse. An illusion.

Shay dropped to his knees beside her, chafing her hand. "Honey, what is it? What happened?"

Kelly lifted her gaze, no longer glazed with pain. "It's her. Keira. She's in horrible, horrible pain. I formed a psychic bond with her. It's as if someone is...torturing her. I felt every single lash."

Dale went still, his pulse racing. A terrible suspicion seized him.

The scars can be removed if the one who placed them there makes an enormous sacrifice.

Fingers unfastening his dress shirt, he opened it and looked down.

The scars were gone.

"Curt, whoa, what happened?" Dakota asked.

Not answering, he rushed to the large mirror over the sofa and stared. He tore off his shirt and examined his torso, the underside of his arms.

Clean, smooth flesh.

"Oh, gods," he whispered. "Please, it can't be so…she couldn't have done it."

He put his shirt back on, leaving it untucked and hanging open. When he returned to the dining room, everyone looked worried. All but Deidre, who looked totally confused.

"What's going on? Is this performance art? Are you guys practicing for a flash mob?" she asked.

Dale waved a hand. "Dakota, wipe her memories, put her in a taxi and send her home."

As the Draicon werewolf scrambled to comply, he turned to the other SEALs. "I want a fifty-mile perimeter psi search, using electromagnetic sweeps for demon energy sigs. Call in Thad."

"He's on leave for ten days," Dallas said.

"It's canceled." He quietly regarded Shay's still shaken wife. "Kelly, I'm afraid I'll need your help to track down Keira, using your link to her."

Shay fisted his hands. "You have me, Curt. But no way, no damn way are you using my wife to find that wolf who tortured you."

Calm settled over him. Dale turned and regarded his SEAL. "Stand down, soldier."

"The hell I will! You nearly died on that table."

"I said, stand down." Steel threaded through his quiet voice.

Raising a hand, he flicked a finger and drew the chair

upright, and forced Shay to sit. "Calm down. You'll be with her the entire time."

Glowering, Shay shook his head. "She nearly killed you, man."

"She also saved my life, and I was too stupid and arrogant to admit it." Such intense sorrow pulsed through him, he nearly reeled from it. Dale kept a grip on his emotions.

He only hoped he wasn't too late.

Twenty-four hours passed. Forty-eight. All his team's finest minds, equipment and scanners resulted in dead ends.

Thad had been found, clinging to consciousness, badly beaten but alive. He'd awoken in the hospital, murmuring about demons and whips.

Ordering security tightened on the ST 21 compound, Dale had a very bad feeling something nasty would soon unfold.

In his office he paced, ignored the phone messages, the stacks of papers requiring his attention. A knock sounded.

"Come."

Shay entered, concern tightening his face. "Someone called 911 the other night, reported a woman screaming from a warehouse near the waterfront. Kel checked it out… we drove by. She felt something…but very, very faint. We think it's Keira."

Dale checked his SIG holstered at his waist.

"Guns and bullets won't stop these bastards, Curt."

"I know. But we're going in with everything we've got. Get the team together. We leave in ten minutes."

Tension coiled his stomach as their Humvees pulled up before a deserted warehouse at the wharf. Rust coated the aluminum-frame building. The entire area reeked of the stench of fish, brine and something foul, like raw sewage. And a far more ominous scent.

The metallic stench of blood.

Dale slid out from the driver's seat. He checked his weapon and gathered his powers as they all crept toward the warehouse.

Holding up a fist, Dale signaled. *Wait.*

He sensed their tension, their eagerness to storm the warehouse and free her, but they were SEALs and knew to tread with stealth.

No telling what the hell lay beyond those doors, or if whatever held Keira would simply cut her throat and be done with it.

Hell of a chance, doing this in bright sunshine, risking not just some concerned Joe Citizen dialing 911, but without the cover of darkness.

Keira couldn't wait until nightfall. All his senses warned him that by then she might be gone.

He pulled down on his fist and they rounded the door. Dakota, point man, shifted into a wolf as Dallas opened the door.

Anyone inside would think a large stray simply wandered in.

Dakota released a low howl, the signal for finding something.

They stole inside, into a small antechamber. Still in wolf form, Dakota growled, pawing at the ground.

Sitting at a wood table, guarding the door to the warehouse entrance was a corpulent man. Plates of half-finished food and empty wine bottles sat before him. He blinked sleepily at the SEALs.

"Ah, visitors. You're late. We expected you a day ago."

"Keira," Dale snapped, training his weapon on the Centurion, recognizing that sniveling voice from the basement.

"Yes, the famous Lieutenant Commander Curtis. Pleasure to meet you again." The demon belched and scratched its groin. "Thank you for removing the slave bracelet so we could send out minions to find her. Tremendous favor you did us. Much better to torture her. All these years we held her captive, she never offered herself in place of another. Selfish little bitch. We searched far and wide for a brave warrior to torture, but the bravest of all was within our grasp. A woman. They always sacrifice themselves. Because of Keira, we are now flesh."

Fury coiled in his guts. Dale held on to his control by a thread. "Where are the others? There are six of you."

"Out, having a night of it. They left me here to guard the girl. What's left of her."

Control snapped. He lowered his weapon. "You fucking son of a bitch…"

Springing forward, he snapped the demon's neck. Surprise flared on its face, then it dropped down, head clattering onto a greasy plate filled with bones. Shay stepped forward and chanted a vanquishing spell.

The demon's body vanished, going straight back to the netherworld.

"Fan out. Comb every inch of this damn place," he ordered.

He had barely taken a step toward the door when he heard a low, strangled whisper. Dakota, in human form, at the door. His eyes wide and expression stricken. "Curt…"

Dale kicked open the door and rushed into the warehouse.

A figure hung, arms outstretched and tied to an overhead beam, the legs spread wide and attached to two supporting poles. Blood slicked the concrete floor below.

She was naked, coated in crimson. Blood, dear gods, so much blood. On the floor near her bare feet was a long whip studded with small silver spikes.

Gorge rose in his throat. Stricken, he stood, immobilized, staring at his former lover.

Unconscious. Thankfully.

Dragging a table over to the column, Dale climbed onto it. He reached for his KA-BAR knife and sawed through her bonds. When one wrist was freed, he tossed the knife to Shay, watching with huge, horrified eyes.

"Cut her down. I'll catch her."

The SEAL did, and Keira slumped in his arms. Warm blood oozed onto his BDUs. Dale's stomach clenched as he buried his nose into her tangled, mussed hair.

Please live.

Low, mocking laughter, burning agony lacing her flesh. The torment stopped, then continued. Moaning, she tried clawing at the air, but her wrists were bound. The demon holding the whip snickered, its round face sneering.

And then the face changed. Clean, defined cheekbones, a wide mouth and intense steel-gray eyes.

Dale laughed as he drew his wrist back to flick the whip once more....

Crying out, she bolted upright.

"It's okay. You're safe now. You're safe," a deep voice crooned.

Squeezing her eyes shut, afraid to open them to find the empty warehouse and the stench of her own blood, she flexed her back muscles.

Skin stretched and pulled, but the searing pain had fled.

Afraid she dreamed, or had died, Keira opened her eyes.

Bedroom, plain white walls, a blue-striped window seat beneath a tall window, shelves lined with books, heavy masculine furniture.

The powerful scent of male and power...

Her gaze swung right. Perched on the bed's edge, Dale quietly regarded her.

"How do you feel?"

Closing her eyes, she fell back against the pillows.

This was a nightmare. Dale had returned to torment her.

A warm palm settled over her forehead. Always so warm, chasing away the iciness inside her.

"No fever. My physician personally took care of you in the hospital. Dakota called in a favor of his people and brought in Maggie, an empath healer. You were very badly hurt, but everything's all right now, Keira."

Keira remained silent.

Worry shaded his gray eyes. "It took all her energy to heal you. Unfortunately, the scars will remain. But your body is healed."

Healed? Physical injuries would lessen, though the cruel scars would remain. But her heart had shattered and she wasn't certain if she could ever mend it.

"Water." Her voice cracked. Dry, her throat felt like sand.

Dale rose and lifted a glass of water to her lips. Hands wrapping around his, ignoring the sudden surge of heat flaring between them, she drank deeply, then licked her cracked lips.

Her throat felt sore. When she spoke, her voice came out as a thin whisper.

"Why can't I talk?"

"Temporary laryngitis." His expression darkened as he set the glass down. "From screaming. Dr. Mitchell says with a few days rest, you'll be back to normal."

"How long have I been out?"

"We rescued you from the warehouse seven days ago."

A full week for the demons to roam through Virginia Beach or even leave the country.

"Too damn close. We cut it too damn close, and almost lost you." His voice broke. "When I saw you there, in the warehouse…"

He cursed and looked away, squeezing her hand. She didn't respond.

Cold, her hands were so icy. It felt as if she'd never be warm again. Dale slid his strong, warm palm over hers. "You're safe now. I won't let anything happen to you. Go back to sleep. You need your rest. Do you need anything? Anything at all?"

She nodded. "Leave me alone. Now."

Turning over, she presented her back to him and closed her eyes, the agony in her heart far greater than the pull and stretch of healing tissue.

Dale returned at noon with broth and coaxed her to eat. Too weak to take the spoon in hand, she allowed him to feed her, only because she needed to recover her strength.

He remained at her side after, as she fell back asleep.

And he returned at dinner. He told her of his team's efforts to track the Centurions, using every method.

"They got to Thad, one of my men, first. Jimali started beating him, but he took the whip and killed her and managed to escape. Unfortunately, Jimali tortured Thad enough to cause one Centurion to become corporeal."

Dale's nearness made her ache. Once they shared intimate times in bed. Now he had become a stranger, a stranger who'd kicked her out of his house and protection.

He removed the tray from the bedside and sat down, stroking her hair. "Keira, why did you do it? One of the Centurions told me you sacrificed yourself."

She shrugged and plucked at the bedcovers.

"You did it for me. Why? After I kicked you out…" His face tightened. "After the way I treated you."

"Doesn't matter now. It's in the past, and I'm not about to make any more mistakes." She looked at him, the hurt and anger grinding through her like a freshly opened wound. "Especially with you. I'm here until I can walk out on my own, and then I'm gone. Whatever we had between us is over."

"Keira." He sighed. "Damn it, I want to tell you I'm sorry, but it seems so…"

"Lame?"

"Inadequate."

"Fine." The knot in her stomach grew. "Then let's focus on the business at hand. The demons."

He became stiff and formal, dropping his hand, the commander assuming control, the man who'd loved her in the dark of night vanished.

"They're out there, roaming the streets, free. We need your help to stop them. You're the only living person with access to their secrets. If those damn things grab innocent sailors…"

She cleared her throat, feeling a little stronger.

"They won't. Ordinary humans lack sufficient strength. Now that they've tormented you, they will only pursue paranormal victims with powerful magick."

"Help us find them."

Bitterness washed through her. "I'll help you find them, because it's the only way I'll free myself. But once the demons are caught and vanquished, I'm gone."

For a moment, a shadow crossed his expression.

"Stephen narrowed the search area for the bolt-hole. The dark pulses of energy radiate close to the Honduran-Nicaraguan border."

"That's where I lived with my pack…when the Centurions attacked and tried to enslave all of us."

"We will get them. *Disperdere malum hoc*."

"'Destroy this evil,'" she murmured.

Dale cocked his head. "You know Latin?"

"Spent many years locked in a cell with the Centurions speaking Latin when they didn't speak English or Spanish. It helped pass the time."

He stood, a determined look on his face. "I can't make up for those years, Keira. But I'm doing everything in my power to ensure it doesn't happen again. My team is focusing all effort on this. In the meanwhile, Sully's sister is here. Cassandra wants to perform a white-light ritual for you. It will help restore your energy balance." He looked intently at her. "Will you allow her to do this?"

Keira hesitated and then nodded.

Orders for deployment came for ST 21, seven months on a mission in the Middle East. Curt sent an entire platoon and the Alpha Squad. They were more than ready.

He needed the Phoenix Force on base to combat the greater threat. In the basement, his team had set up shop, hauling in equipment and taking turns sleeping in shifts.

They desperately needed Keira's help to find the demons. She trusted Sully's sister.

If only she trusted him.

Sitting at the kitchen table the next morning, Cassandra stirred a spoon in her teacup. With her long corn-silk blond hair, large blue eyes and slender figure, Sully's sister was a true beauty. But he only had eyes for Keira.

"The ritual went well. Her inner light was diminished, but it's stronger now."

Dale squeezed and flexed his fingers.

The witch gave him a knowing look. "You're wondering if you can ever make amends."

His jaw turned to rock. "I want to…. There is too much between us now."

"The distance is your pride."

"She betrayed me, in my own house."

"Only your pride was hurt. You threw her out of your house, out of your protection, because of your pride. Nothing more."

He thought of the laughing, vivacious Keira who had

brought new life into his house, reenergized him. Was that woman gone forever?

"She won't respond to me." Dale buried his head into his hands.

Cassandra touched his arm.

"Never have I encountered such pain and sorrow. Keira has suffered a tremendous trauma. Her body has healed, but her spirit is damaged. Badly." Cassandra shook her head. "Such a sweet, brave soul. Her white light was but a flicker, surrounded by darkness. She has survived much evil by clinging to the light inside her."

Dale lifted his head, suddenly filled with fierce resolve. "I don't give a damn if I have to lie, steal, cheat or damn my soul, I'll see her recover."

Keira had embraced life with arms open wide. She was the strongest survivor he knew. Dale slammed a fist on the table, making the empty vase rattle.

Roses, he'd always bought her fresh roses.

Sudden insight struck. She'd appreciated the flowers, but he'd never asked her what her favorites were. Never asked. Simply bought what he thought would please her.

"You are beginning to understand the depths of such a heart." No condemnation in Cassandra's voice, only gentleness.

"She was the vision you saw for me in your crystal."

"Yes. Your redemption. You can be hers, if you will allow it."

"How?" He dealt with weapons and enemies, and bad guys and military bureaucracy. Not anything as elusive and esoteric as inner light and soul healing.

"Open yourself to possibilities, to believing it can happen. Open your heart to her and release your inner light." Cassandra gave her gentle smile. "You are a courageous and noble warrior leader, but you've been deeply wounded, Dale. You must find it within yourself to release the bitterness, anger and pain, and forgive. Only by letting go do we gain."

Despite his massive powers, at heart, he was too grounded and pragmatic for this. He believed in the physical, not the metaphysical.

For Keira, he would do anything, and set aside his belief systems. He wanted her back, wanted to see the spark ignite her now dull eyes. Hear her laughter, sharp and clear as a silver bell.

A shuffling noise sounded in the hallway. Keira trudged into the kitchen in a warm fleece robe Cassandra had bought for her.

The coffeepot was bubbling in the kitchen. She poured herself a cup and stood at the counter, sipping. Dale quietly watched her.

His heart ached. If only she'd open up, and reach out to him. But she was listless and lifeless, an automaton.

The man in him wanted to hold her close, whisper apologies and soothe her heart.

The navy commander had demons to find and a populace to keep safe.

Dale took a deep breath. Could he ever reconcile the two? He hadn't done it in his first marriage. The navy came before all else, even his own family.

It's why Kathy left you. But Keira meant much more to him, had burrowed deep into his heart.

I'm not going to lose her, as well. Not again.

When three of his men came upstairs from the basement, Keira stiffened. She moved away from the counter, went into a corner, like a hurt animal, trying to avoid them.

Shay glanced at Keira. "Sorry to interrupt, Curt. Ran out of coffee."

He opened a door and withdrew an unopened package of hazelnut coffee. Shay stood awkwardly at the counter. Dakota and Dallas shuffled their feet.

He cleared his throat. "Glad to see you upright and vertical, Miss Solomon."

Keira ignored him and stared out the sliding glass doors at the pool.

"Report," Dale said.

"We've narrowed the range to Virginia Beach. Bastards haven't left the area."

Keira set down her mug. "Sooner or later, they'll find me."

She opened the sliders and stepped onto the deck. Alarm pulsed through him. Dale followed, leaving the door open.

Stunned, he watched her shrug off the robe. Beneath it she wore a one-piece red swimsuit. He saw a flash of horrific scar tissue bisecting her back, and then she jumped in the pool. Swimming with strong, sure strokes, she kicked up a small froth.

Dale squatted by the pool's edge. "Get out before you collapse."

"Go to hell. If I don't get stronger, they'll turn me into mincemeat again. This time, I'm fighting with all I've got."

"We'll protect you." He scowled. "I'll protect you. I promise I won't let anything happen to you."

She stopped, and treaded water, fury tightening her face. "Oh? Like you did when you booted me out? Nice protection, Commander. No, thanks, I'll take care of myself."

"Get out of the pool now. We need to talk."

"Screw you. You're not my employer any longer."

Frustration and anger coiled inside him. Dale stood and called on his powers.

Stretching out his arms, he concentrated and pulled her from the water. Shrieks of rage followed as Keira floated in the air to his side. Very gently, he set her on her feet.

"You bastard! You think you can control me? When it suits you, snap your fingers and I'll come running? How dare you manipulate your powers against me! Use all the power you've got but you'll never break me."

Something inside him snapped. He got in her face. "I never wanted you broken, damn it. And if you'd stop being so damn stubborn and proud, you'd see I'm trying to help you, not hurt you."

"Change of heart, because you already hurt me enough when you tossed me out without even allowing me to explain?"

"I overreacted," he admitted, gritting his teeth. "All I could think of was how you nearly killed me and made me vulnerable. And I endangered my team by letting you into my life."

"Because your team is more important than anything else. Even me. You never gave me a chance. Your job comes first, your almighty team."

He didn't like the truth slapping him in the face. Keira's shoulders slumped, her energy expelled, her face pale.

Trembling, she wrapped her arms around her waist. Dale took a shuddering breath and clasped her elbow, leading her to a chair. She collapsed in it, looking as miserable as he felt.

All the anger left, like air escaping a balloon replaced by a growing sense of urgency. Dale put a hand on the armrest.

"Keira. We have to work together on this. I'm sorry…so damn sorry. I can't undo what I did. All I can do is press on and fight these bastards who did this to you with all I've got. Everything my men have. We're a team. I want you to come to the base this afternoon with me and brief my men."

Despair clouded her expression. She shook her head. "All right. I will. But you're part of a team. Not me. I'm all alone."

She pushed up from the chair and shrugged into the

obe. "And I'm better off that way. You can never convince me to join a team, Dale. Because all teamwork's done in the past is chewed me up and spit me out."

That afternoon, she and Dale's SEALs gathered in the team's ready room, the men seated at long tables before her. Dale stood off to the side against a wall, arms folded.

Keira stood at the head of the table after Dale introduced her to all the SEALs. These men had formed an alliance against her when Dale threw her out. Mistrust flared. She'd work with them for a common goal. And once that goal was achieved, she'd be gone.

"Centurions were Roman soldiers," Keira told them. "Executed and condemned by a powerful Mage who fought with them, and then vanquished them to the netherworld for their cowardice. He cursed them to never walk the earth in flesh unless they finally acquired the courage they lacked in battle."

"We need to know everything you know. Even the smallest bit of information can help destroy them," Dale said.

"I know a lot." Keira grimaced and set down the pointer. "The only good thing about being stuck in a dark cell next to Jimali was she liked to talk, and she gave me a lot of information. She was with the Centurions since the time when they inhabited a small village in Nicaragua."

"Why were they in Nicaragua?" Shay asked.

"They were summoned during the Contra war in 1988. The fighting was pretty fierce and Miguel, leader of a small faction of Contra guerillas, was desperate. He had a last resort, a dark book of spells found in a Mayan temple in Honduras. So Miguel selected six of his most loyal and strongest fighters for a ritual to summon the spirit of ancient Roman warriors. He called upon the Centurions to come forth from the afterlife and possess his men with the strength to kill the enemy."

Keira took a deep breath. "The blood rite, combined with the violence from the fighting, opened a bolt-hole into the netherworld and conjured the spirits of the Centurion demons, who possessed Miguel's men. When they discovered they were human, they fled to the village where they began drinking and womanizing. Miguel discovered they deserted the guerilla camp and came after them with a spell to force the demons out. Antony, the strongest Centurion, killed Miguel and confiscated the Book of Spells.

"But the Mage's curse affected them and they began to grow weaker. One by one, they were forced out of their owner's bodies. Before it happened to Antony, he read through the book for a dark spell to become corporeal. By stealing the courage and strength of warriors, they could manifest their original human forms. The demons killed the people they had possessed and stole their courage. They became corporeal for only a few days. But they had more sources."

"An entire army of fighters to sustain them," Dale said.

"They went through both the Contra and Sandinista factions fighting in that area like a buzz saw, stealing their courage and strength until the men started dropping dead. But it still wasn't enough. The bolt-hole into the netherworld began to close, shutting out their opportunity to release more demons and use them to become more powerful. They killed a faction of both Contra and Sandinistas, cursing them to fight forever, the ensuing violence leaving enough of a crack in the bolt-hole for the Centurions to summon other demons from hell. Once the violence builds to a certain level, it becomes a window for the Centurions to use. Only the Centurions can control the bolt-hole."

"But they still needed to be corporeal," Renegade said. "So did they start on the villagers?"

"The weary villagers had no fighting spirit left to siphon. And the war ended. The Centurions were becoming ghosts when my pack came to the village to help the village recover, to plant crops with methods we used from bonding with the earth to replenish soil bloodied by violence. Antony used a slave armband given to him by his lover and empowered it with dark magick to compel me to fight for him, to torture and terrorize brave souls so he and the others could steal their strength."

Dale rubbed a hand over his strong jaw, his gray eyes intense. "Let me take a wild guess. This Jimali was his lover in the village, who teamed with him to do his dirty work."

"In exchange for power and money." Keira sighed. "Antony is the strongest, the commander of the Centurions. He is the first to regenerate and the one who forces me to do his dirty work. He endowed Jimali with special powers to do physical tasks they could not perform when they were not in flesh."

"We know they can be killed in flesh. But how do we kill them as ghosts?" asked Jammer, the SEAL with close-cropped brown hair.

"In spirit form, they can be weakened by siphoning their dark energy." Keira glanced at Dale. "Someone can absorb their essence into their body with the right spell, and hold them captive. And then the demons can be expunged with the right spell and sent straight back to hell. The bolt-hole must be sealed with light energy and white light."

"I'd hate to think what happens to the person who absorbs those demons," Dakota said.

"That's what makes the spell so dangerous. It causes great harm to the person casting it. They become filled with darkness and devoid of white light. Right now they're gathering forces, letting out other demons in exchange for favors. They've formed an effective and lethal alliance."

She glanced at Dale. "This is why I'm not so hot on teamwork. I've seen the results of what they can do."

"You haven't seen the result of what my team can do." Quiet, deadly, lethal force radiating from him, he nodded at his men.

"The bolt-hole is a doorway from this world to the netherworld, controlled by the Centurions. Just like a tollgate, they demand a price from demons who use it to access this world. The longer the Centurions remain flesh, the more power they'll crave. They will return there to open the bolt-hole and allow more demons to infest this world, in exchange for power."

Keira's gaze swept over the men sitting before her. "The worst kind of evil. Including pyrokinetic demons. They'll do what they did to your friend Adam multiplied times ten thousand. No training in your firestorm chamber can stop them."

Blood drained from Dakota's face. He quietly swore.

"We'll find a way to stop them," Dale assured his men.

"You don't know the methods they'll use to get their way." Keira stared at the distant wall.

Dale spoke. "I promise you, we will find and vanquish them. You'll be free, Keira."

Oh, she wanted to believe him, wanted to trust again. She knew the only way to do this was using her.

I don't want to die. But I haven't really been living, either.

Not until she found Dale. And even with all that stood between him, he'd taught her the power of courage and strength.

She didn't know if she could trust him again. But he insisted his team could defeat them, and she had to try.

"You won't find them. Not without me. You need to use me as bait to lure them in."

Silence hovered for a moment. Then Dallas nodded. "Excellent idea. She knows what they look like…."

"No fucking way." Dale's voice sliced the air.

Her stomach twisted in knots. "The only way you'll find those demons is by using me. Either you let me do this or I work alone."

"No."

"Their blood runs through my veins. Until they are destroyed, it will remain."

"We have defenses you can't even match."

"I have my defenses, as well," she said softly. "And mine overpower yours. My wolf is stronger and more powerful."

Dale studied her calmly. "I know. But we're a team that can overcome you."

She hadn't shifted into a wolf since the day he'd thrown her out. The change came upon her swiftly as bones lengthened and fur rippled along her spine. Keira snarled and leaped onto the desk at the room's front, growling, her wolf barely controllable, itching to prove she was far more powerful.

Dale said nothing. Between one breath and another, he shifted as well, into a large gray timber wolf, about half her size.

Keira leaped at him, but in midair, collided with two other wolves as Dallas and Dakota both shifted at the same time. The two Draicon wolves pinned her down as she struggled.

Then Dale, in wolf form, loped over to her. Opening her massive jaws, she struggled to keep her wolf in line, the demon blood surging through her with the compulsion to attack and hurt. But the large gray timber wolf that was Dale did not attack. He growled at the other two wolves, who climbed off her and withdrew.

Dale the wolf tenderly nuzzled her throat, and licked her muzzle.

It's okay, he seemed to say. *It's me.*

Instinctively, her wolf recognized his touch and scent and submitted. She lay quiet and still, the beast at last no longer howling in anguished, emotional pain. This was a good man, a man who did not wish to hurt her.

He eased away, shifted back and clothed himself as she lay panting on the floor. The two other SEALs did, as well.

Suddenly overcome, she shifted into human form, lying naked on the floor. Dale looked at his men and snapped an order for them to leave the room.

When they did, he pushed a hand through her long hair.

"Teamwork has advantages. They were ready to protect me, but I would never let them hurt you. Ever," he told her gently. "Now can you trust me? Just a little?"

She nodded. "You keep telling me how important teamwork is, Dale. Now it's time for you to show me exactly how important."

For the rest of the afternoon, Keira stayed in Dale's office, going over reports he'd compiled to search for any suspected Centurion activity. Dale had grimly informed her he wasn't about to let her out of his sight. She was too important.

Important. Worth protecting because she was the link in a chain they'd use to bring in the demons. But was she important to his life, his heart?

Two hours later, Dale returned to the office with Renegade in tow. The younger SEAL held up the slave armband. Keira recoiled. Seeing it was like glimpsing a live cobra; she didn't want it to bite her again.

Dale's steady gaze regarded her. "Keira, I need your permission to put this on you. It's your choice."

Renegade held up the jewelry, the sparkling sapphire replaced with clear quartz. "I've analyzed the jewel, the source of the spell that controlled you, and removed it, replacing it with a clear quartz crystal. It's embedded with a microchip that picks up negative psi impulses from up to ten klicks away. Acts like sonar. When the waves bounce off you, the transmitter picks up the beam and traces it back to the point of origin."

Dale's expression shuttered.

"And it also works in reverse," she replied. "I'll give out energy waves as well, positive ones the demons can pick up. It will help you find the demons, but first, they will find me."

Dale nodded tersely. "But someone will be watching over you at all times. You're not going to be alone."

The armband pulsed with faint white light. Still, she felt uneasy. "It's safe? It won't compel me to commit evil acts?"

"No, but with the quartz, it might compel you to do something noble and totally reckless, like suction demon souls. You're fine as long as you don't chant any incantations," Renegade said.

"Do it," she told Dale.

Holding out her arm to have her former lover slip on the armband took all her strength. Dale's warm fingers brushed over her chilled skin as he slipped it into place, the metal settling against her skin like a handcuff.

Would she ever be free of it?

"How long will this take?" she asked.

"Depends on how desperate they are to find you. If they're running out of power, it'll be sooner than we expect."

Dale parked a lean hip on the polished desktop. "Safest place for you right now is here. My men are warding the compound so the Centurions can't get in."

Renegade left, closing the door behind him. Unease spiked her pulse, making her heart pound harder. "Guess

I'm a sitting duck until then. How effective is this warding?"

"It acts like a filter and will keep out the strongest demon." He frowned. "But there's a small chance minor demons can slip past."

"Like gnats slipping past mosquito netting?"

"Sort of. I've stationed men around the compound, just in case. Food will be here soon." He glanced at her empty water bottle. "You want anything else to drink?"

"A shot of ginger ale, with a bottle of whiskey and a straw."

Heat licked through her at his slow, sexy grin—it was the Dale who'd loved her long into the night and held her close. "Afraid all I have is the ginger ale."

"Some bartender you are. I'll take it."

At her nod, he left the desk and went to a cube-size refrigerator and bent down.

Whoa, what a view. She craned her neck, admiring the way his trousers stretched over his oh-so-fine taut ass.

Right, Keira. The man is off-limits. Then again, I'm not dead. Not yet.

Dale fished out two ginger ales. He popped the tops on both and sat on the sofa, placing the cans on the table.

Suspicion filled her. She joined him on the sofa, and took a long drink.

"I talked with the admiral. Asked him, again, to tell me exactly what he'd seen in your mind that day when he melded with you. He said the images were a blur, but I should ask you about the family you lost in Nicaragua and the U.S. soldier you met in the jungle."

Stomach knotted tight, she set down her soda on the table. Talk about her family, the family she'd forced herself to forget? But if it helped Dale's team find the bastard demons, then she'd do it. Keira cleared her throat.

"We can shift when we're a month old. My pack leader

betrayed us to the Centurions for his life. Didn't work. They killed him after finding our people. The Centurions began killing us...taking the young away from their mothers, who died bravely, defending them."

Keira's throat closed. "Their courage gave the demons energy to become corporeal.... They siphoned off the white light in their auras, sucking it up like damn vacuum cleaners. I tried protecting Simon, my little brother And I made a bargain with them... If they would let Simon live, I'd become their slave and do their bidding. Because I knew they would not stay in that form for long."

He said nothing, only moved closer, taking a drink from his soda before setting it back down. Condensation rolled off the aluminum can like teardrops. Then she felt the warmth of his palm settle over her clenched hands. Soothing and comforting.

"What happened to your brother?" he asked, his voice gentle.

Fingers clenched tight, she shook her head. "They found another demon to forge an ancient armband to enslave me...and then they killed Simon. I'm the only survivor."

Muscles contorted with the effort to keep grief at bay, she stared at the sodas, fighting the tears. No more. But he came closer, and then pulled her against his broad chest, holding her there, stroking her hair.

Holding her tight, as if he wished to soothe away all her pain.

"All this time, you've had no one to help you, no one to rescue you," he murmured.

A stray tear trickled out of her squeezed eyelids.

"It helps to cry it out. Go on," he whispered.

How many times had she longed to feel the comfort of another while in her dark cell, grieving for the family she'd lost? How many nights had she cried, counting down the days and weeks and vowing not to let the darkness drag her under?

Until she'd met Dale, no one else had held her like this. No one else had urged her to release the emotions she'd held at bay for years.

The tears came in a torrent as she fisted her hands in his shirt and sobbed for all she'd lost. After a while, she finally raised her head and wiped at her face as he fetched a box of tissues from his private bathroom.

"I made a mess of your shirt. Sorry. Didn't mean to bawl on you." Keira took a wad of tissues and blew her nose.

"You had no one to help you, and you fought the demons on your own. How old were you? Eleven?"

"There was a man, that soldier. My memories of him are a little fuzzy, probably because the Centurions messed with my mind. I'd gone mad with grief when I realized Simon was dead, shifted into wolf and went to attack the man. But he refused to hurt me."

He went very still.

"Odd," she mused. "It was as if we shared a moment of connection. He said he refused to return evil for the evil that had been done to me. There was something good and courageous and noble about him. I let him escape, and went back to charge the demons. But they caught me and forced me to wear the slave armband."

Dale quietly regarded her, but this time, his gaze sharpened. "Tell me about your brother. What did he look like in wolf form?"

"About the size of a golden-retriever puppy, with a white streak down his muzzle."

He cupped her face with his large, square hands. "Keira, he's alive. And safe. Etienne, one of my SEALs, and a Draicon, snuck him back into the States."

Hope flared, then vanished like an extinguished candle. "No. It can't be him, I saw him lying in the ditch with the others...."

"He was playing dead, hiding, when we found him. I ordered Etienne to find him a new home." Gaze steady, Dale looked at her. "Keira, I was that U.S. soldier you attacked that day in the jungle. My memory of that moment was fuzzy, until you mentioned it. I think the demons' memory spell erased my recollection of first meeting you in wolf form."

She could not speak, for the rapid beating of her heart and the hope surging inside her. Keira stared at Dale as he caressed her still-damp cheeks with his thumbs.

"Your little brother is alive. Etienne made sure to place him with a Draicon family. He checks up on him once a year and reports back to me how he's doing." Dale dropped a gentle kiss on the corner of her mouth. "He's living with a large Cajun family near New Orleans, and he's in college now, studying to be a physician."

If not for Dale, her brother would have died alone in the jungle. But his team had rescued Simon, who lived somewhere, safe, in the States.

Teamwork did have advantages.

"Thank you," she whispered.

Very gently, he pressed his mouth against hers. Then Dale drew back, his expression solemn. "I know you can't forgive me now, for throwing you out of my house and my protection. I hope one day, perhaps, you can."

He sighed deeply. "I accused you of breaking my trust, but in truth, I broke yours. You trusted that I'd understand and I would be there for you. I wasn't."

An odd pulling tingled in her stomach. She stared at him as he cupped her cheek, trailing a thumb lazily over her skin.

"Dale?"

"Hmm?"

"Something's wrong. I feel…"

Jerking away, she stood up.

Panic filled her as the tingling grew stronger. Suddenly an invisible hand lifted her into the air, leaving her feet dangling.

"Help me," she whispered.

Then the invisible hand picked her up, shook her like a rag doll and slammed her against the opposite wall.

Just as quickly, the violence ended. "It's gone," she said as he raced over to where she lay. "I felt them, but now I don't." She closed her eyes and reached out to search for the demons.

"They're gone. Back to the bolt-hole, thousands of miles from here. I sense it. But there's a presence, an evil that's like a cloud…it's very strong now."

"They can't access the base."

Screams and shouts echoed down the hallway. Dale drew his weapon. "Stay here."

He left, slamming the door behind him.

Icy cold snaked down her spine. A perimeter of safeguards ringed the compound to keep out the strongest demons.

But many more lesser demons could slip beneath the invisible cloak of protection like gnats worming through mosquito netting.

Keira bolted out of the office and ran down the hallway, following the screams, running straight into the gymnasium.

Carnage greeted her.

She ran outside to the firestorm chamber and yanked the door open. Dale, in the antechamber, wrestled with a two-headed demon on the floor.

Rage boiled through her, pure fury. The demon drew back and hissed, its red slit of a mouth showing jagged teeth.

She drew on all her anger, all her fury at the years of imprisonment, losing her family...and pressed the button to release the streams of fire.

"Dale," she screamed. "Throw him toward the chamber. Let's burn the bastard."

As he did, a tongue of orange flame hit the demon. It looked startled, trying to beat the flames out with long, taloned fingers. The fire seared the creature, singeing it, the disgusting stench of burning meat filling the air as the demon writhed and screamed.

Finally it fell over into a smoking pile of muck.

Dale clasped her arms. "Are you okay?"

She nodded.

They went outside and surveyed the damage. Dallas jogged up to them, an ugly bruise on his left cheek and deep scratches on his arm.

"Bastards snuck in through security. We got 'em all. But we lost Rodriguez." Dallas's mouth thinned.

Shay and Dakota joined them. "Curt, there're a few MPs at the gate, wondering what the hell is going on and who let off the fireworks," Dakota said.

Dale's expression shuttered. "Get the wounded all treated. You two deal with the MPs, delay them until we get this cleaned up. If necessary, alter their memories, but only as a last resort."

As he bandaged her burn in the infirmary, Keira felt the weight of Dale's grief and guilt, as well as her own, over the loss of his staff.

"I believed the base was safe from a demon attack." Dale's jaw tensed. "Until we find and seal that demon bolt-hole, there will be more attacks."

"I did this," she whispered as he finished wrapping her arm in gauze. "If not for me, all of your staff would still be safe."

"It's the price we pay to keep civilians safe, Keira. We all know the risks we take."

But his words offered no comfort. People died because of her. How many more lives would it take until this all ended?

Hours later, exhausted and worn-out, she and Dale went home, accompanied by his men. The SEALs went downstairs to the basement to spend the night and discuss their next course of action. No one was returning home tonight, not until they had an extensive debriefing with Keira.

Dale sent Ensign Lees home, and opened the cartons of Chinese food Dallas had picked up on the way over. His SEAL team and Keira sat around the basement's dining table and ate, discussing their options.

"The demons who infiltrated the navy base knew exactly where they were going because of me." Keira's pretty mouth wobbled precariously. "The Centurions have released more demons from the bolt-hole. They're gathering tremendous power. Soon, they won't need to be corporeal. They'll have enough demons to command their own army."

"If that happens we're fucked."

Trust Dallas to cut to the chase.

Dale wanted to keep Keira safe and protected from the world. But for years, she'd been exposed to evil, and knew nuances of that evil. Even their best intel couldn't come close to the knowledge she possessed.

"Keira, you're the only one who can pinpoint the bolt-hole. Stephen found an approximate area, but only you were there when they came from the earth."

He hated forcing her to remember things she'd wanted to keep buried.

Gaze dull, she glanced up at him. "I only remember as a wolf. Scents, sounds, not sights. The memories in human form are too clouded. You can't pull them free. They're buried deep."

"Then she'll come with us. As wolf." Dakota folded his muscled arms.

Dale's protectiveness cranked to overdrive. "No. Too dangerous."

She sat up, face alight with interest. "He's right. In my human form, I'm useless, but my wolf can track the scents. The bolt-hole will carry the scent of the Centurions, and my wolf knows the scent of them instinctively. I could track them through a blinding sandstorm."

His guts knotted. "Keira, we're going to do a HALO drop from 30,000 feet at night and cut through the jungle. We're SEALs, trained to do this. You're not. And you're a civilian. Brass would find out, and cut the op before it even got started."

"She can jump as wolf. Strap a chute on her, let her track 'em," Shay advised.

His men looked at him expectantly. Waiting on his word. He was commander of the best damn team in the U.S. military and always bisected his personal life from his career. Now his personal life stared him in the face and collided with the mission's objective.

They needed her on this op. And every single bone in his body screamed against it, wanted to lock her in a room and keep anything from ever hurting her again.

He hated this. It made perfect sense to take her along as a wolf. Hell, how many drops had Dakota or Dallas done in wolf form? SEALs from other units and other soldiers thought they were highly trained dogs.

But Keira wasn't a SEAL. She'd never trained for a co-vert op, never even held a weapon.

She rested her hand on his tensed arm. "Dale, please. Let me do this. It's our only chance of catching them." Green gaze pleading, she looked desperate. "It's my only

chance of being free, and finally atoning for the bad things
my wolf was forced to do."

Dale clenched his fists. Nodded. "You need a crash
course first on drops. You'll be with me, double jump,
the whole way."

Chapter 23

She'd never jumped from an airplane at 30,000 feet before.

Especially not in wolf form.

Keira had tucked the slave armband into Dale's pack. It would act as a transmitter, honing in on the frequency of the Centurions if they were present. But nothing could pinpoint the bolt-hole.

Except her.

In wolf form, she sat quietly by Dale's feet while the soldiers, non-SEAL members who were unaware that this was a paranorm mission, accompanying them cast uneasy looks her way. She'd shifted, making her wolf form smaller, possible now that the demons weren't there to trigger the slave armband and command the beast. Still, she imagined the sight of a 150-pound black wolf, all fangs and claws, unnerved some.

This jump was HALO—high altitude, low opening—to avoid radar detection and anyone who might look up and see the parachutes opening. They needed stealth for an insert.

With Dale, she'd free-fall for a long period before he deployed his chute.

With Dale, she needed to trust.

Dale reached down and caressed her fur. Green and black greasepaint streaked his face. In his camouflage and military gear, he looked dark and dangerous, someone she'd never want to tussle with in human form.

"Easy, girl. We'll be there soon."

"Big dog," one pimple-faced private remarked. "Sure hope she don't piss all over the equipment."

"She's a soldier, not a dog," Dale snapped. "Respect her as you would respect me."

Keira looked at the solider, her tail thumping against the floor as the private bent down and scratched behind her ears. Dale looked daggers at him. "Hands. Off. Her. Now."

Gulping, the private scurried back to the plane's front.

"Possessive much, eh, Curt," Shay teased.

"Curt's taste in ladies has gone to the dogs," Sully joked.

"The wolves, Sully. Don't insult the lady." Dallas grinned at her. "You just ignore him, Keira. Sully doesn't know a wolf from a squirrel."

The buzzer sounded. Dale signaled the men to don their O_2 masks and then put his own on, slipping a custom-fitting mask over her muzzle, along with goggles.

He strapped Keira on a special harness tied to him, ran a reassuring hand along her hindquarters. She wore goggles and body armor, specially fitted for her.

"I trust you," she'd told him before shifting. "I know you won't drop me."

"Never," he'd replied.

The SEALs lined up as the back hatch opened and the light turned yellow. Outfitted in helmet, oxygen mask and combat gear, she scarcely recognized the men, but all turned and gave her a big thumbs-up. Then the light buzzed green, and they all fell into the sky.

Wind whistled past her. Cold cut through her fur. But she was free, flying! Dale held her securely, then the snap of the chute yanked them upright.

In the starlit night, they floated to earth. Keira gazed down as Dale guided their chute. Never had she seen anything more beautiful.

If she died here tonight, she'd be grateful for this moment. Floating through the sky, secure against the man she loved.

After they landed and buried the parachutes, they set off through the forest. All the SEALs carried weapons, pointed outward as they slipped through the thick jungle. A sliver of moonlight spilled through the branches. With her large paws padding through the undergrowth, she worried about making a sound.

Behind her, the SEALs moved in silence. Once in a while, she felt the reassuring hand of Dale touching her flank.

Sealing the bolt-hole came first. They had to prevent more demons from escaping.

Ribbons of scent assaulted her nostrils, but none associated with nature and freshness. The smell was putrid, the stench of mold and staleness. Evil. The wind shifted east, and the smell grew stronger, along with a thin thread she knew well.

Old wine turned to vinegar and sulfur. The Centurions.

Ears back, she loped toward the smell, approaching a narrow, mud-strewn path dipping sharply down the mountain. Keira followed it and heard the sound of gurgling water.

The path opened up to a wide ravine, where a creek moved in sluggish ripples over rocks, flowing downward. Keira shifted back and clothed herself, the stench too terrible to bear in wolf form.

She squatted, peering at the thin ribbon of creek wending down the mountaintop. The SEALs gathered around.

Dark energy pulsed from granite boulders tumbling

down the narrow ravine. Water trickled sluggishly over
the boulders, forming a small gray pool below. The stench
assaulted her nostrils; decay and rotting flesh, and a blackness no light could ever erase.

As Sully went to examine it, she grabbed his arm.

"Don't touch it. It's poison."

The SEAL tossed her a questioning look. Keira glanced
around, found a small stick and tossed it into the pool.

Upon hitting the water, the dry wood shriveled and
then dissolved.

"I believe we found the bolt-hole," she told Dale. "See
that small black pulsing in the water? That's the entrance
to the netherworld."

He gestured to Shay. "Seal it."

Shay shrugged out of his pack. A white glow surrounded him as he gathered his powers. Throwing out
his hands, he directed currents of white light at the rock
formation. But the oval of blackness remained as he continued the onslaught. Shay dropped his hands and gasped.

"Sorry, Curt. It's too much."

"I'll help you." Dale started to gather his powers.

"No." Keira shook her head, sensing a dark presence
close by. "If you drain your white energy, you'll have nothing left to fight the demons. They're nearby."

His mouth twisted, eyes luminous in the moonlight.
"If I don't seal it now, more demons will leave. Can't risk
it. Stand back."

Shay began the chant, a low, melodious sound as Dale
stood and a white glow surrounded him, silver sparks leaping into the air. A cool wind whipped strands of his silky
hair as he closed his eyes. Dale stretched out his arms and
directed currents of pure blue-white energy at the bolt-hole,
his chants joining Shay's.

Water sizzled as the power stream hit the boulders, dry-
ing up, the oval of blackness finally shrinking and then

disappearing all together. Gasping, Dale dropped his arms, the glow surrounding him vanishing.

He bent over, dragging in deep breaths. "Give me a minute," he muttered.

Sounds of gunfire cut through the night. Dale straightened. "Head for the hillside. High ground. Safer there, until we can assess what the hell is going on."

They climbed the hillside to a tree-lined plateau and sat on the rocky ground in a tall clump of grasses. Intermittent sounds of small arms being fired continued, the acrid stench of sulfur accompanying each volley of gunfire.

"I'm not taking chances with you," Dale said to her.

Keira didn't answer. She dug into his pack and withdrew a granola bar. Moonlight glinted off the slave bracelet as she fished one out for him, as well.

Palming the bracelet, she began to eat the granola bar in tiny bites. "Coming back here brings back a flood of memories."

Dale checked his weapon. "Was the fighting happening while you were living here?"

"We lived further south, closer to the village. There were stories of a haunted forest, of ghosts...."

She broke off in midsentence, staring at the two men approaching each other a few yards away. Dale shoved her downward and pointed his weapon.

But the newcomers showed no interest in anything but each other. The two soldiers raised their rifles and pointed them at each other. Moonlight rippled along their bent, slumped bodies.

Here, the war had not ended. Here, it continued, a curtain into a bloodied past. Dale watched as the two soldiers fired.

The crackle of gunfire split the air. Yet it sounded muffled, as if both men fired with suppressors.

Bullets met their targets. Both men dropped down, their weapons clattering to the rocks.

Dale held up a hand for his men to wait.

A minute later, the two soldiers stood, retrieved their weapons and retreated back down the hillside on opposite sides.

He stared at the dark stains on the ground, blood black beneath the full moon. "They're fighting a war that's been long over."

"Those men are dead," Keira said quietly. "They died a long time ago, and now they're condemned to repeat the same violence, again and again. They're victims to the Centurions, just like I was."

Dale turned to his men. "Sully, I need recon. Now. Find out what you can, what we're up against."

A few minutes later, Sully returned with a dark-haired prisoner dressed in a tattered and bloodstained olive-green uniform. The man had strong features, his well-defined cheekbones hinting of a Mayan ancestry, but his dark eyes were empty.

A zombie, compelled to do the Centurions' bidding.

Sully lowered his weapon and looked at Dale. "This is Juan. He approached me while I was doing recon on the hillside and begged to come with me."

"Who are you?" Dale asked.

"Tell them what you told me," Sully ordered.

The man sat down on the ground and began to share his story.

Juan had once he fought for the Contras. Now, he fought under compulsion of the demons.

"The Centurions killed us and our spirits became trapped, condemned to do their bidding. When the Centurions return and command us to fight, we must pick up arms again and repeat the battle. We're condemned to fight and keep fighting, without purpose or cause, only because we are slaves to the demons. We can never rest. We can never cease. And soon, there will be more of us."

"More of you?" Dale questioned.

"The Centurions have brought Necromancers from the netherworld, to summon the dead to walk the earth."

Keira's breath hitched.

Panic entered Juan's gaze. "I must go. They are calling me."

Moving as if in enthralled, the man returned down the hillside.

"We have to get out of here, find the demons." Dale scanned the area and then signaled to his men. "Get ready to move out. Sully, you remain here with her. First sign of trouble, teleport her out of here."

"No," Keira said slowly.

"The hell you say." He released a deep sigh. "One thing for you to find the source as a wolf, another to remain in this hellhole."

"It's too late." She pointed at the far side of the plateau, where a line of creatures faced them.

They didn't have to worry about finding the demons. Because the demons had found them first.

Chapter 24

Fanged creatures, with claws as sharp as dinner knives, advanced toward their group. Around them floated spectral beings—the Centurions. Keira realized they had allowed themselves to become ghosts, knowing the SEALs were out to kill them.

Dale pushed her down.

"Stay here and stay down," he snapped, then gestured to his men to advance.

Partly hidden by the brush, she watched the ensuing fight.

Skulls and crossbones. The images flooded her mind as Dale fought, throwing bolt after bolt of power. The Centurions danced away, taunting him. Ghosts flew over, around, insubstantial as mist.

One bolt sailed through a demon and slammed into a tree, incinerating it.

Dale was weakening, expending all his energy.

As he and his team fought, their courage unwavering, she knew what would happen. The Centurions had an army of demons to command, an army Dale would never allow beyond these borders. He would die first.

Dale continued to send bolts of white energy at the

Centurions, but deprived of form, they laughed as they dodged the blows.

And then the three forms of mist took shape near the cluster of trees.

Necromancers. Demons who could summon the spirits of the dead and control them. With slits for eyes, flat nostrils and ugly slashes for mouths, their smooth, bald heads sported sharp spikes and they stood more than seven feet tall. Three of them, all waving wands of pure wormwood.

This was the pact the Centurions had made—to summon the dead and force them to do their bidding.

Dry-mouthed, Keira stared at the evil ones. On a par with pyro demons, they could raise armies of living corpses, commanding them to kill, threatening all in their path.

Dale and his SEALs could not fight them. Clouds of evil clung to them, their darkness too great to fight with magick powers.

But the team could kill the Centurions once those demons took form. Her blood, mixed with theirs, might do it. Keira remembered the spell she'd heard them chanting back in the warehouse.

"Sully, give me your blade!" she screamed.

The SEAL tossed her his KA-BAR knife. She slashed her wrist and ran into the fray, targeting the Centurions, spraying droplets of her demon-laced blood at the Centurions. As the blood hit the ghost shapes, she chanted the spell. Suddenly the Centurions materialized into their human forms.

Dale stopped his attack. "They're human. Kill them," he ordered.

Sully dematerialized near one Centurion, the demon's corpulent form quivering in real fear. Keira winced and turned her head as Sully reached out and wrapped his hands around the Centurion's neck. A sickening crack sounded.

As each demon dropped down, Dale and Shay chanted a vanquishing spell. One by one the demons died under the hands of the SEALs. But for Antony, the largest and strongest. Dale ran after him, his knife at the ready. But Antony raised his hands and chanted in a loud voice ringing over the glade.

Horror pulsed through her as the Necromancers emerged from the trees. Dale glanced their way, and that small pause was enough to give Antony time to slip the blade in his hands and thrust it at Dale. Dale dodged, but the blade sank into his shoulder. He grimaced and aimed his knife at Antony, and did not miss. Black blood spurted.

He dug Antony's knife out from his shoulder and cupped the wound. "Report," he said wearily.

"All dead, sir. The Contra and Sandinista armies are gone, as well."

"Keira!" Dale turned, worry riddling his face. Blood streamed from his wounded shoulder. "You okay?"

"They're coming," she whispered. "Oh, gods, they're coming. You can't kill them, they're too strong. There's too much darkness inside them."

The Necromancers advanced, creeping toward Dale. He had no white light left to fight them, expending it all to seal the bolt-hole and in the fight against the Centurions. With wild hope, she glanced upward, but the night sky was clear, no storm clouds near for him to draw more power.

He would die here. And then become a living slave of the Necromancers, a slave as she had been to the Centurions.

She touched the slave armband on her right arm. It glowed with light, a beacon in the inky blackness. Never use it around evil, Renegade had warned. *It might compel you to do something noble and totally reckless, like suction demon souls.*

Incantations... She knew the exact one. The Necromancers advanced. Shay directed beams of power, but the stream was too thin, too weak.

"Get out of here," Dale ordered. "Take Keira and go."

"Curt," Dakota said, his expression tight. "We won't leave you."

"That's an order." Dale drew his blade, stained with blood blackened in the moonlight. "I'm a Primary Mage. I'll handle them."

Her eyes wet, Keira tossed off Renegade's grip and tore off, facing the Necromancers. *"Malorum, malorum, malorum,"* she began to chant.

Dale turned. "No," he screamed. "Keira, don't do it."

"Veniat in me," she continued.

The white quartz on the slave armband began to glow. Keira drew in a deep breath and began to siphon the darkness inside the Necromancers, drawing on their evil power, taking it inside her. Filling her soul with their blackness, watching as a thick black mist streamed out of the Necromancers, floating in the air toward her. The dark power gathered until it became a large, whirling ball.

Her terrified gaze met Dale's. "I'm sorry. I love you."

And then with a tremendous breath, she inhaled the darkness, feeling it whoosh inside her. The foulness of dark power, the stench of evil, filled her spirit, dimming the last bit of white light inside her, extinguishing it until it went out.

And then she felt nothing.

Summoning all his remaining strength, Dale killed the Necromancers with a last bit of white energy. They burst apart, showering the ground with black dust.

Burst apart, because there was nothing left inside them. No power. Keira had siphoned it all.

Sully wiped his forehead with a sleeve. "Last of them, sir. Bolt-hole's sealed."

Renegade shifted back into human form and tore into his pack, ripping open packets of gauze. He ripped open Dale's sleeve and began dressing the wound. But Dale's sight centered on Keira, weaving listlessly on her feet like one of the armies of the dead.

Light had vanished from her beautiful eyes. She said nothing, only stared ahead.

As if she were dead to the world...

One week after their return from Nicaragua, Dale paced his kitchen. Cassandra sat at the table, her gaze sympathetic. Catatonic, Keira sat at the table, as well. The deep scars on her back had healed the moment the Centurions died.

But she seemed dead as well, her empty eyes staring into space. He dropped beside her, chafing her icy hands.

She did not move.

"I called Etienne, and he tracked down your brother. He's on his way, Keira. Your little brother, the one you sacrificed yourself to save."

Still, she remained motionless, staring ahead.

Nothing worked. He'd hired a nurse to care for her, but though Keira remained obedient, performing all the normal functions, such as eating, she did not talk.

"Help her," he begged Cassandra. "Please. She's been like this since taking the darkness inside her."

"I can perform a white-light ritual, but the darkness will remain. The only solution is white-light cleansing and erasure of all her memories of this time." The Mystic Witch looked at him. "It will erase all her memories of all that happened before she met you. She will not remember you."

Stricken, he stared at Keira. "Nothing of me? I'll be a stranger."

"Nothing of you or your time together."

"What if I see her again? Will that trigger memories?"

"She may not react favorably, and avoid you," Cassandra warned.

Dale's insides squeezed. He stroked a gentle finger over Keira's cold, cold hands. "But she will be healed?"

"Yes. And she will remember her little brother. She needs time, Dale, time to heal from her terrible experiences."

Closing his eyes, he remembered all the good times they'd shared, the tender lovemaking, how he felt when he'd found his missing half.

And now, he would lose her.

Too late he'd realized how he'd been married more to the navy than his first wife. He'd expected her to make sacrifices and understand his rigid code of honor. And now he faced an even greater loss.

Kathy had been his wife, but Keira was his heart. He must let her go.

"Do it." Dale raised Keira's hand to his lips and kissed it, barely able to speak for the thick lump clogging his throat.

"I will see to her welfare. She will be safe," Cassandra promised.

Dale stood and dropped a kiss on Keira's unmoving mouth, feeling her lips cold and unresponsive beneath the subtle pressure of his.

He bid goodbye at the door a few moments later, watching them back Cassandra's car out of his long driveway.

Then he watched them drive away. As the tears finally sprang to his eyes and rolled down his cheeks, he did not wipe them away.

Chapter 25

Six months later

After locking Runes and Tunes for the night, Keira got into her little car and headed for the beach.

Working at Cassandra Sullivan's store had been the best thing that ever happened to her, she thought. The kind Mystic Witch had given her a job when Keira's brother arrived, had helped her find an apartment.

Still, something felt missing.

Lately, she'd been compelled to walk the sands, shoes in hand, and gaze up at the stars. And more often, she'd been visiting the beach frequented by navy personnel. Each time she saw a man in uniform, her heart gave an absurd twist.

She was happy. Simon was in grad school at Virginia Tech and doing well. Her salary paid for a small two-bedroom apartment. After years of slavery to the Centurions, she was finally freed. She had no memory of being freed by the demons, only recalled seeing Simon when he arrived. Her little brother was alive and doing well.

When she asked Cassandra what happened, the Mystic Witch hesitated and told her that a courageous Mage had vanquished the evil.

Cassandra said eventually she'd get her memories back. Perhaps.

Keira sat on the sand and watched the surf lick the shore, listening to the crash of waves. Nearby, a tall man walked a large gray dog. The dog resembled a wolf. Silly. No wolves were on Virginia Beach.

Suddenly the dog broke free of the leash and bounded toward her. It knocked her over, licking her face. Laughing, she fended it off and then scratched the beast behind its ears. The dog grinned at her.

"Shay! Stop it. Get off the lady, now!"

The owner jogged up and grabbed the dog's collar, pulling him away.

"I'm sorry," the man apologized. "He's a good dog, but seldom listens to orders."

The wolf/dog seemed to give the man a wounded look.

"It's all right. I like dogs." She gave the dog a final pat.

"I hope he didn't scare you. I was jogging on the beach and he managed to get away from me." The man grinned, and it softened his severe features. "Though you don't look like the type to scare easily. Mind if I sit down?"

Keira considered. "Only if you promise you won't try licking me to death like Cujo here."

An odd look entered his gaze and then he gave a small smile. "Not until we're good friends."

She stole a look. He had short, dark hair, silvered at the temples, and incredible gray eyes. His body was toned with hard muscle. He looked like a man who made a living doing physical work.

"You work at the base," she said suddenly. "I've seen you on this beach before, and once when you were in uniform. You're a lieutenant commander, right?"

Keira didn't know how she knew that, but deep inside, she did.

"Commander. I received a promotion last month." Gray eyes twinkled as he tilted his head. "And you are…?"

She stuck out a palm, and he took it, his hand large and square and warm. An odd jolt of familiarity hit her. "Keira Solomon. I live not far from here."

"Dale Curtis."

He released her hand, slowly, though she had the feeling he wanted to keep holding it. Why did this man seem so…familiar? She didn't know any navy officers.

Compelled to touch him, she placed a hand over his heart. "You wear something. Here. A badge of honor, a pin… It scarred you when they pounded it into your chest during an initiation…."

Where did that come from?

"Yes. We call it a Budweiser. I'm a navy SEAL." His gray gaze held hers captive, searing, penetrating.

Keira dropped her hand, feeling embarrassed. "I apologize. I'm precognitive…and it slips away from me. I work in a New Age shop and Cassandra, my boss, says I'm very aware of others and their pain."

But he looked interested and began asking questions about her visions and her work, and he seemed so easy and comfortable to talk with, she lost track of the time. The sun began setting over the ocean, streaking the blue sky with rose and gold.

He glanced at his watch. "Getting late. I'm starved. Say, I was going to grab some dinner before heading home. Want to join me?"

"What about your dog?"

Dale glanced at the dog, its ears pricked forward.

"There's a place on the boardwalk where we can eat outside. They won't mind him."

"Sure. I'd like that. Only if it's steak, and we split the bill."

He grinned. "Deal."

* * *

Dinner turned out to be a fun night, spent talking for two hours. He asked her out for the next night. And the next.

Every night for the next two weeks, Commander Dale Curtis arrived at her apartment and took her out. They ate at various restaurants or sometimes had a picnic on the beach. Keira discovered he was divorced, no children, and liked to play the piano.

"Once I made no time for it, but someone I knew convinced me I needed balance in my life," he told her.

One Sunday he took her to a spot on the boardwalk and treated her to a special thermos of hazelnut coffee he'd brought along in the truck.

"My favorite." Keira sighed with pleasure as she sipped the brew. "How did you know?"

A wry smile touched his full mouth. "Educated guess."

She liked this man with his quiet manner, assurance and confidence. He treated her like a lady, yet at times, she saw a sadness in his eyes and wished she could erase it.

And then he'd kiss her, and make her forget all else.

After a month, when he still hadn't done more, she began to wonder if there were something wrong with her. Or him.

So when he came to pick her up to take her out for dancing, she bluntly asked him. "What's wrong with me?"

Dressed in a dark gray suit, looking distinguished and handsome, he gave her a quizzical look. "Nothing. You look lovely in that dress."

"I'm not asking if I look too fat," she blurted out. "I want to know why you haven't done anything more than kiss me. We've been seeing each other for almost two months. I've met a couple of your friends, been to your house, even. But you...don't seem interested in me that way."

Heat suffused her. "You know. Why haven't we had
sex?"

Dale pushed a lock of hair behind her ear. The tender
gesture echoed in her mind and seemed oddly familiar.
"Making love. With you, Keira, it would be making love.
And I don't want to pressure you. I cherish our time together, cherish you too much to rush you into anything."

For an answer, she reached up and kissed him. "Guess
what? I'm ready for a little pressure, big guy."

Something dark and sensual flickered in his gaze. "Tonight, then. After the club."

Much as she loved to dance, and the club he brought her
to was a favorite, where they played lots of slow dances,
Keira itched with impatience.

He drove to his house and parked in the driveway. As
the ticking engine cooled, his hands tightened on the steering wheel.

"I want to hoist you over my shoulder, carry you inside and go all caveman on you," he said quietly. "But you
deserve more than that. I can't promise I won't lose control, Keira, because I want you so badly it's taking all my
strength not to take you right here. But I will promise I'll
try to make tonight special."

When they got inside and he locked the door, she did
not hesitate, but slid her arms around his waist and kissed
him deeply.

They barely made it upstairs to his bedroom. Strip-
ping off their clothing, kicking off their shoes. Arms entwined around each other, they fell on the bed, kissing.
His tongue stroked, deep and sure, sparking a distant tug
of remembrance. The man kissed as if he knew exactly
how she liked it.

Heat flared in his eyes as he lifted his head. "So long,"

he said thickly. "I've waited and watched and wanted you for so long."

Dale's intensity frightened her a little, but then he began to kiss her softly, showering her with tiny, hot kisses that made her squirm and ache to draw closer. She clung to him, arching as he entered her in a hard thrust.

"Look at me, Keira," he said softly. "See only me."

Her gaze met his and she saw passion, tenderness, mixed with stark male possessiveness. And something else. Keira looked up into her lover's face and saw a reflection of herself.

He made love to her with exquisite tenderness, as they wrapped around each other in a desperate attempt to become one. Dale held nothing back. Every raw emotion was clearly expressed, from awed wonder to heated desire.

They came together in a blinding explosion of heat. For a long moment he lay atop her, gasping as she pulled him closer, then he rolled off. Keira lay on the bed, staring at the ceiling, feeling oddly shattered and yet overjoyed, as if he'd made love not just with his body, but with his heart. The intimacy they shared left her sated at last, filling the empty spot always inside her these past few months.

Dale drew his hands down her body, as if enjoying the feel of silky, supple flesh beneath the roughness of his calloused palms. Keira turned over and gazed into his eyes, heavy-lidded with satisfaction.

Suddenly memories rushed back in a flood, the wave cresting over her and crashing down. Dale Curtis. The courageous navy SEAL commander who'd given her back her life, had sacrificed everything to save her.

"Dale," she whispered. "Oh gods, Dale, it's you. I remember. Everything."

His expression eased into pure relief. "Good."

"You're here," she said, beginning to cry.

He smiled and stroked her hair, then kissed away her tears. "I never went away, sweetheart. Ever."

"There she is, sir."

The helo pilot spoke into his mouthpiece. Ears covered in soft gel headphones, Dale nodded and gazed at the sand. They'd swept this perimeter twice, but even hovering, it was hard to pinpoint a dark-haired woman with a jaunt to her step strolling on the sand.

She always enjoyed an afternoon stroll on the beach. After last night, he wasted no time. Keira remembered.

She remembered everything. And he wasn't risking losing her again.

"I'll circle around, give the guys a chance to clear an area for landing."

Dale clapped a hand on his shoulder. "Thanks. Owe you one."

"No, sir, we owe you. Least we can do."

He stared at the beach, and felt in his pocket for the small box he'd kept waiting in a top chest drawer for seven long months. Pulse spiking, he waited as the pilot circled around, searching for a clear space to land.

Keira walked barefoot on the sand, absorbed in thought. Dale Curtis was honorable, brave and a good man. Making love with him last night had brought all her memories soaring to the surface.

Along with them, incredible joy.

She wanted this man in her life, and despaired of ever losing him again. But she wasn't certain if he wanted her equally. So much had passed between them.

I'm the demon wolf who tortured him.

And you're the demon wolf who saved him, the same little voice reminded her. *He's the best thing that ever happened to you.*

A couple playing in the surf stopped and pointed overhead. She glanced at the sky.

A helicopter whirled overhead. Several uniformed navy personnel were roping off the beach, waylaying bystanders. An MP jogged up to her, his expression serious.

"What's going on?" she asked.

"Official navy business, miss. Please wait here."

Awe filled her. The uniformed men, expressions serious, functioned like a unit. The power of navy teamwork, she thought, her heart beating faster.

She watched the helo hover and descend. Keira removed her sunglasses and peered at the chopper's window. A man clad in a navy's officer's uniform sat in the copilot's seat.

"Who is he?" she asked the hovering MP.

"Some VIP. Highly decorated naval officer."

"He must be very important for all this fuss."

The chubby-faced MP grinned. "Oh, he is. His men, they'd do anything for him."

Sand stirred at the chopper's blades, sweeping in a wide arc, as the helicopter landed several yards away. The side door slid open and a uniformed naval officer leaped out, jogging on the sand straight toward her.

He wore a dress uniform, with gold bars wreathing the long blue sleeves. A SEAL pendant on his breast winked in the sunlight.

Her heart beat faster.

And then suddenly the serious-looking MP's cheeks became hollowed, his bone structure changed...shifted.

Into the grinning, handsome face of Chief Petty Officer Sam "Shay" Shaymore.

"Please stay here. Like I said, very important navy business."

A few feet away, the uniformed officer stopped and fished something out of a trouser pocket. Lt. Commander Dale Curtis dropped to one knee on the wet sand and held out a small blue velvet box. Sunlight sparkled off the diamond ring resting inside.

"Keira Solomon, will you do me the extreme honor of becoming my wife?"

Tears blurred her vision. Keira nodded. Dale stood, slid the ring on her finger. His mouth was warm and firm as he kissed her. When he drew back, he gently thumbed a tear off one cheek.

She glanced around and heard cheers and several shouts of "Hooyah!" and saw Dale's entire SEAL Phoenix Force standing guard, grins splitting their faces.

"You arranged all this?" she asked him, sliding her arms around his neck.

"They volunteered. It's a team effort," he murmured. "From this moment on, you're the cocommander of the most important team in my life. Us."

* * * * *